GAMBIT

—·—

ISEKAI FANTASY ADVENTURE

PATRICK UNDERWOOD

EDITED BY ELLE WILSON

COPYRIGHT

Contents

CHAPTER 1

— • —

PROLOGUE

The Controller materialized in front of a great and majestic building in the capital city of the Roxannez empire. A massive golden dragon formed next to him, gazing at the nearby crowd of commoners that yelled their cheers or disdain at all those appearing before the senate building's arrival platform.

The surrounding megalopolis was ancient, older than he was, yet it still looked new. The sky-reaching buildings, each made of shining alloys and polymers, sparkled in the afternoon light. As he looked around, no trash existed in any of the streets that he could see. But when you live an existence that requires no material needs or consumption of foods and drink, a lack of debris was to be expected.

The Controller sighed at the memory of his last real meal so many years ago. His oldest friend and he had stayed up into the night, debating the ascension act, his own arguments against it falling on deaf ears. The decision was made, and they had both become some of the first to go through with it.

Ten thousand years came and went since then.

The Controller tossed the old memories aside and focused on what was before him. He would have preferred to appear inside the building itself, but senators could not do things that way. Tradition and law dictated that they appear in the great square in front of the building and ascend the white marble steps to conduct the state's business. This forced them to be seen in front of the people they ruled over, a carryover from the ancient Republic days before the formation of the Empire.

As he studied the crowd around him, at least a part of it cheered for him when he arrived. They were those that supported his efforts to bring his people back to the light that it once had. His goal was to free them of this so-called immortality, return the people to flesh and blood once more, and bring children back to his species. It had been eons since a new one had been born.

This also scared many of the people. They had grown accustomed to their long lives. You could not go back to the flesh and blood and live forever. His species had natural life spans of hundreds of Roxannez years. Some had reached over one thousand before the ascension even, but when compared to time unending, it seemed but a heartbeat.

Those that were against him jeered at his arrival, yelling with voices of hatred while using hundreds of mental data burst transmissions to demand he stop his efforts. They wanted him to let the games proceed on more worlds as the opposing faction wanted, but it would just be appeasing their immortal boredom rather than fixing the problem.

Shyse roared at the crowd, a bout of flame coming from its mouth. His ever-loyal protector did not like the mob's attitude. The commoners nearest to the beast cowered and backed away, exactly what the golden dragon wanted.

"Calm yourself, Shyse," The Controller said to the beast. "They have a right to be angry. They all do."

The great dragon lowered its massive head and shrunk to a size only twice that of the Controller. He still had enough power radiating from him to quiet the onlookers as they made their way up the steps to the grand rotunda. The building itself had been preserved perfectly and was at least a hundred thousand years old.

It was one of the oldest government buildings in the empire. In fact, it was the second oldest still in existence behind only the imperial palace itself.

As the Controller approached the summit of the steps, several senatorial guards came to greet him.

The one in charge bowed before him. "Grand Senator, as you know, your... pet... is not allowed inside the building."

"He was just making sure I was safe from the mob, Centurion," the Controller replied. "You may go now, Shyse."

With a wild roar and in an explosion of light particles, Shyse dispersed, returning to his hunting grounds in the Controller's personal domain on the southern contingent.

"Follow me, Senator. We will now ensure your safety," the centurion said as the contingent of guards flanked the Controller on all sides, forming a diamond.

The Controller studied the building as they made their way to the grand chamber. While it appeared to be little changed over the eons, scans and emissions came from the walls. Thousands of constructs that worked for the various factions were each trying to glean what they could from him as they passed. His own constructs battled for supremacy against the deluge, holding them all at bay.

The sensations passed as he finally entered the Senate chambers. All constructs save one automatically deactivated inside the grand hall. The guards left him at the door, unable to continue further unless called by the Emperor himself, or to protect the Senators inside from harm.

The room consisted of five hundred seats arranged in a circle around a grand dais in the center, which was protected by an energy field surrounding the throne's current occupant.

"Chief Archivist of the Roxannez empire, Grand Senator of the Southern Provinces, and Controller of Fates for the lesser species," the monotone feminine voice of the Senate's construct said as it announced his entry.

Hundreds of peers gazed up at him as he made his way down to his seat. As one of the seven grand senators, he had a place at the foot of the emperor's Dais. Some of them were allies... most of them not, these days.

"Welcome Controller, what mischief do you bring to our chamber this time?" the Emperor said, not bothering to look up at him as he spoke.

"I come only to serve my people, Emperor. I have no mischievous plans that I am aware of," the controller said, a smile on his lips. He had known the emperor since before the great ascension, both boyhood friends from the last generation of children born.

"I do not believe you, but we shall continue anyway. Take your seat, and we can finally get started, my friend."

The Controller entered the main floor and took his seat. To his right sat his nemesis and peer, a scowl obvious on the being's face. The Controller smiled at him. "Ah, Overseer, so good to see you again. How is your latest scheming going?"

"Probably just as good as yours, Controller," he said, disdain in his voice.

"Senators, we have not even begun. Save your theatrics for after the call to order at least," the Emperor chimed in.

"Yes, Emperor," the Overseer and Controller said in unison, both taking their seats.

"The Senate is now called to order. All Senators return to their places and kneel before the last Emperor of the Roxannez," the construct announced to the assembly.

The Controller got up from his seat and took a knee, bowing his head to the only person with more power than him and any single one of his peers. While he and his friend had not always agreed, the Emperor was one of the few beings he still respected this high in the power structure of the Empire.

"Be seated," the Emperor said, still never having looked up towards the gathering once since the Controller had entered.

The Controller took his seat, his Senatorial robes conforming automatically to stay comfortable and perfectly aligned with his body as he relaxed and wondered what games would be played on that day.

"First item on the agenda is decree four-five-seven-one nine. Expansion of the bread and circuses for the lower classes," the construct said.

Before anyone else could speak, the Controller took the floor, standing up from his chair and pacing.

"Emperor and fellow Senators," he began before anyone could object. "I must again remind this body of rulers about my objections to any expansion of the games. The work of the scientific community demands that we keep from spoiling the habitats set aside for study of the lesser species. At least for entertainment purposes. We were promised only one world would be used, which we reluctantly agreed to, under the promise that it would spread no further than this one world."

"Objection!" called out the Overseer, his outburst coming exactly when the Controller expected it. "No such promises were made. Four-Five-Two was simply a test world, and we had not decided one way or another whether it would be expanded, only that we would study its feasibility."

"And that feasibility has not been decided yet," the Controller countered. "We do not know the long-term effects it will have on the lesser races. Or our own kind who descend to the worlds chosen. We have even offered to make new worlds and create constructs for the people's amusement, but you refuse because you say they are not entertaining enough. What else will it take to appease the masses? We have already had deaths, one of yours, if I recall."

"Only ones caused by your agent," the Overseer said, a smile coming to his lips.

"Do you have proof of this?" the Controller asked. "How do you know I even have an agent on Timeria?"

The Overseer slammed his fist down on his chair. "The witness accounts are clear that you have something or someone on Four-Five-Two. We just don't know what or who it is… In fact, why don't you enlighten us with that information so that we understand your motives?"

"So, in other words you have no proof and you simply want me to give out information for free. Is that it? We all know how the games of the Senate are played. We each have our pawns and motives. I recall that your own agent is safe from any monitoring on this world as well. How was that arranged exactly, Overseer?"

The glare from the being in question would scare anyone less powerful than the Controller. Instead of cowering however, he met the hate filled gaze and returned it in equal measure.

"Enough!" The Emperor called out, finally looking from whatever his attention had been focused on. "You two will stay civil in these chambers. Everyone knows that you two are at odds, everyone knows you both have an agenda. For the time being, I will allow the motion to be tabled until the next full Senate while we continue study."

"Emperor!" The Overseer stood up, his anger flaring for just a second as tendrils of power shot along his arms in rage.

The Emperor glared at the Overseer and placed his hand out toward him, crushing his hand into a fist.

The power the Overseer had gathered was gone in an instant, snuffed out by the might of the Emperor like it had never even been there in the first place.

"You will be silent, or I will remove your title, Grand Senator. If you would bide a moment, I was also not finished." The Emperor glared at the Overseer for a long moment before turning his attention to the Controller. "You have until the next session to give us a valid argument why we cannot expand the game to more worlds. If not, it will come to a full vote and no further delays will be allowed. Is that understood, Controller?"

"Yes, my Emperor," the Controller replied and bowed deeply, knowing he had to keep any further arguments at bay.

"Good, half a year, Controller. Then we vote on expansion, or we find another method of making existence more pleasant for our people. Next item on the agenda!"

The Controller bowed his ascent, glancing over to see the sneer had returned to the Overseer's face.

The Controller hoped that his agent followed the right path. It was his only chance to stop what was happening. He doubted his back-up plans would have the same effect.

Chapter 2

Firelight

I sat, staring at the firelight in front of me, deep in thought over the whirlwind that had become my life. Good things were happening, but also many things that were... not quite as good.

I glanced over at Cecil who appeared to be deep in his own thoughts as well. Both of us were exhausted after the heavy jog we had done that day and now we were back in the woods. Hopefully, far enough away from the threats following us or hidden enough that they would not find us.

I considered the fact that it seemed like I had spent most of my time on this world hiding in the woods. The pain of what happened in Hills Crest and the loss of Tasnia's father weighed heavily on me. He was someone who could have been a real friend and mentor to me and his loss in this world struck home.

During our escape earlier in the day, we had found ourselves going more south than east in an effort to lead away any pursuit, just in case someone back in Rivenhold took exception to the damages in the city we left behind. We had finally found a grove of trees nestled in between some large hills and judged it safe enough to start a fire, heat up some food, and get some rest.

The girls had gone with Diane, if that was her real name, to the nearby creek to clean up with some privacy, leaving Cecil and me by the fire with our thoughts. The fight from that day was still fresh in my mind. The power I felt entering me was making my insides feel like they were about to burst.

But that was not what really concerned me.

I was really just sick of being someone's pawn in a game I did not understand, but I didn't know how to get out of the mess I found myself in.

Do I follow along until I see a chance to break out? Or do I keep on the path set for me and hope it's the right thing?

I considered my options for a bit before I realized I still did not have enough information to make a decision. For now, I would have to follow the path as it was laid before me while hoping I made the best decision when it came time.

I really hate that idea.

"How long till we meet the rest of your group?" I asked Cecil.

Cecil was startled out of his thoughts almost like he had forgotten I was around. "What?"

"How long will it take us to reach the others from here?"

He considered this for a moment before answering. "We are taking a roundabout way, so maybe most of daylight tomorrow if we start early and move as fast as we did today."

I nodded. "That works. We make a dash for them and decide the next steps when we meet up."

Silence fell over us for a few moments. I could feel his tension about asking the question I suspected was on his mind.

"Can I ask more about what you are?" he finally asked.

I stared at him for a minute, deciding whether I should answer or not. I even considered putting him under the oath...

I shook my head. No, I was sick of the games, and it was time I started trusting people rather than mind-fuck them. It may burn me later, but damn it if I wasn't sick of the rules these so-called gods had created here.

"This might be hard to believe, but I awoke on this world," I said. "A few weeks ago, now? Maybe a month and a half ago? I am not entirely sure now that the days are all blending together for me. But more or less, I am from another world and time."

Cecil's face went through the emotional range of disbelief, anger, fear, and finally something that might have been acceptance. "So, you are one of them?"

"Absolutely not," I said with force in my words. "I am human, or was... It's a little complicated, but I admit I was put here by what you call gods and given the powers the Demigods have. However, it was not by my choice or doing. I hate everything about what they have done to me and to the people on this world."

I explained a few of the details, telling him about the world that humans had come from and the last moments of it. I told him how I woke up in a body that was not my own. I left out some of the details about me but gave him the gist of it.

"So, what does that make you, then?" he asked.

I laughed. "That is a damn good question, Cecil. I am still trying to figure that out, to be honest."

I stood up and stretched my legs. Glancing in the direction the women had gone but not able to see or hear them return yet. "I have their powers, but I am not like them. I can bind people to my will if they choose to be bound. There is free will to it. Once at least to make the choice, but there is a measure of control once they do. I can also tap into the powers of the Chosen after the agreement and we... seal the deal, so to speak."

"It is if you plan to be like them that concerns me the most."

"I understand that. Believe me. There is an old saying in my world that power corrupts, and I am as flawed as the next person. But no, what they are doing is wrong. Even if I am kind of stuck in the middle right now. I don't want to bind anyone, but then again, I can't do anything to stop the Demigods if I don't. That is the conundrum I find myself in and the struggle I face. I keep going back and forth about it."

Cecil stared back into the fire for a short while before speaking again. "I want to protect my wife and to have children free of this nightmare. I want to believe that you would help us against the Demigods... but like you said, power has a way of corrupting even the good to do evil things in its name."

"I couldn't agree with you more, and I find myself worrying about that. Some of my own decisions I find questionable, even if I thought necessary at the time. You once asked me why Stern followed me?"

He looked up and nodded.

"I freed him of a compulsion that Seir put him under. That is another power I have and one I find most useful. It is the power to free those that were tricked or felt they had no choice. But at the same time, I wasn't sure if I could trust him. Placing him... by his own agreement at least... under a similar compulsion."

Cecil took a deep breath. "I am not sure I could agree to such a thing."

"I honestly don't want you to. Part of me considered it... if just for a minute. But I need to trust people, that is what will separate me from them, without that oath. It will also put me at greater risk, but it's the right thing to do. I feel it here." I tapped my chest.

"And the women you have bound to you?"

"Complicated. I can free them too, though I haven't tested it yet. Or at least most of them. I tried to free Tyla, but she... Refused. She doesn't get a second chance, apparently."

"Why?"

"I wish I knew. Best I can figure out is there is a power struggle with the... gods. They have their own issues and seem to be fighting amongst themselves. Using a set of rules that I don't fully understand."

Why I was trusting this man, I could not tell you other than he fought by my side and spoke honestly with me. It felt right, and not in the 'Vex is fucking with my head' kind of right either. I realized I missed having a guy's perspective, someone to talk to. I loved my women with every fiber of my being, but I could also use a friend from time to time as well.

"I am going to choose to trust you for now. I have my doubts, but I also have hope." Cecil said.

Nodding, I replied, "I hope it is not misplaced, but thank you. I am choosing to do the same."

"It is your own doubts which give me hope. It is something I don't think the Demigods understand. Doubt can be a weakness, but it is also a tool to use to keep from making terrible choices."

"I couldn't agree more."

I heard feminine voices coming from the creek. I smiled at the thought of Tasnia and Tyla. Regardless of the circumstances, they each made me feel happy, and I was relieved to have them by my side.

As they approached the camp, the darkness made it difficult to see, but it appeared they each had wet hair. Tasnia led the group, her smile almost a beacon when our eyes met, reflected in the light of the fire. She wore leather pants and matching top. Her red hair matched the power she wielded, and it flowed freely from its recent brushing.

Tyla came second, her black hair tied in a ponytail, wearing a dress she picked up in Hills Crest. She also smiled at me when she came into view. Both girls came up to me and gave me a kiss as the last of the three figures stayed at the edge of the clearing still shrouded in darkness.

"What's wrong?" I asked the young woman.

"We wanted her to wait before we presented her," Tyla answered for her. "We managed to clean out all the dirt from her hair and found something... astonishing after I restored her health with my healing magic. That's why we were gone so long."

"We wanted to give you a warning before you saw it." Tas took over for her sister-wife. "It is an... odd color."

I sat there and shifted my view between them for a second before speaking. "Confused, but I will play along. I consider myself properly warned."

"Come on over, Diane," Tas said.

The figure walked slowly into the light from the fire. The first thing I noticed was that she no longer wore the dingy and baggy threads from earlier. She had been given one of Tyla's dresses, even if she could barely fit inside of it. Her hips were wider and her breasts, while slightly smaller, seemed to push out from her chest a little further. They almost seemed to defy gravity and her nipples poked out. Probably influenced by the evening air.

I tried not to stare too much as my eyes traveled farther up the young woman's body, it was then I noticed her long hair. It was no longer a dirt covered blond, but bright pink. My jaw dropped at the difference as the girl's face dropped to the ground under my intense gaze.

Her pointed ears stuck out to the sides through the pink hair, which contrasted her grayish blue eyes. She was absolutely stunning right now, and I had to remind myself I was already in love with not one, but two women.

"What... happened?" I finally managed to ask.

Diane looked at my two women for help, clearly uncomfortable speaking out loud.

Tyla answered. "She treated it with some plants in the wood to get rid of the color. Then added dirt and... other things to it to not be noticed when she came into town for food."

"She doesn't remember who she is or how she got there. All she knows is that she had a bracelet with a name engraved on it. What was it again?" Tas glanced over at the shy elf.

Tyla interjected. "Dianeya Do'chatta, she wasn't sure it was her name, and she sold the bracelet for food about a year ago, but she went by Diane since it fit with the humans better."

Diane nodded, face still pointed towards the ground, agreeing with what Tyla said.

"Have you decided to stay with us yet, Diane? I'm sorry, do you prefer... Dianeya?" I said, murdering the pronunciation. Diane smiled and giggled at this at least.

"Diane is fine," she managed to get out with a slight squeak in her voice.

"Come sit with us," Tasnia said and guided her over to the fallen log I had been using as a seat. She sat down and huddled close to Tasnia with Tyla coming and joining a moment later on the girl's other side. "She's had it rough, Love, living the way she had been for a couple years by herself. She is not used to dealing with people, but she said she would stay with us for now."

I nodded. "That's fair, Diane. If there is anything we can do to help, just let us know. The soup should be hot by now. Feel free to help yourselves."

We each dished a bowl and sat down to eat. Pork cubes were added with some dried vegetables and then mixed with some spices that we had picked up in the town we were just in. Cecil had prepared it and it came out pretty good all things considered.

"Thanks for making dinner," Tyla said. "It's quite good."

Cecil nodded at the compliment. "I was an aspiring chef once upon a time. But the guards had a job opening and it was more stable. Lea said I would have made a better cook though."

"How long have you two been married?" I asked.

"Several years now. No children yet, we wanted to wait until she was a full noble at the Lady rank. That might have happened by now if not for..." Cecil trailed off.

"I'm sorry," I said.

"It's fine, Stern got us out. You have my thanks for freeing him of his slavery."

Tyla looked at me with concern, Tasnia joining her.

"I told him most of it. Decided I needed to start trusting people."

Diane looked up at me, the question written on her face, before she noticed that she brought attention to herself and looked back down at her food.

"We will tell you too, Diane, if you decide to stay with us for the long term. Let's give it a few days before you make a decision, though."

She nodded without looking up, and we finished our meal in silence.

"Tomorrow is going to be another fast day till we catch up with the others," I said after we had finished cleaning up our mess. "We can then start making decisions on what to do next."

"Yes, Master," Tyla called out from where she was using a stick to break up the fire so we could pour dirt over it.

"I'll take the first watch tonight, Cecil can I wake you up for the second half?"

"Agreed," he said.

"Love, we can stand watch, too."

I winced as she pointed that out to me. "Sorry, old habit. I know you are perfectly capable. Okay, we split between the four of us. Diane, let's wait before you start doing guard duty until we know if you are going to stay with us."

Diane nodded and went back to washing off the bowls and packing them up next to each of our packs.

"You girls can take the tent. Cecil and I can sleep under the stars tonight until we get things settled."

Agreements were made by all as Tyla came up to me and whispered, "For tonight that will be fine, but I sense that Diane will stay close for a while. She is skittish, and I think we are the first people she has trusted in a long time. I don't think she will want to give that up just yet."

"Okay, just don't go getting any ideas about that just yet about adding her to my... our team... permanently. She is not even close to the being in a place I would consider anything more than a traveling companion." I gave her a serious look.

She smiled. "I know, Master, and in this instance I agree. She needs... to find herself more before we could consider that."

"Good." I leaned forward and kissed her on the lips. "Go get some sleep. Cecil will wake you after his watch."

"Good night," she said with a smile and went into our small tent that was just large enough for three or four people at most.

Tasnia came over and we traded a kiss, an enthusiastic one that made me regret having all these extra people around as she left me... standing at attention when she left. I stood near the now extinguished fire and listened as everyone settled into the tent.

"You are a lucky man," Cecil finally said from where he lay in his sleeping roll.

"I totally agree," I replied with a large smile.

CHAPTER 3

DREAMS

I appeared in my dream world with the blackness all around me as my eyes adjusted. Things came into focus slowly. I was used to this, and while it was difficult to make it appear at will, I had a feeling it would come to me.

The star-scape in the distance was bright now. Not simply dim lights that tried to peek through the darkness, but full-on stars shining their blue light down upon me. What they signified, if anything at all, was a mystery to me.

But that is not what held my attention. The spheres representing the girls were brighter, much brighter than they were last time. They moved around me still, but unlike the lazy way they did it last time, it was now with a speed that seemed like it had a purpose.

They orbited me at opposite ends. The tether of energy burned brightly, at least compared to before, and entered me at my chest to the area just below where my heart should be. As they rotated, though, the ribbon of power seemed to go through my skin and attach at an anchor point somewhere in my center as the two spheres completed their orbit once every few heartbeats. It was like holding two ropes and spinning them around with your arms wide. They seemed almost to counterbalance each other.

The third ribbon I had originally used to join the two spheres together was gone. Instead, a swirl of color that was both red and blue intermingled the main cord. Somewhat like a candy cane with two different flavors. The one going to Tyla was blue with a small red stripe, and the one to Tas was reversed. As I focused on Tyla's sphere, I could see some of the reddish orange hue continuing its spread into her sphere.

Did that mean her control over fire was growing? I honestly wasn't sure.

The same thing was happening to Tas. The bluish energy was invading her sphere, not mixing with the red, but adding to it somehow. I still likened it to water and oil in that it didn't merge precisely but could be combined for a time under the right circumstances.

I reached out to the ribbons and gripped them enough to bring in the spheres towards me. This stopped their orbit and stabilized them in place as I brought them close enough to reach.

As I grasped them with both hands, it overwhelmed me with emotion. Love, warmth, and desire filled me first. These were the raw emotions coming from both of my girls. Tyla's was the strongest of the two, but I could feel Tasnia's growing rapidly, and on its way to matching it.

I smiled at this, since a part of me still wondered if bonding with her was the right thing to do. It had all happened so fast, and my desire at the moment somewhat clouded my judgment. I wasn't sure whether what I had done was right for her, and that bothered me.

Other emotions existed as well. The pain of Tasnia's father's loss was still a great weight upon the young woman. She was burying it deep for now, but I could feel she still mourned him.

I would have to talk with her about that.

A similar pain came from Tyla, she was both angered and sad at the fate of her mother. She wanted desperately for us to free her of the bonds placed on her, and I truly hoped that day would come to pass soon.

Soon the emotions were almost overwhelming to me, and I let go of the two spheres, but not till after I felt that the power they contained had skyrocketed since the last time I felt them.

What changed that?

"You have come far, young human," a voice came from behind me.

I jumped, as much as one can do with a semi-permanent naked body in a space that was not really bound by the laws of physics. I turned to the noise to see a large green bodybuilder looming over me, just calmly staring in my direction.

His bald green head and lifeless feeling black eyes seemed to drill into me as they passed judgment. He was shirtless underneath a brown robe that seemed to enhance his features rather than hide them. He just stood there calmly, as if waiting for a ride share on a corner.

"You're an asshole, Vex," were the first words to come out of my mouth when I recovered.

Vex smiled. "Is that a way to talk to your patron?"

"You're more like my jailer. You put me in this shitty situation where I have to play your stupid game with little choice in the matter. Your instructions sucked, and I have been winging it this whole time with zero support against a literal fucking army of enemies. How the hell am I supposed to win?"

"Be that as it may, you had a choice the entire time. Everyone in this world does. What none of us has is freedom from the consequences of those choices. Each one matters and you should consider them carefully before you choose. Regardless, you're winging it, as you call it, was remarkable if less than... efficient. You removed one of Seir's lieutenants and made the position of my patron stronger in the Senate. I should congratulate you."

"Oh, fuck you, Vex. I didn't know any better last time we talked, but now I figure I am fairly important to your scheming or whatever and that you need me, a hell of a lot more than I need you."

"I could replace you in an instant," Vex countered. "Do not think that your value is worth any amount of insolence," Vex said with some heat. His eyes lit up with power and his hand reached up towards me. A beam of energy came out of his hand to strike me dead in the chest.

But then the oddest thing happened.

The energy hit a translucent field, just beyond the orbs of Tasnia and Tyla that had begun their spinning orbit around me. The field only held for a second before the beam broke through and still hit me enough to rock me back on my ass.

But it didn't hurt all that much. I was on my feet again within a second and saw a surprised look on Vex's face.

"Impossible," he said as he looked at me. "How did you do that?"

I looked down at myself and back up at him and shrugged. "Honestly, not sure."

"You should not have that ability, even in this Sanctum you created within your soul."

So that is what this place was?

"I don't honestly know what is happening. These orbs, this power, the ability for them to share it between them. I have no idea."

"What do you mean, share it?" Vex asked, taking several steps closer to me.

The orbs altered their orbit, so they spun closer to me, rather than hit him as he approached. Vex leaned over them to peer closely at me.

"What has he done?" Vex mumbled to himself. "More importantly, why did he not tell me?"

"Huh?" was my reply, my wit as sharp as ever during the confusing encounter.

"The gift from our patron is more… interesting than I thought it was. In fact, I am surprised even he has this much sway here. Your powers are different from what they should be. You have an element of chaos in you human. You have the potential to be extremely dangerous in this world." He paused for a second. "Eventually anyway, that is, if you do not die first at any rate."

I grasped the bridge of my nose, frustrated with all these half answers. "Please, just tell me what the fuck is going on. Pretty please? With sugar on top?"

Vex gave me a confused glare. "I will tell you some of it, human, but only so that you do not destroy yourself or even this world with your ignorance. The Controller… our patron, has changed the code in you in a way that should not be possible, even at his level in the Senate. Either he did something to this world long before the games which allowed him to do so, or someone else has assisted him. I do not know which."

"What do you mean?"

"Simply? He gave you the ability to change the rules to some limited degree. To break past the laws that govern this world. How far you can take that is a mystery, even to me. But it is beyond what most can achieve even if they are from our race and have the backing of a Grand Senator."

"So, what can I actually do?"

"Unknown… but probably you could bend the rules of this world without outright breaking them completely. Anything more and the System would intervene… in the most violent way. So be careful in what you do and attempt, or it could mean the end of you and anyone you associate with."

I took a deep breath. Even if I wasn't really breathing here, I needed the calming effect of breathing deeply to consider my thoughts. "Is that why I can do things like combine Tyla's and Tas's power, and why I got that rush after I killed Albris?"

"Yes, to the first, the second is a rule of the games. If you kill another of my kind, you get their power. It was supposed to be a way to limit the influence of our kind on this world. A bargain we struck to make it harder for them to achieve dominance and ruin our studies. But the ones that descended instead use pawns and never face each other directly. Playing by a set of... what you would call gentleman's rules."

"So that was the rush I felt when I killed him?"

"Yes, you took a part of his power and probably doubled your own. You would be even stronger if you did not share it so freely with your women."

"Why? They are better off as strong as I can make them." I said, my annoyance clear in my voice. "We won that fight because they were so strong."

"Yes, I am sure Albris never considered that you would have done so. He probably never considered them a genuine threat. I am even sure his bonded welcomed death in a way. It freed them of their torment."

"So, what's next? I sure as hell don't want to be your pawn, but I still don't know the game I am playing here, either."

"That's the beauty of why I selected you, Derrick." Vex said. "You never needed to be our pawn, and simply needed to be yourself. Other than the subtle directions and suggestions I implanted in you and your companions, each of you acted on your own free will this entire time."

I looked directly at the self-proclaimed greenish god before me. "You call those suggestions? They almost feel like commands to go east into the desert."

"Then get stronger and stop whining like a petulant child. Follow them or do not, that is up to you. If you want your best chance for the power to win, take advantage of our help."

I glared at him, wanting to punch this asshole in the face. "How about a little more support than what you are giving me here? I have no idea how this power shit works, and it is too different from what my girls have for them to help me learn it."

"I will consider it. In fact, an idea has occurred to me to do just that. Bide your time and for now, It is time for you to leave. Your power wanes and the morning approaches. As you get stronger, you will be able to form this Sanctum at will more often. There are rules in place to ensure it is not easy to get to. Surprisingly, it is more than almost all of my kind can do in this world and they rely on their own patrons for this type of support. What the Controller has given you is a precious gift that gives you a distinct advantage. You may see me again in time."

The world started to dim before I could speak further, and Vex disappeared from my vision.

"You're still an asshole!" I called out to the fading darkness.

CHAPTER 4

—◦—

REFUGEES

We finally approached the foot of the mountains, and I paused, looking up at the peaks before us. "How are we going to do this?"

I glanced over at Cecil, whose response was just a smirk. "They should know we are here already. This is the spot they are supposed to be watching for us."

I glanced around the small clearing we were in, not seeing anything obvious, and my senses were not screaming at me that we were in danger. So, I closed my eyes and tried to feel around me a little more.

Thinking back to when I was able to pledge Stern to my service and using the same 'feel' I stretched out my... I honestly was not sure what to call it. It felt like listening if I were to describe it, but not for sounds, but instead for a...

I honestly could not describe it.

Maybe like a sensor system. Sending out a pulse and seeing if anything comes back that seems out of place.

As that sensation stretched out from me, it connected to something that seemed a little odd. A wrongness to the background, like hairs standing up on the back of your neck when you felt like you were being watched. I could also tell where it was coming from in a general sense, if not precisely.

I opened my eyes and looked into the shadows of the trees; all I could see was a darkness that stood out to me a little more than the rest. Like it was highlighted to my eyes and not belonging with the rest of the natural shade. "There."

Cecil looked to where I pointed, and he squinted his eyes. "If anyone is there... It's Cecil. The matriarch frowns on tardiness."

I glanced over at him at the odd phrase, having an idea of what it was. "What was that?"

"Pass-phrase that we worked out that lets them know it was all clear."

I nodded. "I approve, what was the one for it not being all clear?"

He looked at me funny. "Yell, It's a trap?"

I chuckled at the old joke. "Nice. Where did you get that from?"

He looked at me as if I were stupid. "I did not have a passphrase for that. They wouldn't come out if I did not give them the all-clear, so why would I need it."

I rolled my eyes. No one in this world would get my humor even if I were to explain. "Fair."

The shadow I had pointed at moved, coming forward during our by-play. Eventually, the shadows moved and shimmered into the form of a human woman. I saw that she held the ball thing that I had given to Stern in her hands.

What was the name of that thing? Shadow's... Mantle?

That was it.

"Lea!" Cecil said happily and rushed up to the woman I assumed was his wife.

She was plain, but in that girl next door sort of way that you could fall for in an instant. Don't get me wrong, I loved my girls, they were what I would call smoking hot in any situation, but there is something to be said for the girl next door.

She had dirty blond hair down to her shoulders and brown eyes. Her clothes were plain and filthy, and her face covered in dirt. But she had smile lines a mile wide when she saw her husband, and that made me sit back and let them enjoy the moment.

She ran to meet her husband, and they came together in a twirling embrace when they met. I stepped back next to Tyla and Tas and grabbed each of their hands as I smiled at the reunited couple. Diane, who stood to Tyla's other side, looked at them and then at us with an expression of confusion.

"I love seeing that," I whispered after a moment as Cecil set down Lea and they kissed.

"They are a cute couple. I have met Lea a few times from my... Mother." Tyla hiccupped only a second at the thoughts of her mother, but it did not dim her smile too much.

We waited in silence for a few minutes while they reunited. Finally, they seemed to notice our presence and Cecil guided Lea by the hand over to us.

"My Love, this is Derk, and his two... should I call you his wives?" he asked. I looked at the girls, who both nodded at me. Cecil saw their ascent and continued. "Wives, and Diane, whom they rescued during the fall of Rivenhold."

Lea gave Cecil a shocked look before smiling at my woman. "It's good to see you again, Tyla..." Then she looked back at Cecil. "Rivenhold fell?"

"Not fully," I interjected. "But it is a disaster zone, and I don't think we can go back. Pleasure to meet you Lea. I have heard a lot about you from your husband. This is Tyla, my... I guess yeah, my first wife and this is Tasnia, my second."

We all exchanged handshakes, while Lea and Tyla exchanged hugs.

"It's so good to see you again," Tyla said as they embraced.

"You as well. I was sorry to hear about your mother. I..." Lea shivered. "I was dreading a similar fate until Stern helped us escape. One minute we were in retreat and the next I was waking up from unconsciousness in the back of a slave wagon. What happened to you?" she asked, looking at all of us.

Cecil looked over at me. "I don't keep secrets from my wife, she needs to be told."

I nodded. "That's fair, but let's not spread it with the others just yet."

Lea traded glances with her husband and me. "Okay, I promise to keep this a secret... but only if I don't think it will harm the others."

I took a deep breath, the temptation of giving the oath once again making its presence known, and I wondered if it was another part of the 'gift' from Roxannez.

No, this was probably just simple human paranoia. We had plenty of problems with giving into temptation before those alien assholes ever showed up.

"Okay, I am trusting you based on Cecil. When someone fights by your side, they earn a bit of that with me. I will warn you though, anyone I consider a threat to me and my girls, I will end that threat. Fair?"

She nodded at me, even if her eyes displayed a little animosity, but I wanted my threat to be taken seriously because I would follow through with it. Cecil glared at me over his wife's head in warning, though he also nodded in understanding.

"Okay, it all began..."

"So, you're telling me you're a demigod, but... not?" Lea asked and glanced at her husband for confirmation. He nodded at her.

"I have seen him do some things that should be impossible." Cecil said.

"And you can't yet manipulate the magics externally yet?"

"No, I was told... by a source I don't exactly trust but whom I think is giving me straight information that it is because I don't steal it from them." I pointed to Tyla and Tas. "Some magics require more power than others, so I can heal inside my body and others that I can physically touch. I can light up a sword I am grasping with fire, but I can't throw a fireball just yet. At least not until we all grow stronger or figure out how to share it more equally between us,"

I took a deep breath, getting my thoughts together. "I saw Albris' women use their powers, if minimally, so it must be possible to share.
"

"That makes some sense," Lea said. "The power needed is much higher for those things. It's exponentially easier to imbue an object rather than cast power. Only the young and the powerful even try." Lea touched Tyla on the shoulder. "How much stronger did you get?"

"Much. I can form water droplets and use some of Tasnia's heat energy power to turn them into frozen shapes as they leave my hands."

"Astounding." Lea said. "You're right, we need to keep this information to ourselves for now. There were several that joined us who I am not sure if I trust yet. They just happened along or were family of those of us who escaped. Some of them feel different than when I last knew them, like they changed. It may have been the captivity, or..."

"Should I test them?" Tyla asked.

"I am not sure how that would go. It is not the most agreeable of groups right now. We are not sure where to go, let alone who we can trust anymore. Several have accused the others of being spies for the Demi's and I am not sure how much longer we can stay together.

"We can settle all that when we get to them. I think I know which way we are going. If we disagree, we can just split the group."

"Okay, follow me, and I will take you to them."

Lea turned and kissed Cecil one more time on the lips before taking his hand and leading us deeper into the woods. I took one last look around the clearing to make sure we were not being followed then went after the girls. They had already fallen into step behind the couple.

It took another half an hour to find our destination. A large rock outcropping formed from the mountain. Before we got too close, I touched Lea by the arm to get her attention. Her entire skin flashed a greenish color as I touched her, and her reaction caused me to delay a bit before speaking.

I shook my head at the sensation. "What kind of Chosen are you?"

She looked at me as if it was an odd question to ask. Though, in her defense, it probably was without context.

"I control the air."

So green meant air affinity. That seemed an odd color for it, but good to know.

"Thanks. I will explain why I asked that later. But for now..." I turned to Tyla, Tas, and Diane. "Let me go with Lea and Cecil first, so we don't cause alarm with so many. You three stay back, and we will call for you."

The girls nodded and hid down by brush as we continued to the outcropping. Leah whistled a bird call as soon as we saw a large bush next to a solid rock wall. A man with a sword at his hip and a bow and arrow in his hands pushed the brush aside and walked out of a cave.

"Orrick, it's safe. These are friends." Lea said to the man as we approached.

He lowered the nocked arrow but did not quite put it away.

He was shorter than me, maybe just about five feet if I were to guess. That put him about in line with my neck. He had a long face with a rounded jaw, an enormous nose, narrow lips. His light blue eyes set wide on his face, which gave a roguish look to him. His face seemed weathered, and he was definitely entering his later years, but he seemed to have a virility that defied it.

He walked with a casual grace that spoke to a lot of time on his feet. The way his green and brown clothes sat on him told me he preferred to do that walking in the woods. Add in the bow he had in his hands that looked well used, and I would place money that he was a scout or hunter.

"Derk, this is Orrick," Lea said. "He was a personal hunter for the Matriarch before the... fall."

The man nodded at me before looking at Lea and Cecil. "This the one Seir said to find?"

"Yes," Lea answered.

He put the arrow in a quiver strapped to his hip opposite his sword then held out his hand. We grasped at the wrist. "Pleasure. I'll introduce you to the wife and others inside."

"Thank you," I said. "I am going to call over some others. I did not want you to be surprised by all of us at once."

The man nodded, and I called out. "You can come over!"

A few seconds later, the three women came from around the trees, Tyla in front.

"Mistress Russel, it pleases me to no end that you made it out of that mess alive. I am sorry about what happened to your mother," Orrick said.

"Orrick!" Tyla called with excitement as she ran over to give the older man a hug. "I worried everyone I knew at my mother's estate was dead."

The man let go of the hug and peered at the other two. Smiling at Tasnia, he did a double take at Diane and her pink hair and elven ears. "Something tells me there is a story here. I haven't seen an elf in... many years. Pink hair, though everyone I have known has been silver haired."

Diane cowered behind Tasnia, peeking over her shoulder at the older man.

"It's a long story," I said. "She has no memory of who she was a year ago. Finding herself alone with nothing. So, we don't have many answers to that I am afraid."

I glanced at her as she smiled at me in relief. "A lot has happened in the past few days and weeks," I added, and she nodded behind Tasnia.

"Let's get you inside and then I will get back on watch. Lea, did you want me to range out while you talk to Cecil?"

"That would be most appreciated Orrick." Lea said as she reached over and grasped her husband's larger hands. Cecil smiled wide enough that you could see his pearly white teeth, which contrasted sharply with his black skin.

"Go ahead and head out now Orrick, I will lead them in and get someone to watch the opening." Lea said.

Orrick put his fingers to his brow as though tipping a hat he wasn't wearing then reached out his hand and took the shadow mantel from her before looking one last time at Tyla. "Mistress Tyla, I am glad you are safe, you will have to tell me what happened later."

"I will, thank you."

"Let's get you and your wives introduced to everyone, Derk."

Orrick stopped mid-stride and turned around. "Wives?"

Tyla reddened a bit while Tasnia beamed at his reaction. Diane just stayed hiding behind her new friend.

"It's complicated, Orrick," I said. "But Tasnia, Tyla and I are together. We had not really named it or had a ceremony, but it feels fitting to say that at this point." I looked at both women, who beamed at me in return.

He glanced at the two, then back at me. "Must be some story, I'm looking forward to it." He turned and headed out into the forest, blending in after only a few steps.

I watched him go, trying to reach out with my senses at the same time. His outline seemed to stand out to me for at least ten or fifteen steps before I lost track of him.

It's a start.

"Let's head in," Lea said.

We entered the cave, completely unlike the one we stayed in a few weeks back. This was not some sanctum for the gods but a naturally built cave. It snaked left and right a few times before coming to a well-lit open area with a fire in the center.

While I liked the cave's ability to conceal you from the outside, my thoughts went back to the entrance to Vex's Sanctum and the lack of getting out through a back way.

That worried me, but I hoped we wouldn't stay long.

Lea led us in, followed by Cecil. There were a few warm hellos, but mostly there was little activity generated by their arrival.

When I entered the room, that changed, as concern grew from the faces of the people just sitting there doing nothing. I had the attention of all fifteen of them, a mix of men and women with no children in sight.

Peering around, the Cave seemed to branch off into smaller openings, at least three in total. The ceiling was high inside this part of the cave, and I looked for any signs of guano or other droppings but found nothing.

Hopefully, bats were not a thing in this world. I hated those little flying rats.

The room smelled of bodies that had not been washed in days, and I immediately hated it and wanted to leave. While someone kept it clean, it was also obviously a home for wild animals when people were not present.

Tyla, Tas, and Diane followed me in. Those in the room gasped when they saw Diane. Questions flew from the mouths of half the people inside, and we just stood there rather than answer them.

"People!" Cecil yelled over the din. "Calm down. I will answer your questions."

No one listened.

After a few more seconds, Lea lifted her hand and snapped her fingers. A high pitch pop that seemed magically enhanced to me screamed out at a pitch that hurt my ears and most of those in the room. "He said shut up!"

That did it.

The crowd stopped and covered their ears, each looking at her as if she had slapped them. All except for one woman over by a large steel pot that came over to us.

"Thank you, Lea," she said then turned to the crowd. "You heard her, everyone. You all knew we were waiting for someone before moving on. Well, here they are, so don't judge them for not being what you expected. Now we can decide what to do next, but first, we should eat. I got the stew almost ready, and we have the last of the bread."

Standing somewhere around five and a half feet, stout with white skin, this woman had a motherly, if not grandmotherly, feel about her. Her eyes were green and kind and her short, frizzy, deep brown hair, which was going gray, sat neatly braided behind her head. Her clothes were plain but well fitted.

She reminded me of my grandmother, if I was being honest, though she was a little young for that in my old world. I would guess that in this world the people aged faster without access to magic.

Speaking of grandmother... Where were all the kids? That seemed odd, but I filed it away for later.

The matronly woman turned to us and smiled. "Now, I recognize you, Mistress Russel, and I am really sorry about what happened to your mother." She faced the rest of us. "I am Estelle, Orrick's wife. Now who might the rest of you be."

Tyla could only smile at the woman as tears welled in her eyes. I guessed that with a couple of reminders now; she was thinking about her mom too much. I walked over next to her and wrapped my arm around her, and she leaned into me rather than answer the woman.

"This is Derrick. He goes by Derk," Lea said on my behalf. "You know Tyla, who is now his wife... this is... I am sorry, I forgot your name, dear."

"Tasnia," Tas said. "I am also Derrick's wife."

"Two wives?" Estelle asked, her eyes raised. "That... is odd."

Ignoring the comment, Tasnia continued, "This is our new friend Diane. She doesn't like to speak much."

"An elf? With pink hair, no less. Another oddity. But regardless, you are all welcome here. Our supplies are running low, but Orrick got a deer two days ago, and it's still good enough for the stew pot. You can find a place to rest until it's ready."

I turned to the woman. "Thank you. Are the caves safe?"

"They go a pretty good way back. You can take the torch and look around, but don't go too far. We haven't marked much past one hundred paces down any of them and they branch off a lot."

"Thank you, ma'am. We will be careful if we do." I looked at my women who were each staring back at me as if waiting for orders, and I smiled. "Let's sit down and rest until dinner first."

We found an empty patch of cave and the girls, and I sat while Cecil went into the back, grabbed a torch, and went on a walk down a dark cave with his wife.

I smiled at my girls as they left.

"I better go watch the entrance to the cave," I said. "I think she forgot to tell someone. You guys stay here, I can use some air, anyway."

Both girls kissed me on the cheek, and I went out to watch outside and get away from the smell.

CHAPTER 5

─── ◆ ───

ARGUMENTS

I stood at the entrance to the cave and took several deep breaths of the clean, cool air that was drifting in. I did not like how cramped the cave felt, and several of the people gave off a vibe that I did not like though I could not place as to why.

It might have been that several of the glares were just downright hostile.

My reprieve was short-lived when a tall and thin man came behind me. "Estelle said to take your place at the entrance so you can get off your feet and join the others for food."

I did not let my frustration show, but I turned to the man and nodded. "Thanks... uh, never got your name."

"Cain."

"Thanks, Cain."

He nodded and moved up to stand next to me, taking my place looking out through the leaves of the bushes that covered the entrance, apparently not wanting to talk to me.

I shrugged my shoulders at him and turned, going back into the cave and pondering what was setting everyone off against us.

Back inside the main entrance, I once again became the object of attention. Fifteen people I still didn't know sat in the large cave near my girls and Estelle. Each of them gave me various expressions of curiosity or dislike.

Cecil and Lea had not come back from their exploring deeper in the tunnels. So, I went over to the girls and sat next to them.

I at least got a smile from all three of them, which warmed my heart to the core. Although Tyla seemed more subdued than the others.

"What's wrong?" I asked her as I knelt by them.

"Just... it's nothing."

"Pretty sure it's not nothing, but I can wait till you're ready to tell me."

She nodded, and I placed my hand on her shoulder as I dropped back against the side of the cave to sit down next to the three beauties.

I glanced around the room one more time before I leaned close to them. "Why does everyone seem hostile?" I whispered.

"Master?" Tyla said, quickly glancing at the others spread throughout the room. The noise of other people talking and the fire in the center of the cave creating a din that hopefully masked our voices.

"You haven't noticed?" I asked.

She shrugged, looking around.

"I think, Love," Tasnia said, her volume matching mine. "That they disapprove of you having over one wife more than of us being new here. Estelle told us most of the women here are Chosen. They are probably used to it being the other way around and do not like change."

Diane stayed silent and just watched each of us as we spoke.

"I guess," I said. "Why are there so many women, though? I count eleven easily and only five men."

Tyla's shoulders slumped. "A few of them I have known came up to say hello to me. I believe most of their husbands had died in the battle or went with the survivors. Just before they fled, they heard that those entrenched in the Maetrine Fortress were begging to surrender but being refused. It is said they are letting them starve to death." Her eyes watered.

"Oh God, that's..." I paused. "What else?"

Tyla let go and tears rushed out of her eyes as a sob wracked her body. I wrapped her in a fierce embrace. Tas leaned over and did the same.

I placed my cheek on the top of her head as she cried. My face was now pointed directly at Diane, who looked out of place next to our affection. Casting glances elsewhere, as though uncomfortable.

"Tell me. Please, Tyla? It's obviously eating you up."

"My... My father... was the one... leading them." She managed to get out between sobs.

I squeezed my arms around her even tighter, Tasnia joining me. Her own tears joined Tyla's.

"I'm so sorry, Tyla. How far is this fortress?" My protective side reared its head as I was suddenly thinking of ways to get there and do something about it.

"No," she said, shaking her head. "The fortress is too far away, and the news is weeks old. They said the army outside was over ten thousand strong. I can't risk you for that. Even for my father... as much as I want to."

That was when it hit home.

She was right. The few of us could do nothing against a force like that. If it was an army, it probably had men, Chosen that were in thrall or sworn to a demigod, and then the demigods themselves.

I just wasn't strong enough to fight that yet. No matter how much my insides burst to do something to fix it.

I thought about my decision to go south and run, reconsidering if that was the right course of action.

A feeling came over me, one I recognized as the 'suggestions' Vex liked to use.

East...

That meant through the desert, but the feeling I was getting told me help would be there... and danger, too.

I sighed deeply. There was no helping this world as I was as that moment. I could not do my own thing and still hope to win. I needed the support of Vex and his backer, the Controller, if I were to have a chance. At least for the time being. That did not mean I had to play by their rules.

Or even like them very much.

I sat there with Tyla crying in my arms and Tasnia wrapped around both of us.

It was time to act. I couldn't confront the Demigods yet, not as I was at least. But I could start doing things that would lead me down that path.

As Estelle used a ladle to pour some of the venison soup into my wooden travel bowl and another in the bowl I had for Tyla, I smiled at her. "Thanks."

"You're welcome," she said as I turned to follow Tas with her two bowls back over to where we had been sitting.

Diane was almost pressed next to Tyla, away from all the others as much as she could be.

"Thank you, M..." Tyla caught herself with all the people around. "My love." She gripped the bowl in her hands and stared at it. Whether to let it cool or she was still deep in thought, I was not sure.

I blew on mine, when I judged it the right temperature, I took a sip. It was actually fantastic, considering it was mostly broth with a few chunks of deer meat. I could not name the spices, but it had a few vegetables in it that looked like carrots. Then there was the small brick of hard travel bread.

I doubt this would stop my hunger, which had been growing daily with all the physical activity I was doing, but I had a few items stashed in my bag that should help with that later.

"You should eat, you need to keep up your strength," Tasnia said to Tyla. She seemed shocked that a bowl was in her hands, and she took a sip of the broth.

Realizing she was hungry, she ate faster, and I smiled at Tasnia and mouthed, "Thank you."

She grinned back, then finished her own meager food.

"You folks doing okay over here?" Estelle said as she made her way over to our group after talking with a few others.

"Thank you, Estelle. It is quite good," Tasnia said around bites.

"Yes Ma'am, thank you," I said. "I am surprised it is so good with as little as you had to work with."

"Thank you, I was planning on being a cook at my family's restaurant before they found out I had powers. Wish we had more to give. But we make do with what we have, not what we want."

"Seems to be a popular profession, Cecil said he wanted to do the same in his youth," I said.

"I can out cook him any day," Estelle said, adding a wink at the end that made me laugh.

"You didn't come from a Chosen family?" Tasnia asked.

"No, child, I would not have called us poor, but we just ran a simple restaurant in the business district of Blackrun. Nothing special, but we were happy. I did not want to go into service to the Matriarch... That was your grandmother at the time, Tyla, some fifty years ago now."

This got a small smile out of her, at least.

Then I did the math and looked at her in shock. She did not look seventy, then I realized. "You have power over water?"

She nodded. "Yes, it helps keep you looking younger, and feeling it, too. Made most of my money after I did my service in healing and helping people keep their youth. That is until the past few months."

No one spoke for a minute as they all thought of their demons. Reminding me again of my need to do something about it.

"So, Orrick is?" I asked.

"Seventy-five," she said,

"Wow... oh, my manners. Would you join us?" I asked.

"Later maybe. I want to check on everyone. My children may be... gone, but I still have the instincts."

She drifted to the next group, engaging them in discussion, again reminding me of my grandmother when I was a kid.

"She is sweet, always has been since I was a little girl," Tyla said, her tone somber. "She was, at one point, a physician in my mother's house. She never went past the rank of Lady, but I think it was more because she cared little for the titles that were forced upon her. My mother once told me she was quite powerful in her day."

"Good to know. We should ask her if she would continue with your studies," I said.

Tyla nodded but said nothing.

After a few minutes, the sounds of people eating and talking died down as Lea and Estelle stood in front of the crowd. I noticed that just about everyone was back, including Orrick. Cain was the only one missing that I noticed...

"Alright folks, it's time to make some decisions," Estelle yelled out to the crowd.

"Gather around everyone," Estelle said to the group and as the people put away their eating utensils and moved into a circle by the fire.

I stood up first and held out my hands for the girls to get up, even Diane, as she stared at my hand as if it were going to bite me.

"He is safe," Tas whispered into her ear before walking past me to the fire with the others.

Diane stared at my hand for a while longer. I smiled at her in return and just held it there.

"It's just a sign of being polite where I am from," I finally said. "Means nothing more than that. However, you don't have to if you do not want to."

She decided and tentatively grasped my hand to let me pull her up. I nodded at her and turned to join the girls by the fire, Tyla and Tas having saved enough room between them for us to join.

I sat down and stared into the fire pit. It was mostly coals at this point, but I watched as someone put a fresh log on the fire and stirred up the coals so it would catch. The warmth was almost too much here as the bodies inside had warmed the cave enough that it was getting quite toasty. But at least the smell covered up the reek of unclean bodies, mostly.

I watched as the smoke from the fire traveled high into the ceiling, rising to the stalactites above us. The longest of them seemed to drop several feet but attached solidly enough to not make me worry about them falling.

The smoke did not build at the top like I expected either, so there had to be a natural escape for the air somewhere I could not see.

Estelle banged her staff on the ground three times, each one landing with a thump on the dirt floor, gaining attention.

"I call this a forum of the Chosen who are present. As the eldest, I will lead. Do we have any who would challenge this?"

I was curious what this was as I looked around at the various women. Not all of them seemed exactly happy with her being in charge, but I did not see a challenge coming from any.

Tyla leaned over to whisper in my ear. "The forum is a traditional meeting of the Chosen. Lead by the senior most amongst us. It's not really about power, as they by tradition do not take sides, it's about keeping the meeting on track and forming a consensus."

I bowed my head in understanding.

"No challenge has been heard, so I will lead," Estelle continued. "We have accomplished the task we have previously agreed to. We are now joined by Mistress Tyla, daughter of the... Former Matriarch of Blackrun," Estelle said, stumbling over those words before she recovered, "and her companions. We have seen a lot of change lately, including the fact that they have turned our Matriarch into a puppet of the Demigods. I am sorry for your loss, Tyla, and welcome to you and your friends."

"Thank you, Lady Estelle," Tyla said through a sniffle that overtook her. "We appreciate your hospitality during these dark times. I hope that someday I can free my mother from her... enslavement."

Estelle nodded but did not comment further. "We have gathered now to discuss our next options. Rivenhold will soon fall, Tyla's group brought word that the condition there has gotten worse. This information was also witnessed by Cecil who was with them. We will not find refuge behind its walls and must flee further away from the threats the Demigods present to us. Or they will do to us what almost happened before Stern freed us from captivity."

The crowd murmured its assent at this, one woman raising her hand.

"Yes Madzia?" Estelle said.

A short, solidly built, tan skinned woman stood, bowing her head slightly at Estelle before glancing around at the crowd.

"I move that we head south. The barbarian tribes have no love for the Demigods, and they may provide us some protection against them. We can hide in their lands and bide our time to hopefully rebuild, or at least survive with our freedom still intact."

Lea, who had been sitting near us, stood, raising her hand. "I would like a rebuttal, Lady Estelle."

"Granted."

Lea stared at Madzia. "You know, as does everyone here, that the Barbarians also have no love for any Chosen in the Matriarchies. Descendants from the great rebellion, they also have a long memory. They would enslave us like they do their own women and use us to fight the Demigods for them. You are asking us to give up one slavery for another."

"What would you have us do?" Madzia countered, a smirk on her face forming as if she knew exactly what she would say.

"East, of course. The rumors of the other noble races fleeing that direction are a legitimate opportunity for us to join them and possibly turn the tide. Or, as you say, hide and survive. It would be difficult for Seir and his armies to march across the desert."

"Rumors," Madzia said with a scoff. "You are talking about traveling through a land with wild and magical beasts, with no force of men to buffer us against them. Hoping to find a land of beings that we do not know exists. That is suicide and stupidity rolled into one."

"Even if the rumors are untrue, there are no known hostile nations there to give up our freedoms to. It gives us a chance."

"With much higher risk and no resources with which to rebuild if you are wrong." Madzia countered.

Almost all the women slapped their hands against their thighs in a repeating sound. Each of them nodded as they did, showing support for Madzia's argument. This was not going well for Lea.

"Only if the rumors are untrue," Lea said, though based on her expression she knew she had lost this round.

None of the women present agreed. Silence governing the group after her response.

"Ladies, let's be civil," Estelle said.

Lea sighed. "Fine then, I can see what the majority wants." She sat down next to her husband.

I stood up and raised my hand. This resulted in the entire crowd looking at me as if I had kicked their puppies in front of them.

"Men have no voice in a forum," Madzia said, almost spitting the words out in her derision.

I hate people like that.

"Look, I'll be honest. I don't care much about your rules. All voices should matter, man or woman alike."

"Derk, please sit," Estelle said, though she did not put any command behind the voice.

"Lady Estelle, I don't mean to be disrespectful to you or your customs, but I am not originally from your lands. Where I come from, everyone has a voice. That may not have always been the case in its history, but things worked much better when they were equal amongst all."

"Sit down!" Madzia commanded.

"Look lady, I'll say my words, then leave. I am not here to argue with you. My girls and I are going east." I pointed at the three sitting next to me. "I can't explain how I know this, but there is something there that may help us. But where you go is your choice. If any of you want to join us, meet us outside the cave at first light. I sure as hell am not staying here tonight."

I turned and stormed over to our gear and started picking it up. Tyla, Tas, and Diane followed me without question. Most of the crowd just looked at us in shock, unable to speak.

Except for Lea, who had a smirk on her face as I glanced one more time at the crowd, and I could have sworn I saw one on Estelle as well before she masked her features again.

Nobody said a word as we went for the entrance to the cavern. "First light," I called behind me as we left the cave of the thousand hideous smells for the forest outside.

We passed a surprised Cain and proceeded deeper into the woods in the darkness.

"Let's set up the tent tonight. I already feel less claustrophobic out here."

"Yes, Master," Tyla said, as she reached for and grabbed my hand, slowing me down from my speed walk.

"I agree with you, Love." Tasnia grabbed my other hand. Diane walked quickly right behind the three of us to keep up.

I took a deep breath as I slowed, glad for the fresh air, as we made our way to a nearby clearing that we had seen earlier.

CHAPTER 6

— • —

ASSASSINATION

We walked from the refugee cave in silence, finally finding the clearing we wanted. The darkness, pierced only by the light of the full moon, did not impede our efforts as we unpacked our gear and the girls set up the tent.

Diane seemed almost as enthusiastic as me about getting out of the cave and back into nature. She removed the pinecones and rocks from where we planned on setting up, singing a song that seemed alien to me.

Guess that world magic only did so much, music wasn't in its repertoire.

"It's not worth making a fire at this point, let's get set up and you girls get some sleep. I'll take the first watch."

"You can wake me up next, Master," Tyla said.

"Thanks. You want the next one, Tas?"

Tas stifled a yawn as she nodded at me.

"Okay, then I can do a double in the morning."

"D... Derrick?" Diane said timidly.

Her use of my given name surprised me. "You can call me Derk."

"Derk," she said, as if trying out a strange word. "I can stand a watch as well. I want to help."

I glanced at Tyla and Tas. "What do you think?"

"She is ready. I trust her," Tyla said then walked up behind Diane and placed a supportive hand on her shoulder.

It was hard to tell in the darkness, but I thought I saw Diane turn a little pink at the praise.

"Tas?"

"I agree. I know it's only been a couple of days, but I think she will fit right in with us. We should show her trust and see how it develops."

Tas raised her eyebrow at me, and I couldn't help but get her double meaning.

I shook my head no at her, but I still chuckled enough that it did not hold any bite. It's not that I was opposed, I just did not know how mentally healthy she was. Until I did, that was a hard pass for now. I needed to talk to them about that in private at some point.

If and when that opportunity presented itself.

"Okay Diane. Last watch, you can wake us up when the sky begins to brighten."

I took out my water bladder and took a long pull on it. The water felt good after the stuffy confines of the cave.

"Derk?" Diane whispered as she cocked her head at an awkward angle. Reminding me she was not human. "Someone approaches."

Without questioning her, we backed into the shadows under the trees. Getting into the darkness to see who was approaching.

I turned to where she pointed, in the cave's direction we had left behind, and listened for what her obviously sharper hearing picked up. Finally, I heard the break of a twig, followed by the outline of two individuals walking towards us.

I dropped my water bladder on the ground and silently pulled my great sword out of its scabbard. Tas pulled her saber out and stood in front of Diane. All in less than a heartbeat or two.

Tyla took two steps behind and away from us, lifting her hands, a hint of a bluish sparkling aura dancing from her fingers as she prepared for a fight. Barely enough for me to see even in such proximity to it. So, I doubt the approaching individuals would see it, but I was proud of her for distancing herself in case a hidden sniper saw the dim light. Even if I did not like the fact that she was making herself a target and getting away from the protection I could provide.

"Tyla, it's me, Lea, with Estelle," a voice called out.

I relaxed and put my sword away while everyone else in my small group relaxed.

"Over here Lea," I called into the darkness, stepping back into the clearing and into the moonlight.

The two women approached our camp, and soon I could make out their faces.

"Sorry to sneak up on you like this," Lea said as she walked within a few feet of us, looking at Tyla.

"Don't worry about it," I said, stepping forward. "What can we do for you?"

Lea looked from Tyla to me, raising her eyebrow. "I... sorry, still not used to your strange dynamic. I wanted to tell you about the meeting after you left and ask a favor."

"What dynamic?" Estelle asked, confused.

"Oh..." Lea said with surprise.

"Like I said before, I am not from here. We are an equal partnership here, man or woman. It doesn't matter," I said.

"Oh, that doesn't bother me." She waved her hands in a throw away motion. "We had to keep up pretenses for years, but Orrick and I are partners too. We listen to each other and each share in the decision. I've never been with another man either. One is good enough for me, and I never needed a harem."

"Thank you, Estelle," I said. "Go ahead, Lea."

"After you left, the vote was almost unanimous. I was the only one that wanted to go with you. Madzia had them fired up against it. She also thought you were a threat and that we should capture or kill you and force the girls to go with us."

"That would be a mistake," I said, fire in my eyes they could probably see in the darkness.

"We talked her out of it," Estelle said soothingly. "No one else will go that far. Mind you, she's still upset that they killed both her husbands in the fighting. So, give her a bit of grace when you judge her for her anger. A lot of them are incredibly angry and lack trust in men after how they treated us."

"It's human nature to get revenge for perceived slights. The men that side with Seir probably think their hatred is justified, too. Look, I like and respect you both in my limited interactions, but I just don't see how it's my fault."

"Honestly, I am not sure why Madzia and the others dislike you either," Lea said. "She has just been bitter since the rescue. I never even saw her in the academy where they had us prisoner, so I do not know what was done to her or the hardships she faced."

That concerned me, but before I could ask, Lea changed topics.

"My point being, Estelle and I talked. We think we want to go with you tomorrow."

"What about the forum vote? What was your choice, Estelle?"

"As the elder, I could not vote... But the old ways are gone. At least for now," Estelle said. "While I filled the role, do not think for one moment I have ever been married to tradition."

I smiled at Estelle. Yup, proper in public, but the same rebellious side as my Grams, too. "I would welcome both you and your husbands to join us." I focused back on Lea. "And the favor?"

"Can I tell Estelle what you told me?"

I thought about it for a second. "When we leave the others, I will consider it. Not before."

"Don't talk about me like I am not here, young man," Estelle said. "I don't know what has Lea so tight-lipped, but I honestly don't care much either. I'm too damn old to be that nosy. I am going east because I actually believe the other races fled there. Without the group, I would not risk it, but with Lea, Cecil, and you four, I think we have a chance of making it."

I laughed at her use of the term too old. I always thought the older the woman, the nosier they became. Guess she had some difference with my grams after all. I know for a fact she would be snooping till she figured it all out, and if she couldn't, she would probably make it up and spread it as truth.

Lea sighed. "Yes, Aunt Estelle."

"You guys are related?"

"She is my sister's grand brat. The worst of the bunch, too."

"I am also your favorite."

"Bah," Estelle said, but I could see her smile.

"Okay, let's get back before they come looking for us."

Estelle walked over and gave Tyla a hug. "Are you happy with him, Tyla?"

"More than I have ever been," Tyla said smiling.

"Good. You ladies have a good night. Orrick will range about later tonight, but I'll make sure he keeps an eye out."

"Sounds good. Thank you," I said.

We watched them walk away, and soon they were out of sight before we whispered.

"What do you think, Master?"

"I like them both. I trust Cecil and Orrick seems okay. Good to have with us on our journey... I hope."

"I agree," Tasnia said.

"What do you think, Diane?" I asked.

"Huh? Um..."

"I want you to feel included. That means your opinion matters too. Feel free to pass on answering this time, but I expect you to speak up in the future."

"Y... yes Derk."

"You girls get ready for bed. I'm going to clean up and walk the perimeter."

I kissed Tyla and Tasnia goodnight and waved at Diane as they stepped into the Tent. She stopped at the entrance and hesitated.

"Derk?" Diane asked.

"Yes?"

She looked at the ground when my eyes went to her.

"N... nothing."

"Diane, no matter what it is." I walked up to her, not touching her but putting my head down so it was in her line of sight. "You can tell me without fear. I will never judge you or tell you those things have no merit. Okay?"

She nodded. "It... it was probably nothing, I just felt something... odd while you were talking and not sure if I should say anything."

"Could you be more specific?"

"No... something just felt out of place, like a haze in the corner of my eyes. I thought I saw someone standing near you, but it was gone in an instant."

"Hmmm," I said. "Not sure what that is, but it could be anything. I will keep an eye out just in case."

"Th-thank you," she stammered.

"Hey, it's fine. Thank you for trusting me."

She smiled and went into the tent with the girls.

"I told you he would treat you well..." I heard Tyla whisper before I walked out of range.

I went over and picked up my water bladder from the ground where I tossed it earlier. The cap did not sit correctly and had leaked a little of the water.

"Huh, good thing we can produce our own water in the desert if that keeps coming loose," I said to myself. I took a long drink of water and attached it to my harness. Then I started making my rounds of the camp.

I did another round of the camp to stay awake, my exhaustion from the day of moving and my dealings with the refugees taking its toll and I was sluggish.

I stopped briefly by the tent. The occupants were quiet other than the light sounds of snores I heard from them.

A smile crested my face as I considered how lucky I was to have them in my life now. I never had to worry about being alone again here on this world. The stress of losing Jessica back on Earth had eaten away at me before I had come here. The feeling of being whole once again lifted a great weight from me. The fact that there were two women in my life who loved each other as much as me only made it better.

I considered what I had endured to get here. A life nearly ruined on earth when I was dropped unexpectedly from the colony project. The wormhole collapsing followed by an alien invasion destroying everything I knew. Not to mention my first day on this planet in a body that was not mine originally.

Part of me still hated the Roxannez for what they did, but at the same time, I was not sure I would change it now that I considered all that I had gained.

But I was sure as shit not going to tell Vex about that.

I loved Tyla and Tas, knowing beyond a shadow of a doubt that it was not some alien mind fuck doing this to me. I could feel it in my bones now that I knew the difference between what they artificially did, and what I really felt now.

I realized I had stopped moving and my eyes started closing, my thoughts drifting rapidly from memory to memory. So, I shook my head to wake back up and got moving again. I had not had this much trouble staying awake since my first day of boot camp in the Marines back on Earth.

I slowly meandered around the camp, occasionally stopping and jumping in place to keep the blood flowing. All the old tricks I learned to stay awake. They were not helping me now, though, and I wished once again that I had coffee.

Snap

A noise in the distance made me go to alert. I gazed at the direction the noise came from but could see nothing. As I tried to focus and cast my senses out into the woods, my eyes wanted to close themselves despite my best efforts.

This is... odd.

My thoughts were becoming muddled, almost like I had been drinking heavily.

The world even started the spin it does when you drink too much alcohol and hit that point past the buzz and into a severe drunken state. Something was very wrong.

Fear shot through my body, the pump of adrenalin helping me for a short time to regain my senses. I could not close my eyes to focus, that was too dangerous right now, but I tried to reach down deep into my core for the healing ability that Tas gave me.

I struggled to find the problem, searching... feeling inside my body for something that was causing this. I ended up dropping to a knee to keep balance, as my feet became wobbly. I used what little focus I had left to find what was affecting me.

Some kind of poison. My mental image of my blood stream showed me a red glowing substance coursing its way through my veins and spreading rapidly. I did not know what it was, but I applied the water element to purify it from my body.

This slowed the spread, but the problem I faced was that I couldn't remove it fast enough.

It was overwhelming my system, and against my will, my eyes closed yet again. I struggled with all my might to open them again just in time to see the ground rushing at my face as I collapsed forward.

I heard the thump as my face struck the ground. The pain I should have felt was dulled, but I clearly heard the crack as my nose hit the dirt. I could taste and smell the grass and soil entering my half-open mouth, and I could not move my numbed tongue enough to eject it.

I tried to call for help, but my voice would not work. My body was getting harder and harder to move, and my arms barely responded.

I used the last of my strength to flip my head to the side, a monumental accomplishment in my current state. My eyes had stopped trying to close at least, but that was not necessarily a good thing. It was as though they were frozen in place, and I could not close them if I wanted to. I could see the forest in front of me, noticing I was now facing away from the tent the girls were sleeping in.

I tried to fight to get my willpower back under control in one last attempt to get this poison out of my system before it was too late. I found the glowing red substance again and began working slowly to clear it. This time focusing on my head to clear my thoughts.

A flash of movement in the forest distracted me, I could see an outline of a woman stalking towards me. It solidified into the face of someone I recognized, showing me a chilling image of Madzia holding a large dagger in her hands, smiling wickedly at me.

Then she disappeared again, vanishing right in front of me like she was holding the shadows mantel.

Fuck!

I redoubled my efforts, the fear of helplessness threatening to subdue me, but I could not afford to give in to the sensation or I would be dead.

"Nooooo!" screamed a woman's voice and a flash of light filled the clearing we were in. A shadowy visage of Madzia became visible again directly above me, the dagger ready to strike.

Then a flash of pink hair slammed into Madzia and brought her to the ground. The impact made her fully visible once more.

More sounds came as my girls rushed out of the tent. All I could do was watch as Diane pummeled the woman who a moment before, was about to end me with a dagger to the heart.

Diane punched and kicked and displayed a savagery that I did not know she was capable of as she beat the solidly built Madzia to the ground.

I felt a hand on my face and another on my chest, a cool tingling sensation ran through my body. Tyla pumped all the power at her disposal into me to combat the poison wreaking havoc on my body.

Still unable to move, I watched as Tasnia pulled Diane off the now bloody and broken woman off the ground. Tas's own face was a mixture of concern and anger. Diane resisted at first as she continued to desperately punch and kick several more times before she finally let Tas pull her away.

Finally, Diane relented, allowing Tasnia to pull her up and spin her away from the mess she left of Madzia. However, just as I thought it was over, Tas spun once and kicked the unconscious woman in the side. "Bitch!" Tas cried out and tears sprung forth from her face as she backed away and came over to hover over me.

"Here," Tyla said through clenched teeth, as one of her hands left my body, the other still on my head. I heard her rustling around inside of something but could not see what it was. Finally, she handed Tasnia a leather strap. "Use this."

The power collar. I didn't even realize we had kept it.

"Put this on her, then bind her wrists and feet." Tyla commanded as she put her other hand back on me and continued to fight off the poison.

"Okay." Tasnia said and went to the woman and fastened it around her neck.

I could feel that the effects of the poison were lessening, but I could not get myself to move.

"Diane, watch her while I get something to bind her with." Tas said.

Diane was sitting on her butt, huddled in a ball as she cried. She looked up at Tasnia and nodded and stood over her. The anger returned to her tear-streaked face.

"Don't harm her yet." Tyla said through clenched teeth. "We need answers. Remember, only Tas can give her order's since it was she who placed the collar."

Diane slowly nodded her head as she stared down at the woman, who did not move in the slightest. She just kind of laid there bleeding.

It took a few minutes before I could even clear my thoughts enough to help Tyla with my own power.

"Master, this is Vescallum poison. It is very tenacious. It will take some time to remove. Help me as much as you can now that you are able."

I tried to nod, feeling a slight motion in my head, but not much else.

Frustration at my uselessness made me lose focus on the healing for a moment before I redoubled my efforts to combat the poison. Finally getting my way back to the mental image of my body. I saw the red glow again and saw what Tyla was doing to fight it.

She had created a filter in my bloodstream right before the blood entered my heart. She attacked the substances there, removing the majority before it could travel back out into the rest of my body. I realized that was what I should have done from the beginning, rather than focus on my head like I did. So, I did the same, focusing on what was leaving, getting the poison that Tyla could not, and clearing the blood as it flowed back into the cells.

"I have already removed it from your stomach, we just need to cleanse the blood now." Tyla said.

I finally could close my eyes just as Tas began tying Madzia up with leather cords she found. Trying my best to tune out all distractions as I worked with Tyla to fix my body.

Sounds of people entering the clearing threatened to undo that focus, but I persevered this time.

"Come no further!" Tasnia said. Even with my eyes closed, I could see the bright orange red light as she summoned her powers.

"What happened?" I heard from a voice I recognized as Cecil.

I stopped listening further, trusting that Cecil was not there to kill me too, ignoring the heated exchange to focus on healing.

In degrees, we slowly made progress. Finally, the poison filtered out of my body so that I could move my extremities. As I finished the last, Tyla focused on getting my cells back to working order.

After a few more minutes of effort, my body was exhausted, and brain felt fried. I gave into sleep right there on the ground rather than getting up.

I came to sometime later; It was still dark, so I hoped it was only a couple of hours, and not a day that I lost. I was on the bedroll in our tent with Tyla on her knees leaning over me, smiling at me from a few inches away. Part of me noticed the dip in her shirt and the tops of her perky breasts on full display. So that was a good sign for my prognosis.

"Master, I am so glad you are awake... I can see parts of you are feeling better," she said as she tilted her head down at my crotch. Her hand coming up and gently cupping my rising manhood. "Yes, healing nicely."

"What happened?"

"She filled your water bladder with a Vescallum. It's a nasty drug humans got from the elves when we first arrived on this world. It is actually a medicine for surgery, commonly used when a town is too small to have a Chosen with the water ability and must do normal surgery."

"I... could not move and the feeling went away in my body before I knew it. Never even saw it coming."

She nodded, massaging the bulge in my pants. I groaned, almost giving into it before reaching down to stop her. "It's probably not a good idea to do that right now."

She pouted. "Probably right, later then." She kissed my lips quickly and patted my shaft, as if promising it she would deliver it the attention it deserved.

"Tell me about the poison," I finally said.

"It is a pain suppressant and immobilizer. Its key problem was that it took an hour to get to work. Which is why it became used as an assassination drug more than a medicine. Given before someone's bath and they drown or something similar. It's banned in most of the civilized communities."

I nodded. "Yeah, that seems a very human thing to do. Find a way to turn everything into a means to kill one another or end your rivals."

I got up slowly, my body still a little sore, but not as bad as I expected.

"I healed most of you, Master, but I did not want to use up all my power. It took... quite a bit of my energy to get that poison out of you."

"It's fine Tyla. I know you did your best. I am both thankful and proud of you."

I closed my eyes, the mental image of my body coming much easier now that I wasn't succumbing to the Vescallum.

I used my power and healed the sore muscles and the last of the swelling on my forehead and the bruise on my nose caused by the fall.

"Do you still have the water bladder with the poison in it?"

"Yes, it's right there." She pointed at it lying in the corner.

"Where are the others?" I asked, getting up and moving over to the bag of water. I picked it up and extended my senses into the bag.

"Outside, they took Madzia back to the cave, bound and tied. They promised to watch her when she woke up. She was... unconscious when Diane was done with her. Marylyn healed her. No one knows why she did it."

I nodded, keeping my focus. I finally saw it. When I extended my senses into the bag, I saw the red glow infecting the water now like what I saw in my body last night.

I set the bag down, stepping away from it, trying to get my senses to reach into the bag from a distance. However, it didn't work.

"Going to have to remember to check everything before I eat or drink it now."

"What do you mean, Master?"

"Huh? Oh, I can push out into the bag when I touch it like I can inside my body. I can see the poison in it now that I know to look for it. Can you do that?"

"Yes, I can sense into the water, but I never considered looking for poisons before... but now that you mention it, I think my mother's food testers did that for her."

"That should keep that from happening again, I hope. As long as I remember to check. Going to practice on other things to be sure it all looks the same, or similar, though. Who is Marylyn?"

"One of the water chosen in the group."

I nodded. Not sure who it was. "Tas and Diane?"

"Outside the tent with Lea and Estelle."

"Let's go." I started but stopped.

Turning to Tyla, I encased her in a hug, holding her tight before leaning down and giving her a long and deep kiss.

She returned it with passion, her arms going up and down my body, pressing against me tightly. I groaned as she rubbed up against me, my manhood going back to full mast once again as I considered changing my mind about taking the beautiful black-haired woman in front of me here and now.

"Derk?" Lea called from outside the tent. "Diane said you were awake but wanted me to give you a minute. I would like to talk to you sooner than later though."

I took a deep breath and sighed. Moving away from the tempting woman before me and we smiled as we looked into each other's eyes. "Thank you for helping me. Rain check?"

"What is that?" she asked playfully.

"Uh... never mind. How about until later, then?"

"You have no idea how much I am looking forward to this... rain check then."

My little brain screamed for me to forget Lea and get to work, but instead we walked through the tent opening and greeted the pink morning light just before dawn. It disappointed me we were not leaving as intended, but no plan survives first contact with reality.

I let it go, we needed to adapt and overcome it. Instead walking over to Tas, kissing her on the lips deeply and giving her a hug.

"Thank you," I said after the kiss, looking into her eyes.

She nodded. "I... feel almost like we let it happen. We should have... I don't know. Stopped her somehow."

"She slipped by us all. Well, Diane warned me she felt something off, but I never expected it either. It's not your fault. We live, we learn, we grow. Okay?"

She nodded, tears threatening to come out once again.

I hugged her tightly. "It will be okay. I love you."

We squeezed tightly one more time and then I let her go, walked right past Lea and Estelle without acknowledging them. Stopping, right in front of the pink haired young woman sitting on a tree stump looking miserable.

I picked her up under the armpits and lifted her up to me. Giving her a great bear hug, twirling her once, then set her down, kissing her on the top of the head.

"Thank you." I said when she squeaked in response. "I owe you my life and I won't forget it."

She turned a bright pink from the attention and couldn't speak, just giving me another squeak and an embarrassed smile.

"You are welcome with us. Always. For as long as you want," I said, leaning over so our eyes were even as I stared into her pretty bluish gray orbs.

I wanted her to know that I meant every word of what I was saying.

She nodded, tears forming. I reached out and patted her on the shoulder, squeezing it once. Giving her one more smile before turning away and facing Lea and Estelle.

"Okay, your turn. What happened?" I asked.

"Orrick saw the flash of light, woke us and we raced over. Everyone is back at the cave now."

I nodded. "Where did the light come from?"

Tyla smirked and pointed at Diane. I faced the woman and the pinkness she had on her face easily tripled in intensity. It was an odd color, not a reddish hue like a human, matching her hair in a way that made me think of cotton candy.

"Well done, I doubly owe you then." I said to her, then faced away. Figuring she was getting enough attention, I walked to the other side of the group from her. This way, they were looking at me and not her.

"What do you plan to do?" I asked.

Lea sighed. "I don't know. It's not like Madzia, she had been different lately, but we assumed it was stress."

"Think one of the Demigods bound her to them?"

Estelle shrugged her shoulders. "We have no exact way of finding out. We believe you can sense it if you are strong enough in water, but I have not experienced it myself."

Lea gave me a look. I turned towards Tyla, and Tasnia and they both nodded at me.

Sighing, I decided to add another to the circle of trust, not the timing I wanted, but you had to learn to take a chance on people sometimes.

"I... might have a way."

"How?" Estelle asked.

"What Lea wanted me to tell you about. I am going to trust you because I have an idea and will need your help to get the others to allow it, I think."

Estelle looked at Lea in confusion.

"I have not seen it. He only told me about it yesterday, but Cecil trusts him so don't overreact to it." Lea said.

"You better tell me what's going on right now, young man."

"Brace yourself, Estelle," I began, taking a deep breath to tell my story again. "I have the same powers as a Demigod."

She gasped, putting her hand to her chest. Lea came up to her side to brace her. "It's alright Aunt Estelle, let him finish."

So, I told her my story. Well, most of my story.

CHAPTER 7

QUESTIONS

We walked into the cave entrance, all five of us in a single line. Estelle leading, with Lea right behind her. I followed with Tyla, Diane, and Tas bringing up the rear.

Overall, the conversation went well. Estelle's shock was quickly replaced with concern, but she was giving me a small amount of trust that I would not be like the Demigods she knew.

It was a start.

The problem was that I realized that my desire to trust humanity was going to lead to an increased risk of this happening again in the future. I wanted to be different from the Demigods, I really did. But I also would never win if I blindly trusted everyone around me. I could almost hear Vex laughing at me from whatever place he chose to be when he wasn't giving me problems.

Fuck you, Vex.

I needed to decide whether I was going to use these powers to bind those around me or not with oaths like Stern. I doubt it would have changed anything here, none of them would have followed me just walking into the cave as I did. But maybe there was a way to get an oath, without taking advantage of people like the Demigods did. I would have to think more on this later, I had things to focus on now.

We entered the cavern they were using as a living space carrying all our gear, having broken down our camp so that we could depart as soon as we finished here.

A woman from inside walked up to Estelle. "She is still sleeping. I healed her as much as I could. We don't know what to do next though."

"Thank you, Marylyn," Estelle said. Marylyn was hefty with a caramel-colored skin. I would not call her fat, just well-built and large, even if she was shorter than most women. It almost made her look like what I always figured dwarf would look like. Short and wide. I wonder what a real dwarf looked like and if I would ever get a chance to see one.

"We will attempt to question her," Estelle said. "I will bring Lea, Tyla, and her companions with me. Derk has the right under matriarchal law to question his attacker, make sure we are not disturbed."

"Yes, Lady Estelle."

"Would you like us to accompany you?" Cecil asked, walking up to us with Orrick in tow.

"No," Lea said. "But thank you, husband. Keep us from being disturbed, though, if you would."

Both men nodded, and we continued past the others who just sat around the cave. It bothered me that none of them had prepared to leave like we had discussed. Almost all of them had their gear unpacked and laid out like they were going to stay another night.

If they came with us, we needed to change things.

We grabbed a couple of makeshift torches and lit them in the still going fire. The smell of smoke actually makes the cave smell better. If they did not have so many with the water element, I would be concerned about disease rearing its ugly head in here.

We continued down one of the cave offshoots, its path marked with white marks made in the wall, until we reached the end. Cain was standing over the motionless Madzia, his arms crossed and facing her.

"I have this for now, Cain," Estelle said. "We will call for you when we are finished questioning her."

The man nodded and silently stalked off. Not a word spoken the entire time. Maybe he was just quiet and did not hate me? Probably a bit of both if I was being honest.

"Do you want to wait for her to awaken? Or would you like to wake her?" Estelle asked.

I glanced down at the woman. Her body was still, her breathing steady, the perfect representation of what we think someone asleep should look like.

"She's awake. Probably waiting for Cain to drop his guard," I said.

"How can you be sure?" Lea asked.

"Can't really, I guess," I said with a smile, "but I'll just stick her with this torch. If she jumps before it burns the shit out of her, then we know."

I went up to the woman, holding a torch in my hand and lifted the empty one in her direction, my senses now tuned to look for things odd about her. When I got within arm's length, I could see a strange energy coming off her. Kind of like the haze you see on a hot day when staring into the distance, there... yet not.

It seemed dark and foreboding if I were to describe it. Something just like an egotistical, self-obsessed being that lived too many lifetimes wanting for nothing would do to someone.

I poked her bare arm with my finger, careful to keep my distance. She flashed the yellow that showed she was empowered with the power of light. At least with my minimum experience of witnessing it. But it was much different than Diane's. As the aura around her glowed, it seemed muted, with dark lines that reminded me of a spider web streaked throughout. The feeling I got reminded me of my encounter with Stern, but much more powerful.

My experience with bound women was Susan, and those that followed Albris. But each of them was either dead, or I was actively fighting them before I really had a chance to examine how they would react to me. So, I never noticed how they reacted to my touch before.

But I was sure that the woman in front of me was bound to a Demigod. I knew it in my soul to be true.

I dropped my hand and slowly reached the torch out to her arm.

"Derk..." Estelle began, but Tyla shushed her.

Just as the fire was about to touch her arm, right about the point that the heat could be felt, Madzia pulled it away and rolled to her side.

"See," I said. "Awake. She is also bound. I can feel it on her."

The woman sat up. Her mostly healed face had an angry expression. "Masaki will kill you all when he arrives."

"Who's Masaki?" I asked.

"My Lord and Master," she replied, pushing herself up to the back of the cave abruptly, like she was about to stand up. She reached for her collar and just as she touched it, pain wracked her body as she let out a scream.

"That was stupid, Madzia," Lea said. "You know, removing those collars equals pain."

She hunched over as the pain stopped and took several deep breaths. While I hated the idea of the collar, they had a useful purpose. Another thing I was going to have to come to terms with. Just because it seems wrong to me doesn't mean it isn't necessary. I needed to alter my perceptions of right and wrong in order to succeed here. Just another thing added to my to do list.

"How long have you been... in service to Masaki?" I asked.

She recovered and looked up at me, staring at me rather than answering. I doubted she was going to tell me anything. These bonds were too powerful.

I asked a few more questions as she sat there seething, not saying a word to any of them.

I blew out a breath in frustration, turned, and faced the group. "Lea, a word?"

Lea joined me on the far side of the small cavern.

"Can you explain to me how your power over wind works?" I asked. "Tyla mentioned something about a sound barrier or something?"

"Yes, I can create pockets of air that keep sound from traveling. Why?"

"Good, I am going to try something. It's going to take a lot of my power and still may not work. It is going to cause her a tremendous amount of pain, and I don't want the others to come in when she screams. Can you set one up?"

She studied me for a second. I had not explained that I had the power to break bonds yet, for a few reasons, but mostly I had never proved I could do it. I did not want to set up a false sense of hope until I was sure. This seemed like a good chance to test it out.

That, and I needed to help if I could.

"What do you hope to do?"

"Help her, I hope. Let me see if it works before I tell you the details. I just need you to trust me a little more."

Lea glanced at Madzia then at me. "Okay... She is no longer the Madzia I knew, but I still care for her. If you harm her permanently..."

"Won't be permanent... at least it shouldn't. I actually hope to fix some of the damage they caused her. It is painful, but it is also up to her whether it works. She has to be willing."

"Fine. If you can help her..." Lea trailed off as she raised up her hands and faced the cave opening. The very air became visible for a second as she created a barrier over the entire opening. A line of sweat came down her temple. "I can hold this for a while, but hurry just to be safe."

Nodding, I turned to Madzia, who had been watching me the whole time. A scowl on her face that let me know what she thought of me.

That would change in a minute, or so I hoped.

Rather than play it out, I rushed forward to surprise her. I gripped her bound hands with one of mine and tore the collar off, not sure if it would hinder my attempts or not.

I threw it to the side and placed another hand on the top of her head and pressed my power into her. I heard a concerned scream from Estelle as she was restrained by my girls. I focused on Madzia as we sunk together into my inner Sanctum.

A flash and I found myself back in the room of darkness, my vision only taking a second to get used to the new surroundings.

"Where... where am I?" she asked, looking around? She tried to move but couldn't. She found herself covered in glowing bands that prevented her from moving even an inch as she struggled against them.

"My world Madzia. My rules. I have you immobilized for now. I am going to give you the chance to be free." I left out the part where it was more of a hope.

I walked around her and studied this version of Madzia. She had thick chains covering her body underneath my own bands. I could see a thick rope of power coming out of her core and going out into the starry void that surrounded my sanctum, escaping through the black nothingness beyond. I wasn't sure if I should be concerned with that or not. Could that give one of the Demigods access to my sanctum?

No sense in worrying about it now, let's focus on the poor woman in front of me.

Her body battered and her face bruised, she reminded me of the severe abuse victims that I encountered in Boston when I was a cop. She had the same look on her face as those who would not want to press charges, even if they were bleeding in the back of an ambulance, against those that harmed them.

I always hated that part of the job, not being able to do anything because of the constraints placed upon me.

I let a small smile form on my lips. Those constraints were no longer a factor in limiting what I could do. I could help here in ways that I could never help back on Earth.

But this is what it looked like to be bound to a Demigod against your will. It disgusted me that a race of advanced beings would allow a travesty such as this to occur. They made themselves feel better by making it a choice of free will, but someone could always trick people into making poor choices.

I hated them all.

Then I froze, a brighter thought wondering what Tyla and Tas would look like here. If I could experiment and bring their physical forms here, I might be able to see if it was truly their choice or not. Maybe I could do nothing for Tyla, that chance had passed, but I could release Tasnia if she looked even remotely like this woman before me here.

People always seem to forget that when they got power, others around them were affected by it. When you think of yourself as the center of the universe and consider everyone around you as objects, you can damage them in unintended ways. Even though I could release any woman I bound to myself, the potential for them to end up like Madzia was more than I was willing to pay.

It had to be an honest choice, made with full understanding of what was happening for it to be okay. I could live with binding women to my soul, but not like this woman in front of me.

"What do you mean, release me?" she asked after a moment's thought, for a brief second. Hope showed on her face, quickly followed by pain. She was obviously still connected to her master even here.

"You will see in a second. But I warn you, this is going to hurt."

I reached forward and grabbed the chains that bound her. My hand passed through my own bindings as if they were not even there. I forced my will into them to break them apart.

Power surged through me as I put all I had into it.

I felt them unraveling, the links breaking, and joy flooded into me at my instant success. But something sensed me, and soon I felt another power push in through the connection that was feeding off her in an attempt to reinforce her bindings.

I stumbled, dropping to one knee, not able to counter the increasing amounts of power from whatever was repelling me. I knew then that I would not win this fight. I was not ready for this, and it was becoming clear that I had made a mistake in the attempt when I had no idea what I was doing.

I vaguely heard Madzia's scream coming from the real world. However, my own ragged voice started joining in as well in its own scream. The pain reverberated inside me as I struggled against the hold over her very soul as my bindings began to unravel with all my focus going into fighting against whatever I was battling.

Just as I was about to give up, a new source of energy joined my own, matching the force that was resisting. I was no longer losing ground, and it momentarily confused me where it came from.

It felt pure. The first was cold and liquid, like pure chilled water on a sweltering summer day - infused with a love I recognized from when I felt it in our bond.

Tyla.

She was giving me her power, and my heart soared in response. I was no longer losing ground against the force that resisted me.

Then another joined in. This one blazed like the sun but didn't burn. At least, not me, it didn't. Whatever was resisting me recoiled at the inferno that assaulted and lost ground instantly. It was filled with love and passion, feelings that I knew without a doubt were Tasnia.

Now I knew I was going to win. The love and power of these two basked me in a confidence that we would never lose to anything as long as we were together.

I used the space created from Tasnia's entrance to gather my own remaining power in one giant ball of force. I held it as long as I could before I threw everything that I had left at the chains locked around Madzia in my inner world.

With a burst of bright light, they shattered into nothingness, a thousand motes of darkness spread out and evaporated right in front of me. Finally freeing the woman in front of me as she collapsed on the floor of my inner sanctum when I released her from my control.

The power of it all was so intense that it threw me out and back into my actual body as I collapsed on the floor. I opened my eyes to find Tasnia and Tyla had fallen on top of me, both with their eyes closed and unmoving.

Diane rushed forward and checked us as I faded in and out.

Damn, almost didn't pass out this time. Guess I'm getting better at this.

Those were my last thoughts as I faded and I entered oblivion once again.

I awoke, startled, but it all came back to me quickly.

Diane was still above me, and Tyla and Tasnia were both next to me with bed rolls, still in their travel form, under their heads.

"How long?"

"N... not long." Diane said and noticed my look of concern. "Both of your women are fine."

I nodded, relieved, then looked over at Madzia, who was being tended to by Estelle. Lea was by the entrance to the cave, sitting down.

"I ran out of power but kept it up long enough. You both were screaming for quite a while," Lea said.

"Didn't feel that long to me." I glanced over at Estelle. "How is she?"

"Sleeping. For real this time," Estelle said.

"Good, that was a lot tougher than I thought it was going to be, and I am a realist. So it was pretty bad."

"What exactly happened?" Estelle said, now fully turning to me. She placed the collar back on the woman, touching the little crystal and willing a small amount of power into it.

"Well, let's say I hope the collar won't be necessary. I think I broke the hold that this Masaki had on her."

"You what?" Estelle asked, her voice increasing in pitch with each word as she stopped everything that she was doing to stare at me.

Her voice was mirrored by Lea behind me. I chuckled, but it was an exhausted laugh. Their perfectly timed question came in stereo from both their mouths at the same time. Almost at the same tone and pitch too.

Definitely related.

"I uh... was holding off telling you this, did not want to get your hopes up, but I can break the bonds between Demigods and the Chosen. Given to me by one of their kind... Well, you call them gods. But as you can see, it's difficult. I... doubt I can do that again for a good long while. My power, I can feel it, is just about depleted. I learned some things, but I don't want to repeat that until I gain in strength. It almost didn't work. Her former master was fighting me."

Lea and Estelle stared at me for a while, their jaws open. Neither of them moved.

Estelle finally recovered first. "Young man, do you know what this means?"

"That there is a chance... A chance to win against them, to free those that are enslaved. I know. I need to get much stronger, though."

"I swear on my life that I will help you, if you promise to free all my sisters that have been taken," Lea said in a whisper as she approached me and knelt next to me.

Power welled up inside me and tried to reach out for the woman. I was lucky that in my weakened state, I was able to stop it before she bonded herself to me in some way.

"Don't..." I said with my eyes closed, trying to keep it from escaping. "Say stuff like that around me. The Roxannez... I am sorry, the gods have made it where things like that have meaning and power around them. You almost just bound yourself to me as a servant. Please... don't do that again," I said with my teeth still clenched.

"What?" Lea's face went white.

"The... gods created this world, or changed it, have power over it in some way. I am not sure. Now they send their least desirables here to keep them from causing trouble in their own world. There are a lot of them, an entire civilization worth. Billions, I would guess at least. Each varies in power from what I understand. But they all live forever and want more than what they have."

"What does that mean for us?" Estelle asked, even the aged and experienced woman's voice cracking.

"That we are just entertainment for their outcasts. I know little more than that, just that there are two sides to it. One that wants to expand it to all worlds where us... they call us lesser species live. Then the other is set to stop it, the side that thinks that it is wrong... or at least I hope that they do. I am backed by the latter."

"It's true..." Estelle said, sitting on her butt with a flop. "I believe you that it's true. It's incredible, and I should doubt it, but I don't."

"Yup, and we need resources and allies to stop them. I think that I will find that in the east, but I can't be sure." I turned and glanced at Diane. Her face was white, and her eyes locked on me. "I know this is probably a lot for you. I understand if you want to escape and run away from all of this and make your own way. We will miss you, but you have to make your own decisions with full knowledge."

She closed her eyes, shaking her head. "I... I feel my place is with you as well. For now, at least."

"Heh." I chuckled. "Might be better if you do the opposite. The gods like to place suggestions in people's heads."

Diane just shrugged as Tyla moved at the same time as Tasnia. Each of them making noises of regaining consciousness. I got up with a stretch and kneeled next to my beauties. "How are you two doing?"

"Mmmhm, excellent Master. Weak, but good, the backlash was... actually kind of pleasurable."

"Yes, I was overwhelmed when I felt her bonds break. It went through you and into us. It almost felt like when we have sex," Tasnia added.

"Huh, for me it was painful. Figures something like that would happen, but I am very glad you did not have to go through what I did." I let them lie there and went over to Madzia. Estelle backed away, and I placed my hand on the woman, closing my eyes.

"Seems fine physically," Estelle said. "but I don't know about mentally. She... went through a lot. She seems off... her powers are gone, like she is still wearing the slave collar."

"Damn, I forgot. Part of the process that removes the bond also removes their power forever."

Both Lea and Estelle looked at me with concern.

"That is horrible," Estelle said. "But between that and slavery, I think it is the better option. What do we tell the others?"

"Did you mention to any of them that she was bonded?"

"Not directly, as we did not know for sure, but the rumor of that is probably going around."

I nodded. "Okay, we will try to convince her to go with us then. I don't want this getting out to anyone that does not go with us. Put the collar back on for now. Hopefully, when she wakes, she'll think it is the collar doing it until I can explain it better to her. Too much of a risk otherwise. This could give us problems, but I had to help her, the risk be damned."

I could not let someone be a slave when I could help it. It was just not going to happen.

"I hope she understands," Lea said, looking down at the woman in question.

"Estelle," I said. "You and Lea try to convince the others she is not enslaved. It will be tricky, and they may not believe us, but it's better than them knowing the truth for now."

"We will head out there now. What should we tell them?" Lea asked.

"Maybe a mental break or something. Trauma from all that happened made her hate me. We will join you," I said. "I'll carry her out to the group to show I don't hold her responsible."

I placed the collar around her neck, this time it didn't power up when I snapped it in place and touched the ruby. But I honestly wasn't sure how the thing worked. I should probably ask more about it when I have a chance, so I added it to my mental to do list.

We got up, and I picked up Madzia, following the rest of them as we made our way out with the group.

"What happened?" a tall red-headed woman asked as we made our way out.

"She is sleeping now, Tricia," Estelle said. "We do not know what happened, but we are almost certain she has not been bonded."

Several members of the group started asking questions, but I could understand none of them.

"Quiet!" Cecil yelled as he came over and stood by his wife, with Orrick standing next to Estelle. They grabbed bookends to help provide some intimidation for the others.

"Look, all of you," Estelle said. "I scrutinized her thoroughly. Her mind is her own, but we are not sure what caused her to do what she did." She glanced at me and added, "It might have been the mental stress from her captivity."

I saw the confused looks in the group, the disbelief, but they would just have to deal with it.

"I will take her from you," Tricia said as she approached.

I glanced at Lea, who nodded. "They are old friends."

I handed Madzia off to the woman, and they went over into a corner where she sat her down and she kneeled next to her. I briefly touched Tricia, and she glowed in a reddish hue before it disappeared again.

Fire Chosen.

"We need to decide what to do now," Estelle called out to the group. "Do we still want to head south or do we go to the East with D... Tyla and her group?"

I stood back and watched as the fireworks began as everyone argued. I wasn't hopeful in the slightest that we would get out of there soon.

The arguments went on for a while and I lost track of what they said. I sat on the floor with the other men as the women argued. Feeling like a kid at the children's table at a family meal, waiting for the adults to let us go play. A sizable part of me hated this.

But then Cecil nodded to me, and Orrick gave me a smile as we did the thing all men have done since the beginning of time when women argue amongst themselves. Or at least the smart ones did.

We shut the fuck up and hoped not to be noticed as the cats fought.

Diane, Tyla, and Tasnia soon joined us. None of them concerned in the slightest what the others chose, getting bored quickly with the concerns of their so-called elders.

"We need to go south. The east is too dangerous," Tricia said, almost yelling to be heard above the others.

That's odd, who was watching...

I looked over to where Madzia was laying earlier to see an empty spot on the bedroll Tricia had put her, a pack nearby had its contents spilled out on the floor nearby.

I stood up and walked over there, catching the attention of Estelle. "Derk?" She asked.

"Where is Madzia?"

Silence gripped everyone in the cave as they looked to where she was.

"She was sleeping there just a second ago," Tricia said.

"Quick, grab a torch and everyone check the caves, she couldn't have left, or we would have seen it," I said.

I ran to the corner where the nearest torch was and grabbed it, the girls joining me as I led the way.

We walked back to the cave I had used to break her chains, following the white marks on the tunnel sides, thankful it was still well lit from the lamps they had set out earlier.

As we walked into the small opening of the hollowed out dead end where she was imprisoned before, that was where we found her. A long dagger in her hand pressed to her heart. Her red-rimmed eyes filled with tears as she clutched it.

I froze. Not wanting to scare her into reacting. Estelle wasn't here to use the collar to command her. I lifted my hands, palms facing up and out as not threatening as I could after I handed the torch back to one of my girls. "Madzia, how can we help?"

"It's gone, I feel so empty that it's gone."

"What is Madzia?" Tyla said.

"My power, who I am, you took it from me didn't you?"

I was at a loss. She somehow knew it wasn't the collar that did it. She must have felt it when the bonds broke. "It was the only way I could free you. I am so sorry," was all I could say.

"I... I... Thank you for freeing me. I do not blame you," were her last words before she shoved the dagger deep into her heart with all the strength she could muster, throwing herself forward so that the force of her own body weight helped it pierce through her chest.

Tyla and I rushed to her side. Pulling her back up to see that most of the long knife was lodged deep in her chest. Quickly placing our hands on her, using what little power we had left after freeing her earlier as we tried to keep her alive.

Estelle joined right behind us. Where she came from, I wasn't sure. She placed her hands on the other side, and the three of us joined our powers, trying to save her.

I sensed the knife had pierced her heart. I wasn't sure we could fix it if I pulled it out, but it was just damaging itself further as it attempted to pump blood around the foreign object, and we couldn't fix it like that.

Tyla met my eyes, her head shaking silently. I glanced over at Estelle who looked down at Madzia, heartbroken.

I braced myself then pulled the knife out, at the same time trying to stitch together the ripped cells in the heart wall. Tyla and Estelle joined me, and I could feel them closing the knife wound she had opened up in her chest as the blood flowed out. The knife had shattered parts of her ribs as she shoved it deep into her chest and the impact that followed on the ground.

Tasnia yelled for help from the others, hoping other healers could get there in time to help us save her.

"I..." Madzia choked out blood at her lips. "... I... Can't live with what he did to me, not without my powers. Please let me have some rest." Her voice sounded like it was gurgling water.

A quick check told me that it was filling up her lungs.

My heart broke for this woman, I could never know what horrors she had been through. Her dull brown eyes gazed up into mine as she pleaded with me to let her die.

I finally nodded, as I stopped trying to repair the damage. I glanced up to Tyla, her own eyes filled with tears as she did the same. Estelle never gave up. I could feel her trying until the bitter end.

"Don't, Madzia. Do you know what hope this man brings for all our sisters?"

"I... so... ry," she said with a gurgling voice.

Tears mixed with blood streamed down her face.

With a final sob, Madzia let out her last breath. It sounded like a thank you as we watched, holding her poor soul in our arms as she died.

"May you find peace in the next life," I said.

People filled the room and saw the woman laying lifeless between me and Tyla. They saw the bloody dagger in my hand and the last of her still warm blood dripping off it.

"You... You... killed her? Estelle?" a woman asked.

I did not look up to see who. I honestly didn't care right then.

"He did not!" Tasnia yelled. "She killed herself, you idiot, and they were trying to help her."

I looked up just as the blond woman recoiled from Tasnia and hid behind someone else. It was Tricia who had said it as she put her hand over her mouth, tears streaming from her eyes as she processed the fact that she was supposed to have been watching her.

"She..." I began. "It was too late. She pierced her heart and I... Tyla and Estelle couldn't fix it. She would have found a way eventually regardless, I think." I tried to say something to make the woman feel better without giving away my secrets. Not sure why I cared, but there had been enough pain and suffering already that I did not want anyone else to feel more.

The collective mood of the group was destitute, and no one made a noise, other than the whimpers and cries of the women who had known Madzia.

"Let's..." Estelle began before clearing her throat. "Let's pack up, give her last rites, and leave quickly. I don't think any of us want to stay here any longer." The woman looked sad, but she kept glancing at me.

For the first time since I had entered the cave, absolutely no one argued with her.

CHAPTER 8

—— · ——

INTERLUDE: MASAKI

Masaki rested in the camp chair his servant set out, enjoying the sensation of one of his thralls mouths on his manhood as she pleasured him. He held the cup up to his mouth and took a deep swallow of the golden liquid and savored the pleasures of his life.

The physical form held so much more than the partial existence of life as a supposed god. He was sick of the rules put in place to keep him tied down to the lower castes. Never able to rise and live like his overlords, even if he had the power to rival them.

That changed the day he entered this world. He risked much, his very life in fact, but the pleasures of the flesh were worth it to him.

A smile overtook him as he thought about how much power he had here. Here he lived like the Patrician in Roxannez society, well above his plebeian roots that had strangled his ambitions for thousands of years. Even after ten thousand years, he had not risen at all from where he was before his ascension.

In fact, if he had his way, he would soon replace Seir as the elite in this world. The current opportunity before him would be a major step on that path. Not the ultimate step, but he was patient.

"My Lord, would you like me to rub your back while Joyann services you?" Oralie asked.

"Yes," he said as he glanced down at Joyann. Her eyes locked on his face just as he always demanded while she was performing these duties.

"Faster," he commanded.

Her head bobbed up and down faster, her eyes never wavering as she obeyed.

He lifted his arms while Oralie removed his metal plated leather armor from over him then removed his undershirt. When she was finished, he sat back in the camp chair and let her drip oil over his back.

He had bonded with five women now, each of them selected for the power they could offer. However, only four were with him at the moment. He would reunite with his favorite soon however, returning Madzia to her proper place at his side.

He found he missed her. She was one of his most attentive of his women, always supplying him whatever he needed or wished.

After he broke her and convinced her to join him that is.

Oralie's hands caressed his back, slathering the warm oil and gliding her hands up and down as he enjoyed himself and her sister thrall. The tingling sensation joined in as she used her power over water to relieve the tension built up in his muscles.

It had been a long road to catch up to Madzia. For two weeks he had been marching his men hard from the capital of Nitre. She had been at the academy in Blackrun with the other prospective Chosen, looking for his next conquest to add to his harem, when she joined the group freed by the traitor Stern.

When he was told of the escape, he jumped at the chance to impress Seir. Between the messages she left as they made their way south, and her connection to him, it had been easy to follow them so far.

Seir would be most pleased when he brought them back. So much so that he would likely reward him with his pick of women to finish out the last two places on his harem. It was his chance to become the top lieutenant to the overseer's chosen agent. Letting him increase his personal guard to one hundred men.

The power and status he would receive, even if they forced him to return to heaven eventually, would let him climb out of the plebeian caste. Maybe not to the Patrician's, but at least to account as one of the wealthiest members of his own.

But he had to ride hard and force his personal company of men to the brink in order to make it to her before the others could. They had made excellent time, and he felt that he had earned this relaxation after a hard day's work of forcing his men to move faster.

He glanced over to the nearby camp his men had made, after they set up his own of course. This was the first time they had rested in several days. He had finally been forced by his lead guard to stop and let them rest even if it was barely after high sun. Most of his men were now dead asleep on the ground. They did not even bother setting up tents, instead just sleeping on their arms where they landed.

He had over fifty men in his personal company. A mercenary company of well repute whom he had gotten to swear oaths of loyalty before he changed their terms. He still paid them, of course, but only half of what he had promised.

In full view of the few men on guard, Masaki grabbed the head of Joyann and pushed her face as far down his cock as she would go, climaxing inside of her.

"Mmmhhm," she mumbled as he released his seed down the back of her throat.

"Well done, Joyann. Join Oralie on my back now."

Joyann swallowed hard, "Yes... my Lord."

The petite blond woman got to her feet, used some of her air magic to get the dust off her knees, and walked behind Masaki to join Oralie.

Her hands, now also covered in oil, started messaging his left shoulder while Oralie switched to his right. He relaxed into their touch as he considered his next move.

They were only about a day away from where he felt Madzia to be. He closed his eyes and felt for the connection between them. Weak but there, confirming to him he was about a day away at a solid march. Near the mountains to the southeast, on the border of the wretched city of Rivenhold that Seir's army would soon sack.

He would have to push his men even harder once they had their short break.

Then his connection to Madzia changed.

"What?" he said, his eyes widening in shock.

"My Lord?" Oralie asked, confusion in her voice.

"That should not be possible." Masaki said.

The connection was fraying, like rope coming apart at the ends. Somehow, the connection was breaking away.

Masaki tapped into his own well of power and sent it through the connection, trying to repair the damage being done. Giving back the power he normally took from his women.

"She must be wounded or dying," he said to himself. "It's the only possibility."

"My Lord, how can we help?" Joyann said, alarm in her voice, afraid that Masaki would get angry at her. Both women had removed their hands and took several steps back from the now angered Demigod.

"Silence!" he declared and focused on the connection.

Something was trying to break it, but what it could be, he did not know. It should not be possible, even with her death.

He stabilized the connection with his own power. He felt it as he started winning the war against whatever was causing this.

He could save her and bring her back to him. He would not lose what was his.

A surge from the other side traveled back to Masaki, the power so great that it caused him to curl in a ball as he screamed from the pain. At first it felt cold, like an icicle from the great southern permafrost on his home world.

Then came heat, great heat that was like the core of a star. It felt like fire had engulfed his entire body.

"Arrghhhhhh!" he screamed as he fell to the ground.

Men from the camp went on alert, forced by the bond to respond to their Masters screams. The remaining three of his harem rushed to his side. Oralie placed her hands on his bare chest and tried to heal him, but before she could, he reached forth and drew all the power he could from his women to prevent the power surge from overtaking him completely.

All four of his women collapsed at his feet, unconscious before they even hit the ground.

But it was not enough.

The connection snapped. He could no longer feel Madzia under his power. The tie that bound them had shattered into a thousand pieces.

"Dead," he sighed, staring up into the blue sky. "She must be dead."

He slowly climbed back to his feet. He could still feel the pain throughout his body as he stretched himself out.

"Julian!" he yelled, staring at his women, still collapsed at his feet, each barely breathing.

One of his soldiers, the captain of his personal guard, ran over to his side. "Yes, my Lord?"

"Prepare the men to march."

"Sir, you promised them the rest of the afternoon to recover. They have been going non—"

"Silence." Masaki said as he back handed Julian to the ground. "Get them moving. Pick up my women and put them in the back of the cart until they recover."

"Y... yes, my Lord," Julian said and scampered off to carry out his orders.

Masaki seethed at what happened. Someone killed his property, and whoever was responsible would die for it, or wish they were dead. Either way, he would have his vengeance.

CHAPTER 9

MOUNTAIN TRAIL

"Are you sure you don't want us to help?" I asked Marylyn, as we were ready to leave.

"No, we will burn her body, do the rights, then leave as well."

"Marylyn—" Estelle began.

"It's fine Lady Estelle. We have chosen our path. We will go south, and you will go east."

"It's not too late for you to come with us," Lea said.

"There is too much..." Marylyn began, before shaking her head. "No, our place is not with you. We will run and hope to be forgotten somewhere in the southern parts of the continent, far away from all this nonsense."

"We understand," I said, "Good luck. I strongly urge you to leave as quickly as possible. I have a feeling that pursuit is not far behind."

Marylyn nodded and then turned back into the cave. We had watched as they wrapped Madzia's body in cloth and covered her in flammable oils. From where, I wasn't sure. They planned to light the body on fire and leave the cave before it was completed.

I sighed and turned to my girls. Tyla and Tasnia were on either side of Diane. The smiles they gave me were genuine, if burdened with sadness at all that had happened. Lea stood next to Estelle, with Cecil and Orrick on either side of them.

"Ready?" I asked.

Acknowledgments were given, and we left the cave, walking eastward, away from the entrance to the cave.

"How long should it take us to get to the desert?" I asked Cecil.

"A few days. The map I have is old but should still be good. No one has ventured the deserts in years to my knowledge. There is a small town on the way there, but I do not know much about it."

"Hopefully, we can stock up on supplies before we get to the desert, then."

"We have about three hours of daylight, Master."

"We should be able to get far enough away to find a place to sleep safely," I said.

"Why do you call him Master Tyla? Does he force that upon you?" Lea asked.

Tyla turned red, not noticing her slip in front of the others.

"I... ugh," she began.

"I tried to get her to stop, actually. Now I don't even notice it. It was originally a side effect of the bond, but now it feels more like a pet name to me more than anything."

"Yes," Tyla said simply.

"Tasnia, do you call him Master too?" Estelle asked.

"He wishes," she said as rolled her eyes at me. A sweet smile formed on her lips right behind it, though. "I love him with all my heart and yes, I will bend my will to him if he demands it. But no, that is not how I think of him. More of a pillar to lean on than someone who wants to control me. I would do anything for him because I know he would never treat me poorly."

We clasped hands as we walked.

"Thank you." I gave Tas a bump on her shoulder.

"Hey!" Tyla said, a mock look of shock on her face.

Laughing, reached over and grabbed her hand with my other one. "I love you too. You are my first, after all. Even if you are a hopeless submissive."

"Only to you," she mumbled.

"She's right," Tas added, "with us, she is right bossy."

"I am not!"

"Yes. You are," Diane said from behind us. I looked over my shoulder at her in surprise.

"I didn't think I was that bad," Tyla said.

"It's your right, Tyla. Like he said, you were first... and noble born too," Tasnia said.

"I will let you guys hash that out. But I Love both of you and will treat you equally. I will leave all that other politics between you. Got it?"

"Yes, Master."

"Yes, Love."

Estelle just shook her head as she walked out in front of us. "So different."

"Different is good, Estelle," I said. "The old ways failed. While I am not saying that men should run the world instead or anything, I think we need more balance to thrive here."

Estelle never answered, and that conversation died soon after as we began taking the steeper steps up the hills. We made good time, if not as quick as I wanted because of Estelle's and Orrick's advanced age, keeping us from breaking up the journey with occasional jogs. I just did not want to push them like that even if they seemed spry enough for it.

"Think they will be alright?" Estelle finally said, looking back in the direction we left the others.

"I'm not sure," I said. "Keep getting one of those feelings I get when... the gods want me to do something. Telling me to head east with a feeling of danger behind me. I just hope they listened to me this time when I told them to get moving."

"I feel responsible," Estelle said.

"Don't, dear," Orrick said as he reached around his wife's shoulder with his arm. "You tried. Most of them are too stubborn to listen. Even with all that has happened. They just are not in a place to want to give up control yet."

"He's right," I added. "You can't force people who are used to being in charge to make the right decisions. Most will be stubborn unless all their hope is dashed before they submit to another. You can only try and reason with them and hope they make the right choice."

Though I did not feel certain of those convictions as I said them. Especially since I struggled with my own concerns about being a pawn for the powers that governed this world. I realized I needed to blaze a trail on my own and was still unsure how best to do that.

I hated feeling like I was only reacting to things, following the cheese like a mouse in a maze. Every time that I thought I was getting ahead, something would happen that forced me back on to the path I was told to travel.

An idea started forming in the back of my head, still too raw to be acted on. But I wondered if there was a way that I could change things around in this circumstance I found myself in. Get some of my own personal power back.

I continued to dwell as we walked. The problem was that I did not know what I would be getting into to justify the risk.

I held my hand over the wood, trying but failing once again to get the fire to leap out of my hand from a distance.

"Not yet, plus I am tired," I mumbled to myself as I reached forward and placed my hand directly on the kindling underneath the wood.

I used some of my still depleted power to transfer the heat directly into it.

It started burning in a second, and I marveled as the small flame danced over my fingers, feeling warm, but not quite burning.

"Some level of fire resistance now, at least. This feels like a game world in a way. Fuck Vex and the lack of instruction manuals."

"Who are you talking to?" Diane asked, standing over me and looking down at my hand.

"Myself mostly. I am figuring out how to do things, just not the why behind how it works. I could really use one of those cool interface tracking systems like we had on the video games back on Earth."

"Those words, they were... strange. What do they mean?"

I sighed. "Nothing, just not much of an equivalent here that you would understand. How are you doing?"

"Lost," she whispered. "I am not sure I am doing the right thing. I was used to being alone for so long. Then there were so many people in that cave. Part of me was thankful only a few came with us."

"Yeah, most of them didn't want to make the leap of trust and come with us, too much for them to handle after Madzia's death, I think. At least you seem to feel comfortable talking to me finally. That is a start I am happy with."

"Tyla told me to come sit over here while they finish setting up the tents for the night. I think she wants me to talk to you."

"She does that." I smiled as I said it. "You are welcome with us for as long as you want, but any more than that isn't required nor expected."

"Thank you," she said,

"So, tell me about yourself."

She nodded. Sitting down on the log we rolled out from the forest around our makeshift camp for the night. Orrick and Cecil were trying to scrounge up dinner, so we did not have to dip into our meager rations.

"I..." she began. "I woke up about a year ago in the woods outside the town you call Rivenhold. Alone, with just the clothing I wore and the bracelet I told your women about. I wandered for a while, living off a few things I learned that did not make me sick in the woods, until I found the city that is."

"So complete loss? Like you had to learn to walk again? Or did you remember how to do certain things?"

"It is hard to describe. I never had problems walking or eating, but I did not know where I was, why I was there, or how I had gotten there. I had some feelings about what I should do, but nothing I could think of for examples on how to do it."

"Did you have any wounds or bruises on your head?"

"Not that I remember," she said, shrugging her shoulders. "I remembered my words when I encountered my first human, a small child that ran from me screaming when I came out of the woods and surprised him. It was then I hid myself and studied the humans going into the city on the main road."

"Makes sense," I said. Not wanting to press too deeply, just letting her continue.

"When I felt confident enough and hid my features, I eventually snuck into the city and sold the bracelet. It was worth several of your copper coins from a man I met in the market. Now, of course, I know he took advantage of me. The gold in it was worth much more than the copper coins he gave me. It allowed me to eat more than I had since I... awoke. So, I was happy at the time. It was then I started to distrust all those around me."

I resisted reaching my hand out to her. Other than when I hugged her, I had tried to keep from scaring her off with physical contact until she was more comfortable.

"And you lived like that till we found you?"

She nodded. "I lived in the forest. Only coming to the city to steal..." She looked at me. "Take what I needed to live. I took little, just things that allowed me to make living in the forest easier. My home was there; it felt right. I tried to pay for things when I could afford to."

"Tyla tells me that most elves live in forest homes, so it makes sense."

She stopped talking and instead just stared into the flames of the now fully engulfed fire. There was more, I could tell, but she seemed to be done for now.

"Diane, I won't pry... but if you ever feel you want to talk about the rest, I will be here. Or the girls. We will be here for you."

"Thank you," she said,

"Master, tents all set up," Tyla said, coming over to join us.

Tasnia was only a few steps behind her with Estelle and Lea coming from the other side.

"I'll get started on something resembling dinner," Estelle said. "See if the other boys have any luck bringing us food."

"You should know me better than that," Orrick said, entering the small clearing like a ghost. He held two fully dressed rabbits in his hands. "That should get us through the day."

"Perfect. I can do a lot with that," Estelle said, taking the rabbits from her husband's hands as he wiped off his hands with a towel he had.

"You girls take the tent tonight," I said to Tyla, Tas, and Diane. "I can sleep outside, so you have privacy."

"No," Tyla said first. "We discussed it. There is room for all of us, if a little cramped. Diane said she can sleep in the tent's foot, and we can put our bags outside. That way, we are all under cover for the night."

Both the other women nodded, even if Diane looked a little pink when she said it.

"You sure you are okay with that, Diane?" I asked.

"Y... yes. I would feel more comfortable staying with Tyla and Tas, if you don't mind having me. I can stay outside as well if it's a problem."

"It's fine," I said.

Estelle soon placed the prepared rabbits onto a spit to roast the rabbits as Cecil set up some sticks that would hold them while we talked. I was amazed at how fast she did that. My own skills were much cruder in comparison.

"Anyone have a preference for keeping a lookout tonight?" I asked.

"I will go first," Cecil said.

"Second," Orrick called out.

"Fair," I said. "But let's get rid of this system where the men do the work. Let's call the era of the matriarch dead in our little group and everyone pulls their weight equally. That way, we get more rest every night."

"We have agreed to follow you. We will comply," Estelle said, coming over with the rabbits prepared for the fire.

She stuck them on Cecil's apparatus to let them cook then started turning it slowly as the seasoned meat began to heat up.

"Good," I said. "On that note, I can take the third watch."

"No, I can take it. Estelle can be after me. If you approve, that is." Lea said, glancing over at me. "Then tomorrow night you and your girls can take all the watches and we can get a full night's sleep."

"Works," I said, noticing that she referred to Diane as mine, but I did not say anything to correct it.

"I told the others about what you could do. I hope you don't mind." Estelle finally said, and the conversation stopped.

"No, this group here should probably know. What do you all think?"

"You told me you did it, but even then, part of me didn't fully believe it until Estelle told me Madzia's last words. But to lose one's power." Lea said, as she shivered.

"I heard them all," Estelle said. "All of her words, she was free of the bonding. I... you could not fake what she said in that cave at the end. I wish we could have saved her. The hope it would have brought to the others, we could have convinced them to join us."

As Estelle trailed off, the others became silent as well. Each was deep in their own thoughts of having a tool to free their sisters and the tradeoff it meant. Finally, I could not take the awkward silence anymore.

"If you don't mind, I am going to meditate for a bit, see if I can get into that sanctum. My power has not come back as fast as I thought it would. Still feel empty."

"I also feel weaker than I should." Tasnia said.

"Me as well." Tyla added.

"Interesting. So, you all feel drained, too?" Lea said.

They nodded. Tyla spoke up, "I feel my power returning, but not as fast as I had been accustomed to. Not as efficient as it was before we met, Master. I am not sure why."

"Even more interesting," I said. "Another reason to get back to my inner sanctum place. I need to know if it is because we have more power and it just recharges slower, or if there is a downside to the bond between us. Just another thing to figure out because no one tells me anything. Alright, I'm going to go find a place to do that without distraction. Come get me when the food is ready."

"Tell me more about this bond of yours, I find it fascinating to discuss when I am not worried about being bound myself," Estelle said as I walked away from the group. Starting a conversation between them that I was thankful not to take part in. People expected me to have answers when I just did not have them yet. It was frustrating all around.

Heading a short distance away, I sat down like I learned in school all those years ago, crossing my legs and trying to get comfortable. I was not an expert on meditation or anything, but I figured it was time to try and give it a shot. I started regulating my breathing like I read about in those fiction novels that were popular back on Earth. Maybe this power was like the cultivation stories that became popular in the west for a time.

"Master, it is getting late."

I opened my eyes, frustrated that I could not enter the Sanctum that seemed to come so easily sometimes. Just appearing in my dreams when I...

"Power. I had always made significant gains in power when I entered it."

"What, Master?"

I glanced at Tyla, smiling in the darkness, not even sure she could see me. "Nothing, I just had an idea, but no way to test it. My power has barely come back. It's like a garden hose trying to fill a lake. Hoping sleep does it."

"A what?" she said. "Never mind, just hurry, we are tired."

I got up from my spot with sore legs. While in reality I had not been at it too long, I had never been one for sitting around doing nothing with my body. Dinner broke me from my first attempt. The rabbit Estelle made was good. I didn't know where she got the seasonings, but it was not just plain rabbit meat.

I entered the tent, taking my boots off just outside. The small candles in the brass holder lit the inside as I lifted the tent flap, which seemed bright to me after sitting in the darkness for so long. Diane was lying down at the foot of the tent so that I had to climb over her to get to the spot in the middle that the girls had left for me. I tried my best not to land on her, but a muffled grunt told me I was less than successful.

I quickly covered myself in our shared blankets and removed the uncomfortable clothing that I hated sleeping in, leaving me in just my wool small clothes. Doing my best to fold my outerwear and place them on top of the girls in the corner of the tent set aside for such things. The pile already there seemed rather large, but I let it go. The space was tight, and we should have gotten a bigger tent now that I thought about it.

The armor and our weapons were left outside, and that just would not do if something happened again. It was set in a way that we could get to it quickly, but it still bothered me not being able to see it with my own eyes.

"Wishes and horses," I mumbled.

"What Love?" Tasnia asked, lying almost completely under the covers to where only her head and face could be seen.

"Nothing. Old saying. Are you guys ready for me to get the light?"

"Can you leave one candle burning?" Tyla added.

"Sure, any reason why?"

"In case I have to get up. I don't want to smash Diane in the dark."

"Fair. Didn't help me much. Sorry Diane."

"It's fine. You didn't hurt me," she said.

I sat up high enough to open the small glass case that sat over the candle holder, blowing one of them out and shutting it once again. The light dropped enough that I could still see, but it wouldn't bother me as I tried to sleep.

I lay down in the modified camp roll we set up to fit three people and sat my head on what we could loosely call a pillow. Really, just a small square of fabric stuffed with feathers. Just enough to be padding on a hard surface, but not so much that it made it hard to pack, either.

"Good night, everyone," I said, as I tried to get comfortable.

"Good night, Master, Tas, you too Diane."

The other girls said the same, and I closed my eyes. Both of my girls cuddled into me from each side, each plopping a leg over on top of me under the cover.

Wait... Why were they naked?

Hands slowly began rubbing up and down my chest on each side, eliciting a response regardless of what my mind cried out about propriety in front of our guest. I debated saying anything to them about it, but I stopped myself. Whether that was because I did not want to make a big deal out of it, or my desire that they would continue, I couldn't honestly say.

Probably the latter.

Honestly, part of me was interested, even if my big brain thought we shouldn't be putting Diane in this position so soon. The little brain was screaming out to be a caveman and claim these women before I exploded. It had been a couple days since we had been together sexually - right before we entered Rivenhold, actually.

When you get used to sex with two beautiful women each day... and night, and morning. Well, your body wants to override propriety and tell it to be damned.

Before I knew it, Tyla's hand brushed away from my side, caressing over my stomach and, rather than go back up like she had been, went farther down to the tip of my woolen underclothes. Her smooth fingers slid under the woolen pants and curled around my hardening shaft, giving it a firm stroke to encourage it to harden faster.

On my other side, Tas brushed her lips softly against my chest and trailed several kisses to the crook of my neck, where she nibbled against me just below my jaw. I shivered from the pleasure their joint efforts sent down my spine.

I lifted my head and glanced down towards where Diane was sleeping and saw that she was facing away from us on her side. Tyla picked that moment to speed her stroking, going up and down on my cock with her hand, making my eyes roll back and then close. Soon she joined Tas in kissing the other side of my chest, working her way up to my neck.

I tried to keep from groaning at the sensation of them fondling and kissing me in such a way. I reached and placed my hands along their backs, eventually reaching around to grope the base of their gravity defying breasts. Soon I was teasing their nipples into becoming hard with my thumb and forefinger after I finished handling their globes.

"Mmmmm," Tyla let out. Just barely a murmur, but it was enough for us to slow for a moment to see if there was a reaction from our tent mate.

After a few heartbeats of hearing nothing from Diane, the girls quickly continued their explorations. Working together, they grasped with their fingers and pulled down my woolen small pants to the base of my thighs just above the knees. Their movements seemed calculated and silent as they drove me insane with need. It took all my willpower to not mount one of them then and there.

With a little more effort, soon the pants were around my knees, they each caressed back up my thighs, like they had practiced this together for years. They were so perfectly coordinated I wondered if the link that bound us also let them share their thoughts and desires. Their hands soon returned to my aching manhood. Tyla stroked the rigid shaft while Tasnia cupped my balls, causing my hips to rock up to them against my will.

Rustling at our feet caused us to freeze again as this time Diane rolled over on to her other side, now facing us. Her face in the dim candlelight showed her eyes were still closed as she repositioned the small bunch of cloth she used as a pillow. We froze in place, like deer caught in a headlight, none of us sure if we should continue.

I let out a frustrated sigh. It was not fair to Diane, who did not know us well enough yet. Last thing we should probably do is start having crazy sex and drive her away. I patted the girl's arms who then looked up into my eyes to see me shaking my head.

The cuteness of them almost made me change my mind.

Tyla immediately turned over in a thump, and her completely naked ass pushed into my hip. Then she reached back, grabbed my opposite arm, and pulled me over to my side and wrapped my arm around her like I was her personal blanket.

Tasnia made me her little spoon and filled herself in behind me. Her rock-hard nipples pressed into my back as she pushed up tightly against me.

The problem obviously being that my rigid shaft was now pressing right into Tyla's ass. The desire that welled up inside me almost made me take her right there as I closed my eyes to get my needs under control.

Deep breaths followed as the girls adjusted into me to get comfortable. Not helping my rock-hard problem in the slightest.

I was about to reach down and adjust myself when Tasnia's hand guided slowly down my side. I could tell what she was about to do, but I was almost unable to resist as she forced her way through the crevice between Tyla's rear end and my groin to wrap around my shaft with her hand. She gripped me tightly, moving it left and right, rubbing it between her sister-wife and me for several seconds.

The sensation sent stars in my head as all the blood went elsewhere. I no longer cared if we woke Diane, but the sensuousness of the encounter and the pleasure it gave made me keep my noise in check as I embarrassed the sensations going through me.

Tyla adjusted her ass slightly away from me, creating just enough room for Tas to reposition the head of my cock into her tight and wet opening. When Tyla felt the tip, she slowly backed up as I entered her inch by inch.

Tyla's breathing hitched as she wiggled her rear end more and more, finally impaling herself fully on my member. She started gliding forward and back, doing all the movement as I lay there and felt her engulf me repeatedly.

Tasnia reached around under the blanket, past me and over to Tyla. I saw her arm trace its way up her side and stop at my black-haired beauty's left breast. I pulled down the covers to enjoy the sight of her circling Tyla's nipple with her fingers, occasionally stopping and pinching them.

I freed my left hand from Tyla's hip and slid it behind me, between Tas and myself. I teased her opening gently before plunging my middle finger into her, grinning at how wet she was for me. Tasnia let out a contented sigh as my finger entered her soaking slit and rubbed back and forth between us.

Before long, Tasnia moved her hips in time with my motion and Tyla sped up her hips to the point that we were starting to breathe heavily. all worry about noise seemed forgotten. Tyla reached back and cupped my ass, pushing me into her harder and faster.

"More," she whispered, and I began thrusting to meet her need while my fingers shoved their way into and out of a moaning Tas.

"Mhmmm," Tasnia let out as she rubbed herself on my fingers, lifting the blanket up to her mouth and biting down.

All of us were close.

More sound of movement came from our feet, but this time we did not stop. A quick glance down showed me that Diane's eyes were wide open, and she was watching us intently as we continued.

To my surprise, I could see that she had reached under her own blanket. The way she bit her lip at a single point between her teeth, and how the blanket rises and falls, tells me she's rubbing her clit with great vigor to match our pace. The erotic view of her getting off to us exited me, and I was even closer to release.

Her other hand, also under the blanket, seemed to grasp at her own breasts and shifted back and forth and fondled them madly as I saw the woolen blanket rise and fall. Then suddenly, our gazes locked, her cheeks flushed as she realized I had caught her, but neither of us stopped our activities. Her hands kept moving, and I kept pumping and rubbing, if anything, we both became more frantic in our movements.

It also only made my rod that much harder inside Tyla. I was so close to popping!

I bucked my hips faster, getting a low but deep moan in response. Tasnia spasmed in my hand behind me, grabbing my hair in her hands as she came. Her whole body becoming rigid for several heartbeats. I followed a moment later, slamming into Tyla hard several times as I filled up her insides with my seed and she joined Tasnia in rigid bliss.

My body relaxed, still deep inside Tyla, as I breathed heavily. I glanced back at Diane in time to enjoy her own blissful expression as she brought herself to orgasm.

None of us said a word. Simply lay there as we enjoyed the sensations. Our breathing slowly coming under control. I felt energized, like my core had refilled and my power had returned. It was probably just my imagination, a feeling of elation mixed with the joy of getting laid for the first time in a few days.

Tyla slowly pulled me out of her, and I fell flat on my back. Both girls resumed their original positions on each side of me and I stared at the ceiling, enjoying the sounds of their breathing in our afterglow. Within a few minutes, I could tell all three women were sleeping contently by their light snores, and I joined soon after, forgetting about my now full core of power.

CHAPTER 10

— • —

SANCTUM

Arriving in my sanctum was a surprise, but a welcome one. The darkness greeted me with the two balls of colored light that represented my women orbiting me.

I smiled. Now it was time to make sense of all this. What could I really do here?

I walked around the perimeter, Tyla's and Tasnia's representations following me like loyal puppies on their leashes. I stepped to the edge to see what would happen, but they just passed through the edge like it was not really there. Nothing happened at all.

Curious.

"What I need is to sit down and think." My mind drifted to my apartment back on Earth, the ratty old chair that I used to sit in to watch sport or shows on. I could almost feel the old suede couch as I thought of it.

"This was my Sanctum, right? Kind of like a lucid dream, I should be able to do what I want here. I could control the body of Madzia, after all, while she was here. Why not other things?" I thought aloud.

"Let's give it a shot," I said after a moment's thought.

I held up my hand like I was a wizard in a book and closed my eyes. Using the same ability that let me naturally break the bonds of that woman earlier that day. I wished for the chair to appear in front of me while I pictured it from my memories. I imagined everything I could remember about seeing it and feeling it when I sat on it. I stood like that for several seconds, not feeling a single thing happen.

My shoulders drooped, and I opened my eyes, expecting failure. However, right in front of me was the chair.

"Holy fuck... It worked."

I went to the chair and sat down carefully, not wanting it to be figment and falling on my ass. Even in my own mind I would like to avoid that kind of stupidity.

But what met my ass as I sat down was heaven. My favorite chair, as cheap and second hand as it was, was back in my life. Even if it was just in this room I could only seem to visit after I killed a demigod or got laid.

"Speaking of, why did I get here tonight? I did not add another woman to my harem. Or at least I hope I didn't. Diane never actually participated or agreed to anything that I could notice."

I should probably stop talking to myself, but it was just me here, so I disregarded it as unimportant, instead thinking about the chair I sat in.

It was a start. Deciding to try again, I pictured my old Ultra definition flat screen television I had on the wall back home. Without even closing my eyes, after a few seconds it appeared in front of me as though hanging in the air.

"Sports channels!" I called out, hoping that I also re-created the virtual interface that went with it.

This time I was disappointed, as the black screen did nothing. I mean, where would the channels get their broadcasts from? I could probably remember a few things, but not enough to get me the details of a movie or show. Maybe I could ask Vex if they have any of the old broadcasts, like how he transmitted Jessica's last message to me into my head.

A small pang of loss hit me as I thought of her. Another thing I wanted to ask about was how she ended up. I have had two conversations with that alien asshole and both of them seemed rushed and full of nothing that I actually wanted to know. Just cryptic warnings and threats.

What I could really use was one of those video game interfaces I kept joking about. That would help me figure out what the hell things mean here. give me a status screen so I could see how I was leveling up or something.

"Wait... Why couldn't I?

I looked back up at my vid-screen. Reaching out with my hands, mostly because it felt like the thing to do, I waved in the direction I wanted, and saw the screen increase in size to my demands.

"Nice, went from a forty inch to a four hundred inch. Wish I could have done that back home."

I laughed as I thought of what every man in existence would do first with the power to enlarge things at will.

Moving on from that thought, with the giant screen in front of me, I tried to power it on. I thought back to my childhood, and the video games I stopped playing when I joined the Marines. I was never a huge gamer, so I kept it simple.

I thought about the image of myself and my body that I had been living in for the past month and a half or so and watched as it filled the middle of the screen. I guess it was me now, not someone else. Though the lack of mirrors and glass in this world had not really given me much opportunity to get used to it.

I shrugged. No time like the present. I studied the image while I wondered how I could get all the powers to represent themselves so I could understand.

The picture was lifelike, the current uncut hair, the small beard still growing, but not at the rate I was used to when I was on earth. I still looked young, about twenty or so, but my muscles had grown a lot in my time here. Too bad I couldn't find a gym or something and get some weights in.

"Hmmm," I mused, wondering.

I needed to keep it at the crayon eating simple level. I had friends that gamed regularly, ones I served with. But that was never me or what I did to pass time. That usually involved booze and bars until I accidentally got Kate pregnant when I was twenty-two. I ignored that thought before I started thinking about my first kid from Earth. That would not be what I needed to focus on right now.

Getting back to it, I figured I would need to create an interface of some sort. But I was not a number crunching genius. Would the interface help me? I wasn't sure.

Probably should not count on that.

Then it hit me. "But, like any Marine, I can at least count to ten." I said, laughing as I held out my hands and wiggled my fingers. "Let's see if the system, or whatever it is, is smart enough to help me with it."

I pictured something simple, a picture of three wavy lines that represented water to me and placed it above my head. Nothing fancy, just made it blue on the otherwise black screen.

Underneath, I tried to think of a number scale up to ten, but nothing happened.

"Damn." I said as my first attempt failed. Maybe I could not video game my way out of this after all. "Or I am just thinking about this wrong."

I was surprised when the spheres that represented my connection to Tyla and Tas just disappeared right in front of my eyes. Fear shot through me at what that could mean, but then I was even more surprised by the voice that came from everywhere at once.

"You are thinking about it like an idiot, Derk," a cool feminine voice said as a chill went down my spine from the familiarity that I had with it. "You don't have that kind of mental capacity to track it, and the interface will not do it for you... and don't worry about your connections, I can almost read your thoughts. I am going to manage those for you from now on, so you won't see them anymore, but they are still there."

"Who..." It was almost a cough.

"Hello Derk, I missed you," it said.

My heart started pounding in my chest.

"Jessica?" I finally whispered.

"Sorta?"

"Explain."

"Let's see, I guess you could say I am part of an interface created by Vex to assist you in equaling the innate knowledge of your competitors. A stretch, but technically within the rules that say each denizen is supposed to have an equal chance between the competing factions. That you are not, in fact, a member of the Roxannez species is the stretch part."

"Where are you?" I had so many questions, but I desperately wanted to see her.

"At this time, I am not... corporeal. Your sanctum and power are not yet strong enough for more than an audio interface."

"Yet?" I asked but put my hand up in front of me. "No, wait, too many questions. Why did they pick you? And how?"

"I do not have access to that information," she said, almost robotically. "Ouch, that fucking hurt. Apparently, there are some sort of nasty firewalls to information I am not supposed to tell you. Sorry Babe."

My heart warmed at the old nickname she had for me, but I stopped. "How do I know it's really you?"

"Well, I could tell you about our first date at the coffee shop back in Boston. That blind date we set up on the dating site we used. That you had a white chocolate mocha and called it a large rather than a Venti to the poor barista... But given the power that Roxannez has, that would prove nothing really. They could have access to the security cameras or something."

"Good point," I said. Not sure what to do to verify it further. It felt like her but... "Do you remember... what happened?"

"I... remember everything until just after the message I sent you. Then it's... ack! That hurt again. Apparently, that is classified information. I am sorry Babe. I actually want to help, but there are some restrictions in what I can do."

"It's fine Jess, honestly... real or not, it is good to hear your voice," I said, a tear threatening to find its way down my cheek.

"I know, you too, even in that young hot body you are in now, I still know it's you. I can... I guess you can say I can feel it."

"So, how will this work? Are you going to be here now, or eventually?"

"As much as I know or can say right now, I will only be here in your sanctum. It's kind of small and not very functional yet, but on the bright side, it appears that you are dilating time while you are here. So, when you manage to get here, not much is going on in the real world other than a couple of missed snores from the girls."

I laughed. "That's... interesting. I mean, this is better than I hoped for... Jess, I will be honest here. I have felt lost since I woke up in this body, like a rat in the maze with my eyes covered and I can't figure out which way to go."

"I know, babe, I think Vex actually has a soft spot for you though. From what I can tell, I am some kind of mix of what Roxannez calls a construct with my stored personality in control over it. Other than these pesky firewalls or whatever they are. It's really weird. I don't even have a body, I can just... see everything in this small room and around you in the real world."

"What do you know about my life here?"

"Everything Derk. I... I'll admit I am a little jealous, but I wanted you to find someone else and I am glad you did. Not as hot as I am obviously, or was, I guess. But they are smoking hot in their own way."

I laughed. "You were always a little overconfident. Hell, I wondered what you saw in me back then. But If I knew you were alive..." I trailed off.

"Stop, babe. I do still Love you and that will never stop, but I am glad you found someone after me too. At least a part of me is. The other part wants to start a cat fight, tell them you are my man, and rub myself all over you while they watch me claim what's mine."

My smile was ear to ear at that. "I get it. But too much has happened, and they are with me now. You know the rules here?"

"Yes. Full access to them. I am allowed to tell you anything that a Roxannez would know about how things work here. However, as for their politics going on outside this world, there is a block in place on most of it. Though..." She trailed off.

"What?"

"I am getting some strange information about something chasing you. It's not from Vex. He is following the letter of the rules if not the spirit, but something else..."

"His boss?" I asked.

"Maybe? Whatever it is, it's something that no one in this world should have per the rules. Everything Vex programmed into my construct side says to shut up and accept it without question. Which makes me even more curious, but I can't do anything about it without hitting a block."

"That's fine Jess. Don't do anything that will hurt you. Wait... you said you can tell me what a Roxannez would know. Why do things work differently for me here? Why can't I project power like the ones I have faced?"

"That's easy. That is where you are screwing up. Well, the Roxannez construct part of me thinks you are screwing up, the human part of me thinks you are doing it right."

"What do you mean?"

"So, think of it as a two-way street of power. Well, it is when you get strong enough. For now, it's a one-way street. You have the same capacity a Demigod has when they get here on day one. Super strength compared to a mortal, speed dilation when in combat, and the capacity to bond one of the magical women here in this world into your service. Just at level one like a video game. It takes a while to work up to the shared power part."

I nodded. "Okay."

"Now, the Controller gave you some bonuses, but other than the ability to break the bonds, they are mostly passive. The way to get power here is to get more Chosen to bond with you and use theirs... Wow, this is one sexist world. I wonder if they have a reverse world for women or something—"

"Jess! You're sidetracking."

"Right, sorry babe. Anyway, a typical Demigod at first transfers most of the power from those chosen so that they can use it. Giving their women only the merest amount that is left. As they get stronger, they leave a little more behind for them and the bond makes the women think they are still just as strong, if not stronger than they were. Total lie by the way... You, on the other hand, seem to have given all the power to your women and only kept a little for yourself. That is why you can't throw fireballs."

"No shit," I said, thinking. "Can I make it an equal trade instead?"

"Eventually? You are not strong enough yet to control it on that level. You pretty much either take it all or almost none. When you get stronger, you should be able to control it better. Or at least, I will control it better for you. Right now, I don't have access. The fact that you combined their power, so they get a bit of each other's is supposed to be impossible."

"Vex said as much. How do I know how strong I am?"

"I would say that after everything you have done, you are still probably at a level five of one hundred. Making up a number system from bullshit that is. It doesn't really work that way and is rather complicated. But let's just say that Seir is likely at level fifty or more. Hard to be sure."

"Fuck."

"I wish," she joked. "Seeing the three, no four of you together was a little hot and bothering tonight, if you know what I mean, and I can't do a thing about it until you give me a body. So, hurry up on that, please. I need to get off."

I chuckled. "I missed you, Jess."

"I know. I kind of got a running video of your time here. Seeing everything, including when you thought of me," she said, a sadness in her voice.

"Any chance I can bring the girls here to meet you?"

"I think so," she said. "But remember, you should not have been able to create this place. You should never have been able to bring Madzia or even Stern here. A Sanctum is not something that most Roxannez can get except maybe Seir and those with high-level patrons. But with whatever the Controller gave you, and the ability to break bonds, you have a significant advantage over your rivals now. Even if you are still too weak to use it properly. You will have to try it and see."

Finally, I had information that was useful to me. I almost took back everything I had ever said against Vex.

Almost. The guy was still a dick though, so fuck him.

"Okay, what was the strange information you were getting? Can you tell me?"

"Not in detail, but someone is on your trail, and they may be about to attack the group you left behind. It's basically telling you to run for the east and start a base as quick as you can. If I understand it right."

"Going after the others?"

"I... think so."

I thought for a minute. The smart play would be to run like it said. "Okay, any details of what is chasing us?"

"Not really, just a feeling more than actual data. Doesn't seem like a large force, maybe fifty to one hundred? It's hard to be sure," she said. "Oh, also your time is running out. At your power level, you only get so long in here and then it's back to the real world."

"When will I see... hear you again?"

"They based it on how much power you have charged up. Oh, and I can tell you that this world was set up by what amounts to horny Roman-like space gods. So, you recharge fastest through sex or your orgies from last night. Orgies are fantastic, actually. Sleep, not to mention just time, works, but when you bone other girls, you get a bonus. Fucking bastards, they are."

I could not help but smirk at her attitude. "Hey, it's not so bad."

"Of course, you think that. You are a young guy again with a giant dick. But for us women, it is not the best thing that could have happened to us. Well, the mental enslavement side, at least. You know how I was in private."

"Insatiable." I laughed. "Ugh, I agree with some of that. I mean, I love Tyla and Tas, but the way they set this world up is going against all my morals from Earth."

"I love you Derk, and while I feel that way too, it's also time to get over those hang ups and do the job. If you don't start adding more women, you are going to lose this little war you are part of. Then all the Chosen of this world are going to live a life of slavery and mind control forever. You need to stop this, which means becoming more like them. Even if a few must sacrifice for the whole."

"I know," I said as I sighed deep. "It has just taken me a while to get used to it. I don't like the way this works. I keep thinking I want to be different, but realizing it puts me at too big a disadvantage."

"Adapt and overcome. That is what you always told me when we were going through colonist training."

"You're right. I agree and have been telling myself that. I'll work on it. I need to start growing an army, I fear that the only way to do that is with the oaths. Especially after Madzia."

"Good. You have to fight on their level. You can always set them free after. A few more seconds."

"Thank you, Jess. I was still a little lost here on what to do. Talking to you helped, even if there is a chance it's not the real you."

"You're welcome, Babe. I don't know what is real or not anymore either. Does it matter? I mean, it feels genuine enough to me... other than I don't have a body or can't get laid anytime soon. You're right. Vex is an asshole."

I laughed deeply as the Sanctum began to fade away.

"Oh Derk! Remember, be careful what you say outside your Sanctum. They obfuscate you from your enemies, but nothing is safe..."

Her voice faded away before she finished.

Fuck.

"Derk?" a feminine and sultry voice whispered into my ear.

"Hmmm?"

"Tyla said we could have some time alone, but we have to hurry," Tas said.

She slid her naked body over mine, bending forward to kiss me on the lips.

Need clouded my mind as I reached up to hold her close to my body. My morning wood needed no further motivation as she reached down and inserted it directly into her waiting entry.

"Mhhhhmmmm," Tas groaned as she impaled herself sitting upright and placing her hands on my chest. "I needed that after last night. I wanted my turn, but we fell asleep."

"Did you?" I asked, smiling up at her.

"Yes." She bucked up and down, her perky chest heaving up and down as she closed her eyes and rode my cock like it was a wild stallion.

It only took her a few moments to get into a rhythm as she leaned forward on me for leverage. Slamming her soaking entrance down on my cock repeatedly.

"Fuck, fuck, fuck," she mumbled softly as she went faster. This was pure need on her part, and I did not argue in the slightest. I needed it too, and I answered her by heaving my hips up in time with her and grunted in response to her motions.

I reached up and grabbed her tits, massaging them as she moved, and I could feel my end coming quickly as she slammed herself down quickly.

"I'm coming," Tasnia moaned softly as her body convulsed with an orgasm. Her end sent me over the edge, and I joined her in ecstasy, filling up her insides with what felt like never ending spasms of my own.

Tasnia fell forward on top of me, and we lay there breathing heavily for a few minutes. No words said as we held each other tightly.

"Good morning," I finally said.

"Morning Love. Nothing like a quick morning romp to start the day. Hopefully, we have time for more... vigorous activities again later."

The tent was barely lit, the reddish hue of the morning light just enough to let us see by. The candle must have burned out in the night, for the lamp was still dark. But I felt almost fully charged.

"I missed waking up to it the past few days. How are you doing on power?"

She gave me a confused look for a second and thought about it. "I feel almost full, I was doing pretty well this morning, but now I feel like I am about to burst."

"Sex charging," I said, thinking.

"What?"

"Apparently, for the bonded, sex recharges are power better than anything else. I mean... I don't really mind that much if I am being honest. Not for us. But it is just another bit of crap from the so-called 'gods' of this world."

"OH, we need to tell Tyla. That would explain why she was bouncing around with energy this morning."

"Means we need to do it regardless of company, need to warn Diane."

"Oh, she loved watching us last night. Did you see her?"

"Umm... Yeah, I saw her. Still, we should probably talk to her about it."

"Tyla and I will, Love. Don't worry about it. We will come to an arrangement."

"God, I love you."

"I know," she said, using her index finger to bop me on the nose.

She rolled off me and sat up. Leaning over to grab our clothes as I admired her pert ass and gave it a quick smack.

"Hey!" she said, smiling back at me as she threw me my clothes. "There will be more of that later. Let's go join the others for breakfast."

Leaving the tent, resisting the urge to whistle, the others had gathered around our small campfire.

"Morning," I said as I kissed Tyla on the top of the head. She handed me a bowl of nuts and berries with a hard travel biscuit to go with it.

Breakfast of champions.

"Sorry, breakfast is plain. We need to ration before we go across the desert in case that town doesn't have anything." Estelle said as she handed a bowl to Tasnia.

"It's fine... and about that. I think we need to have a change of plans."

That got the group's attention as everyone stared at me. Holding up my hands, I silently asked for a minute to explain before the questions started.

"I got... some information last night."

"In your dreams again?" Tyla asked.

"Yes, and part of that is that I need to be careful about what I say in public soon. So, I may not be able to explain everything to you. But on the brighter side, I am finally getting information that will help us."

I told them about the highlights from my experience last night, along with my intentions. Without saying how I got it and leaving out the parts of who gave me the information. Though I would have to tell the girls about it. It was wrong to keep that from them. I just wasn't sure how I would do it when we could be under observation.

"So that is what you want us to do?" Cecil asked. "Seems risky."

"Yes, but it's time to start acting rather than reacting. Plus, I need to get stronger, and this is one of the two quickest ways available to me." I said, purposely not looking at Diane.

While I needed to come to terms with bonding for power, I did not need to rush people into it. But it wouldn't bother me to take from my enemy's power and turn it against them if I could do it right.

"Anyone have thoughts or alternatives?"

"No," Lea said. "I agree with you, actually. Even with the risk."

"Good. We will need to do some scouting, but I think we can make it work. The trick is to get them separated. Anyone want to stay behind? Diane, you still have a choice to leave or stay back."

Diane looked up at me, staring into my eyes for a good several heartbeats before shaking her head. "No, I will come with you."

"Good, then it's decided. Let's get moving."

CHAPTER 11

INTERLUDE: AMBUSH

It was approaching evening and his forces were in position. His scouts had located the runaway encampment earlier in the day.

Masaki sat on his horse in a ravine far enough away that his prey would not hear his men. He could barely make out the small glimmer of light rising out of the small ravine the refugees camped in.

"As soon as it is dark, move your men out, surround them, and rush in. I want as many people alive as possible."

"Yes, Lord." Julian said, standing next to him. Masaki's mark is almost glowing on his forehead from the power in it, keeping him awake.

"You disagree?"

"No, my Lord."

"I can tell when you are lying, Julian. You are on the verge of triggering pain."

"If I may speak freely, Lord?"

"Granted. I am magnanimous and listen to my servants."

Juliane's shoulders relaxed as the minor bond released him to speak. He controlled his features rather than give offense to the Demigods comment. "I think we are making a mistake, my Lord. The men are exhausted, the scouts are about to collapse. All of them kept standing only because of your power. Moving only because you bade them to. They will make mistakes."

"They will have their rest soon. We had to beat the others here. These people are no real threat to us."

"But my Lord..."

"Enough," Masaki commanded.

Julian hunched over as the bond overwhelmed his will. He dropped to one knee as he fought to keep upright. "Yes, Lord."

"You had your say. Now do as I command you, for it is almost dark."
Julian slowly got to his feet, nodded once, and walked over to his men.
"Tsai?"

"Yes, Lord husband?" his Earth-witch said as she walked up to his horse.

"Go with them, take Joyann and Julika. Ensure they have enough
magical support."

"That will leave you unprotected, my Lord."

"I will have Oralie with me and be close by. I will be in the shadows and
come when you secure the area."

"I understand," the dark-skinned woman said as she left with his two
other bonded.

"What would you have us do?" Oralie said after she coaxed her own
horse next to his.

"Watch, intervene if needed. Let the men take the brunt of their
resistance and have your sisters follow up. No need to risk ourselves just
yet. Normal human men are easily replaced."

Masaki watched as Julian organized the fifty men under his command
into groups of ten. Giving the commanders of each group instructions on
what to do by drawing a crude map on the ground.

When they finished, Julian walked back over to Masaki. "Lord, we are
ready to move out. The scouts are in position."

"Proceed."

Masaki got off his horse to follow his troops, leaving most of their
supplies and gear behind and stalking silently to where the runways had
camped. He decided to leave no one behind, Julian was right that the
men were exhausted. So, he wanted them all present to make up for any
lapse in judgment by one or two.

His men moved into position, each only wearing the basics of leather
armor to be silent as they moved through the hills to their ambush
points.

The refugees had camped for the night in a small canyon in the hills.
While out of direct sight, it was stupid in that it left them no place to run
against his forces. The sides were not a sheer cliff, but the hills were steep
enough that it would be difficult to run up them to get away. Leaving
them only two options if they needed to flee.

Masaki found a small rise to stand on that was just high enough to see
inside the ravine at the group of runaways. Fifteen or so of them could

be seen. Mostly women and none of them had thought to place a scout on one of the hills to keep a lookout.

"Pathetic," he said.

"Yes, Lord," Oralie replied, her face passive but visible in the pale moonlight from above.

He watched as his men climbed the hills to either side while another of the groups went around to the far side of the canyon to prevent a simple escape.

The group of people sat around the fire. While from the distance it was hard to tell, none of them appeared to be talking. Most of them just sat on the ground staring at the pot that was probably cooking their dinner. None of them were aware of or even looking for the trap that was about to fall on them.

Two of the groups of ten mustered just out of sight at the entrance to the canyon, with three of his women in their midst. He saw as Julian stacked them in a single file line on each side of the hill and glanced one more time in the distance towards Masaki.

Masaki raised his hand and waved it forward.

"Go!" Julian shouted, his voice barely heard by Masaki due to the distance, and his men rushed into the ravine. Two more groups came down from the hills on each side after they heard the signal, followed by the last coming from the other side Boxing the refugees inside.

A perfect maneuver, even if the men were exhausted. It even impressed Masaki to a degree.

"We will reward them when this is done. Four hours of sleep before we march again."

"Yes Lord."

The refugees, for their part, were completely surprised. Only one woman managed to do anything when the blond woman cast a fireball at his men coming down the hill engulfing a single man in flames.

She went down immediately when Tsai cast a spear at her, using all her considerable earth-based strength to fling it at the woman. The spear, almost making a boom when it flew, went through her midsection at such speed the woman flew several feet back before landing into the ground. The spear sticking out with the blond woman impaled upon it slowly sliding down to the dirt as it went through her chest. Her body never stirring again.

The rest of the group surrendered, raising their hands in the air and offering no further resistance. Masaki could see the women crying from here as he smiled.

"Let's move up and finish this," he said as he started walking forward down the hill he had been observing from.

He heard a meaty thwack come from behind him, followed by a thump when Oralie tripped on her way down. Oralie let out a muffled cry in pain as she hit the ground.

"Heal yourself and get up, do not let them see you on your...." He stopped talking as he turned around.

Her eyes were wide as an arrow protruded from her throat as she struggled to breathe. Blood poured from her wound as she tried to heal herself.

"What?" Panic flooded through him, he looked up from her body at a blur coming to him.

He tried to dilate time so that he could match the threat, but it was too late as the sound of steel passing violently through flesh sounded in his ears.

The last thing he remembered was looking up at the sky... then seeing his body fall over his face as it followed his head to the ground.

CHAPTER 12

DECISIONS

The power flooded into me, but I was ready for it this time. My knees buckled only for an instant as the death of the Demigod saturated my core and spread from me to the girls. I felt it as my power core, or whatever it was called expanded and became larger inside me.

"Masaki. So, this was Masaki," I said as the name came to me.

I glanced down at the corpse of my foe as it fell on top of the head. My sword extended in a single hand as the blood dripped off the edge ever so slowly, having not let go of the time dilation just yet. The face of the Demigod looked surprised just before his body landed on top of it. Part of me was amused as the Demigod in question got to watch his own crotch land on his face in wonderment of what just happened.

I felt like I should say something cool, like 'eat a dick, asshole' or similar. But I refrained from it, if just barely. I guess I would never have a place in show business on this world.

I placed the Shadow's mantle stone in my right pocket, releasing the shroud that made me difficult to see and let time flow normally once again.

I reached down and wiped the blood on the sleeve of the fine silk shirt the man wore under his armor. Not like he would care, nor would I ever wear the man's clothes.

"Nice shot," I said behind me as I surveyed the field before me.

"Thank you," Lea said. "That was a lot easier than it should have been,"

"Overconfidence. A lesson I have to keep in the back of my head, so I don't make the same mistake."

I glanced over to where the others had gone. The women that Masaki bonded had fallen where they stood, dead when the strings to their master severed.

"Why did his men collapse too?" I asked, confused. "That didn't happen with Albris."

Most of the men that had surrounded the refugees had simply fallen to the ground, only a few were still upright and struggling. Making this battle much easier than I expected it to be even with the surprise.

"I don't know." Lea answered.

"Let's go find out." I said, as we marched our way over to the others. Tyla and Tasnia stood guard over the area, having rushed in as soon as Masaki's Chosen had collapsed. Tyla planned to play crowd control for any that tried to fight or escape, with Tasnia watching her back from any other threats.

None had even moved one way or another.

Estelle rushed over to the refugee who had a spear impaled through their chest. I doubt she could save the woman, but I would not stop her from trying. Orrick and Cecil moved over to check on the survivors, who seemed almost in shock from all that happened.

If I were to guess, their will had fully broken in this latest thing to befall them. Part of me thought that might be a good thing if I needed to go that route. But I would leave that part up to them. The men laying on the ground was a different story.

By the time I got close, all but one of the enemy troops had fallen. As I passed, I noticed they were all still breathing.

"What happened?" I asked the last one, who was on a single knee struggling to stay upright himself.

"Exhaustion," he croaked out. "Been awake for days. Only Masaki's power kept us going. We surrender. Please take my life and spare my men."

"I will not harm you or your men until you are awake. That is all I can promise you right now. But until that time, you will meet no harm and we will watch over you."

The man nodded, never answering, and just collapsed where he was. Asleep before he even hit the ground.

"Shit," I said, looking around. "Cecil, make sure everyone is okay, then get everyone working on stripping these men of their armor and weapons, bind their hands for when they wake up. Do not let them be harmed."

"Yes, Derk," Cecil said without question.

"Estelle, do you need help?"

The older woman was walking down the hill, she bowed her head and sighed before she answered. "No, Tricia is dead. There was nothing I could do."

I walked up to the older woman, placing my hand on her shoulder. "I'm sorry. I didn't know her well, and we didn't get along, but I did not wish her ill. Let's get everyone working and we can give her and those that were bonded to Masaki a proper send off before we leave."

"So that was the one who corrupted Madzia?"

"Yes, his name came to me when I killed him."

"Do you want us to burn him, too?"

"Nope, I have plans for him. Leave that to me."

I glanced down at the group of refugees, now only nine women and five men. None were moving, just staring at me. "Get moving. I know you are all tired and in shock. But we need to get the enemy troops bound, the bodies ready for their last rites, and leave before the next problem shows up."

"Who put you in charge?" a tall but overweight woman said.

Her name was Eileen, if I recalled correctly.

I pinched my nose.

I really have had enough of this crap.

I glanced at the woman. "I did, and I also saved your ass from going back to a life of slavery when I killed that Demigod asshole back there. So, I would truly appreciate it if you would kindly shut the fuck up and get to work like I asked. We can deal with power issues later."

Her eyes widened in shock, and her expression changed to anger as her fists tightened.

"Eileen!" Lea yelled. "He's right, and I agreed with him being in charge. Stop being a bitch and get to work."

The woman broke from her anger and stared at Lea. "You?"

"Yes, he is our one chance to fight back. Listen to him or run away. We won't be saving you again."

"But... how?"

"Later. We will discuss it all later. Just for now, let's get this place cleared," I said.

The others finally broke from their stupor and did what I asked. Eileen eyed me for a few seconds longer than the rest, but in confusion, not anger now. Finally, she nodded and got up, going over to one of the nearby sleeping soldiers, removing the weapon from him and loosening his armor.

I stood there for a few seconds, watching my girls and Diane walking over to me.

"Are we going to let them come with us this time, Love?"

"If they want," I said. "but it's time to make some changes. We can't hope that people will do the right thing just because it's in their best interest. I trust the four who joined us, but after that? No, it's time to do what I didn't want to do." I trailed off.

"What will you do, Master?"

"Only what I have too. But it might not be pretty."

"We trust you Derk," Diane said.

"I am glad to hear that from you Diane. I will try not to let you down. All of you."

"We know Master, we love you."

Tasnia nodded in agreement. Diane stayed neutral in her expression, but she didn't disagree, either.

"Thank you," I said. "I love you all too."

"What do you plan, Love?" Tas said as we finished placing the last of the bodies on the soon to be funeral pyre.

"I... am going to give them a choice," I said, almost sighing as I did it.

"We support you," Tyla added while wiping the sweat off her forehead.

The three of us hugged, holding it for a couple seconds before Tasnia reached over and brought Diane into it. "You're in this too, pink hair," she said. Diane tried to hold off her smile at being included but failed miserably as she turned pink in the face while doing so.

"Okay, let's go," I said after a few more seconds. We walked over to where Masaki's men laid bound, about three feet from each other in a line. All of them lying on the ground asleep. I did a quick count at forty-three of them in all.

"This all of them?"

"Several did not survive. They just stopped breathing as they slept. We didn't notice until it was too late," Tyla told me.

"Fuck."

Estelle walked up and joined us. "The others are all resting for now. Cecil and Orrick are scouting. Lea is keeping the group away from us, as you asked."

"Thank you, Estelle, we can't stay here too long and I want to give these men a chance to live." I sighed and looked down at the sleeping guards. "Two hours will have to be enough sleep for now."

I reached down and shook the man, who seemed in charge. He awoke groggy, his eyes opening and closing as he looked around. He struggled against the bindings holding his arms behind his back and I could see alarm on his face. "Relax, you will not be harmed... yet."

He glanced up at me, his eyes struggling to focus before relaxing against his bonds and placing his head on the ground. "Yet... So, you will kill us later."

"That remains to be seen. I do have some bad news. Several of your men died. We did not cause it, but we noticed it too late to help them." I said, standing up and walking around him, glancing at his men.

The man nodded. "He pushed them too hard. The human body isn't meant for that abuse."

"I am sorry for your loss. But I am also going to be honest with you... what is your name?"

"Julian," he said.

"I am going to be honest with you, Julian. I can't take the risk and leave you behind me alive. It's too risky for me and those I need to protect. There is another option, though."

"Are you one of them?" he asked.

"I have similar abilities, yes. But I am not one of them."

"Will you require us to serve you like we did Masaki?"

Estelle came up to my side and leaned forward. "What do you plan on doing?" She whispered, looking around to make sure none of the other refugees were in range.

"Like I keep saying, giving them a choice."

"Is that wise?"

"It's the only way. I can't afford to trust so carelessly, as much as I would like to. We talked about this at camp this morning."

She nodded. "I know, I just want to make sure you were sure. I actually agree with you, but you have seemed so... uncertain before."

"That's because I am trying to shake the morals of my old life. That officially ends today." I looked back down at Julian. "What do you say?"

"I do not wish to serve a monster anymore. Death would be preferable... But if it's the only way I can keep my men alive? So be it." His shoulders seemed to drop in shame.

I looked into his eyes and saw the conviction, the selflessness. "Well, I just hope that I am not nearly as bad a boss as your last one. There will be clear rules set, if you agree to them, that is."

"Get on with it," he said, seemingly resigned to his fate.

I bent down so that our heads were level. "Do you agree to serve me as part of my personal guards, upon pain of death, for any betrayal through action or inaction?"

Julian braced himself for the extreme pain, taking several breaths before nodding his head and saying, "I agree."

He closed his eyes hard but nothing happened. Reaching up to his left arm with his right hand, he lowered the tunic he wore and saw the new mark on his arm. "It... didn't hurt."

"That's because they are being dicks about it. Never had to hurt. They just like to remind you of the pain of betrayal and who the boss is. I think that is bullshit. As you can probably tell by now, I don't do pain, but if you betray me in any way, you die. Quickly. Painlessly."

Julian nodded. "I see. I understand, my Lord. I will ensure the men understand and swear to you." He almost seemed... happy?

"No need to call me that. Derk is—"

"Lord Derrick, a word?" Tyla asked, cutting me off.

I raised my eyebrow at Tyla's weird use of the words and took a few steps away from the man. Estelle and Tas were coming with us too before I called back, "Diane, free him, please."

"Yes, Lord," Diane said, copying Tyla.

"What is it?"

"Keep the title, Master, or something like it. You will never get the respect of others without it in this world."

I considered her words and had to admit she had a point. Rank was important. I had learned that lesson in both the Alliance Marines and Boston Police. I kissed her on the lips. "Thanks, my love."

I returned to the man. "Julian?"

"Yes, Lord?" he asked as he massaged his wrists.

"Start waking your men one at a time. If they agree, we can do the same oath all at once. Tas and Diane here will watch, though, to make sure they don't run or fight."

"They won't, Lord. I promise. Once they find out the terms you give compared to Masaki, they won't," he said.

"Very well. I hope you are right. See to it."

"Derk," Tyla whispered. "What about the refugees?"

"I am not sure. I don't want to leave them behind, but without an oath, I am not sure I can count on them if they come with us."

"Can you do the same bond? Even with the Chosen, without the... other stuff?" Estelle asked.

I laughed. "Without the sex? I think so. When I think of it, the name, the term 'Minor Bond' comes to mind. I think the only reason the Demi's don't do it is because to them it is a waste of potential power. I get nothing from these types. In fact, the minor bond takes only a small bit of power from me and stays with the person forever that I can tell. Or until I release them. Honestly, not sure how it would affect a Chosen, but it feels to me like it should work."

"So, what do you want to do?" Tyla asked.

"Give them the choice, same as Julian and his men, if they come with us. Otherwise, they can go where they please and are no longer my problem."

"Will you kill them if they refuse?" Estelle asked.

"No, they haven't earned that. Certain lines I can't cross. But we need to ensure they have as little information as possible. That might already be too late, but we need to try."

"I have an idea, if you will trust me," Estelle said.

"What's the idea?"

"I think it would be better if you do not know ahead of time."

I looked at Tyla. "Thoughts?"

"I have known her since I was a girl. I trust her, Master."

"Fine, you can talk to them first, before I ask them."

The three of us made our way over to the refugees. They looked battered and near broken, from what I could tell.

Hopeless, if I had to call it in a single word.

"Lady Estelle," Marylyn said as she walked up to us with Lea. "We are at an impasse on what to do. We all agree that nowhere is safe, but we do not have the power to stand up to the Demigods on our own." She leaned forward so close that I barely heard her whisper. "They are desperate."

Lea nodded and leaned over to me. "They will want to come with us now, I think."

"Good," Estelle said and looked back at me. She gave me a nod and approached the others. "Everyone, let me have your attention, please."

The men and women huddled around the fire, all turned in her direction. Orrick and Cecil had joined them, so we had the full group.

"I know you are all scared and tired," Estelle said. "It has been a long road and you do not know what to do next. The Demigods are too powerful to fight, they have bonded our sisters and mothers against their will. Each is stronger than the mightiest of our matriarchs with such power at their fingertips. What can we do against that?"

Sad nods greeted her as I wondered where she was going with this.

"What if I told you there was hope?" She asked, which got their attention. "That we could match the strength of the Demigods themselves? Even possibly break the bonds of our sisters?"

"How could we do that?" Eileen, the woman from earlier, asked.

"By bending our knees to a person with the same power as a Demigod. One that is on our side, one that will not bond us into slavery forever."

The crowd was silent, with shocked expressions on everyone's face other than Cecil and Orrick.

"How could you trust one of them?" Marylyn asked.

"Part of it is trusting my own instincts and the other part is taking a chance. We have no hope without it. The old ways are dead. It is time to embrace the new." Estelle answered.

No one spoke for a while as they digested the information. Finally, a short and wide-bodied woman with ruddy skin stood up. "What would you have us do?"

Estelle smiled and glanced around at each of them before turning to me, placing a knee on the ground, and saying "I, Estelle Halton swear fealty to Lord Derrick Schultz, I promise to follow his orders and any betrayal through action or inaction will mean my death."

The power welled up inside me and rushed towards the woman standing six feet away. Slamming into her and forming the minor bond. I slowed time to think as I reached into that power to change it before it fully took hold.

Happy with my modifications, I restored time and saw the surprised faces of all those before me.

"I... accept your oath," I said.

Estelle rolled the sleeve of her dress up and bared her arm to show the others. On it was the simple design I had created originally with Stern, a stick figure of an Eagle, anchor, over a circle since I couldn't get a laurel and shield in there right. It looked almost childlike to me, but at the same time it was mine now. Influenced by my past but steeped heavily in my present. That elicited some pride in it.

"What have you done?" Eileen asked as she touched the symbol.

"Put my trust in a man that I believe will never mistreat us or expect us to serve in his bed," Estelle said. "In fact, the oath is quite clear that the bond will break if he ever tries." She glanced over at me. "You added that?"

"I did."

Silence once again reigned over those present. Most of them just stared at me as if I might grow a second head and start killing everyone.

"I, Lea Ursula Hutton swear fealty to Lord Derrick Schultz. I promise to follow his orders and any betrayal through action or inaction will mean my death." Again, the power welled up and bound itself into a willing soul, connecting them to me just like Estelle, the same modifications in place.

Then more took a knee, taking similar oaths. The voices overlapped as they swore their fealty to my command. Even Cecil did, which surprised me, followed by Orrick.

The amount of power that left me made me stumble. Tyla caught my arm and held me stable while I adjusted to those that just swore their lives to me. I had a feeling all my newfound power would soon be depleted, but it was worth it.

It wasn't an army yet, but it was a start.

"Thank you," I said, as Tyla once again caught me before I hit the ground. Another forty-three people just swore themselves to my cause. "That's it. I have little left. They tapped my power dry, even with what I got from Masaki."

"Master, you need to rest and regain your strength. I can feel you pulling at my power for more."

"Yes, Love, rest."

"Just give me a minute. We need to get out of here, and with this many people on foot. We need to make time."

"My Lord?" Julian asked.

"What is it?"

"Masaki left the camp unguarded like the fool he was. We can use the horses and carts to make better time."

"Shit, I knew I was forgetting something. I was going to ask about that and forgot," I said. "Take your men and... Damn, we have a small army now. Okay, first let's huddle and get things situated. Get Estelle, Lea, Cecil, and Orrick and have them gather around."

I closed my eyes and sat down on a nearby rock. Trying to keep my head from spinning. Tyla and Tas squeezed in next to me to hold me up. Diane standing right near us. I must have fallen asleep on Tyla's shoulder because she was shaking me awake a few moments later.

"Master, they are here."

"I'm awake." I said, shaking the sleepiness away from my head. "Damn, I need coffee."

"Masaki had a small supply in his wagon, my Lord."

"Julian, you just earned your keep, and if I ever have money, a raise. Save that for me when we get to it."

"Yes, my Lord."

"First up, I am not a micromanager, and I am tired. I need people in the right place for now. That may not be the place where they stay though, and it may change as we go. But this is down and dirty until we figure out more later. Julian, tell me about your men."

"I have forty men at arms and three scouts left, Lord."

"Stop, I get we need honorifics for morale and discipline, but when we are in our meetings, just call me Derk, Sir, or nothing if that is easier. Got it?"

I got a round of nods from the group. Estelle even did a curtsy, which got an evil eye from me.

Man, I was tired.

"Julian, keep charge of the Men at arms. Scouts, go to Orrick for now. That work for you, Orrick?"

"Yes, L... Derk."

"Will the scouts have issues with that, Julian?"

"I will make sure they do not."

"Great, next. Estelle, you and Lea take all the Chosen. Get them situated for now. Eventually, we will need to figure out some kind of order of battle... command structure if you didn't understand that. Do we have any archers?"

"Derrick," Estelle said. "Archers are usually Chosen who can imbue the arrows with power. Other than the scouts, men usually fight with sword or spear and shield. Protecting those with power."

"That explains why no one ever has good range support, at least," I said, thinking. "Okay, for now, no changes to that. But that does not sit well with me. We will work on archers down the road. Let's just get everyone moving with you in charge of the groups of Chosen. Cecil?"

"Yes, Derk."

"Do you know the skills of the men that were with the refugees?"

"Homemakers mostly. No skills that would be of use in combat that I am aware of, but I will check. Most serve in the militia in their youth so they should have some skills."

"Most of them did their mandatory militia training, yes." Estelle agreed.

"Fine, I want you to take charge of them. We may throw them in with the men-at-arms later, but for now, let's keep them training separate. I don't want to add new folks to Julian's team until we have had time to work together."

"What do you want them to do?"

"Odd tasks for now, till we think of something better. There are only five of them so it's hard to decide. For now, maybe cart drivers if we have enough stuff at the camp."

"Understood."

"Okay, that is a start. Figure out more later when we leave this place. Let's get to work."

"Julian?" Tyla said.

"Yes, Mistress?"

"Can you send a cart back for us after you gather the supplies? I want Lord Derrick to take a nap."

I started to protest, but Tasnia placed her hand over my mouth, and I didn't have the strength to stop her.

"Yes, ma'am," Julian said with a chuckle.

"Thank you."

I watched as all the folks that now followed my banner, or whatever it was that I had, moved off to carry out my tasks.

"You want me to sleep on the ground?" I asked.

"No, Master."

"What then?"

"I believe that you told Tas this morning about sex recharging your power?"

"Uhm, I did mention that didn't I." Though I had not yet told them about Jessica. "There was more, but I don't want to say out loud yet, just in case."

"That is fine Master, we trust you," Tyla said as she stood and began unfastening the leather armor she wore when everyone was out of eyesight. "Diane. Can you keep a lookout while Tas and I recharge our beloved Master?"

"Yes Tyla," Diane said as she walked up the incline to have a better view of the surrounding area.

"Keep your eyes out there and not on us this time, please, Diane. You can have your own private time watching us later," Tyla said with a smirk.

I glanced up at Diane, who turned a solid shade of pink but did not bother answering.

"Take off your pants, Master. Tasnia, get him started and we can make quick work of him before they come back."

"I would love to do that for you Tyla," Tasnia said, an evil grin on her face as she strutted over to me, snapping her hips in her form fitting leather pants.

I watched as Tyla finished stripping out of her clothes, while Tasnia got on her knees in front of me and untied the strap to my trousers.

Damn, I was a lucky son of a bitch.

Chapter 13

Eastward Bound

"Better than walking, I guess," I said as I looked out the little viewing window facing forward.

I opened the little glass port, barely big enough for a child's head to fit through. "Cain, you okay out there?"

"Fine," he said, not a single note of emotion in his voice.

"Great chat buddy," I said and closed the window, fastening it with the iron bolt and then closing the curtain to give us some privacy.

"He does not like me," I said as I sat back on the mattress that made up the bed at the front of the coach.

"He doesn't like anyone. He is Norma's brother," Lea said.

"The other wind mage?" I asked.

"Yes."

I glanced around the cabin of the carriage. It was kind of like a coach you would see in the old west on earth. Though it was round instead of square, which gave it the feeling of being much roomier than a box would in a way.

It had a bed big enough for four to sleep across, which was a lot for most people, but perfect for anyone that had multiple wives like I did. Or its previous owner, I guess. The bed itself raised up about halfway so that it sat in the widest part of the circular cabin. Underneath was a place for storage you could access from outside, though there was a latch on the bed you could lift and get to it from there too.

The girls all lay next to me up against the flat part at the front of the cabin. Diane was asleep and Tyla and Tas sat between me and the open space in the rest of the Cabin.

"We will need to break and camp soon. Give the men a rest." Estelle said, sitting across from the table that was attached at the foot of the bed. While it could slide underneath the bed to create an open space and be out of the way, we kept it out so that Lea, Estelle, and Cecil could keep notes of our impromptu meeting.

"Soon as we meet up with Orrick and the scouts, we will call a halt for the day. I think we got enough ground in the last day to give us some leeway, provided our earth mage is doing her job."

"Miho knows how to bend the earth so that it looks unbroken after we pass," Estelle said. "A tracker could probably still find us, but between that and our wind... mages as you call them, it should make it difficult and buy us time."

I laughed. "Sorry, easier to roll off the tongue in my language to say mage rather than Chosen. I'm sure the world magic will turn it into Chosen in your head before long."

"Indeed," she said.

"Let's bring this meeting to order," I said. "Here is how the organization will play out for now. Estelle, you are too experienced for me to put anyone else in charge of the other Chosen. So, they all go through you. However, even saying that, Tyla and Tas only work for me and carry my voice. Diane, while not my wife for now, only works for me. I want her trained up but not in the field just yet. I know you and Lea are senior in rank to them, so I hope you don't mind."

"I understand," Lea said.

"Yes, Lord," Estelle followed.

"Yes, Master," Tyla added with Tas, nodding.

"I want it divided up into two groups. Lea, we need archers. I know we have two more wagons of supplies. Is there enough of those long bows to fit out your women?"

"I think so," Lea said. "We have nine of the longbows, and five women who could use them to full effect. Four wind and a single fire Chosen. They are usually the best with them in separate groups."

"Why is that?" I asked.

"Fire is easily empowered within the arrow and does not affect its dynamics in flight when used with magic. With the right training, you can heat it up several hundred degrees and send it in flight with enough protection that the heat will not burn the arrow until it strikes an object. Using the enhanced magical strength to send the shafts farther than men could."

"And the wind?"

"You can make the arrows shoot faster and longer with pinpoint accuracy."

"So, snipers?" She nodded. "That's what I thought, especially after seeing you take out Masaki's woman yesterday. Okay, start training the four of those women to be as good as you if you can. Can any of them fly with that power?"

"Wind is the most common power amongst humans, but flight is the hardest thing to learn by far. Taking years," Lea said. "I have just begun to master it myself but cannot stay aloft for more than a few minutes yet. It is... was, the final obstacle to achieving the rank of Lady for me."

"I want to learn a lot more about that, but not now, since we can't use it. Let me get back to you for more information later?"

"Yes," she said.

"Thanks, I am guessing fire for mass and crowd control and wind for sniper duty on the arrows?"

"That is how most armies are built, yes.

"Tas, I know you are good with the sword. Can you practice arrows with them as well? We only have one other fire mage left after Tricia's death and I want options."

"Yes, Love."

"Good. What about the others?"

"Earth Chosen are better for being swordswomen. They can use their enhanced strength to great effect if the men start to get overwhelmed. We lack the armor to properly outfit Miho though, and she is our only Earth... Mage," Lea said.

"Does Miho have training for that?" I asked.

"Some, but she is young. She just started going through training at the end of the war."

"Better than nothing. Can we get the gear for her?"

"Not as it should be in modern warfare, but we can put something together from the extra leather armor from Julian's men and make something that should work well enough."

"Tas, can you work with her on using the great sword? I can help with that as well, if needed."

"Yes, Love."

"Chosen with the Light element are usually used as scouts and assassins," Tyla added before I could ask. "Neither Kameyo nor Mahalo still served at the end, but they were both trained for scouting when they worked for my mother years ago."

"Understood. Can they also start training Diane?" I asked. "When she wakes up, anyway."

"I am awake Derrick, just listening," she said, never opening her eyes.

"I know... when you stopped snoring, it clued me in, but I wanted to let you have your pretenses."

Diane turned pink as the rest of us laughed, her gray-blue eyes opening to glare at me before burying her head under the pillow. It took a minute before Tas took the pillow off her head and smacked her with it, which caused her to join the rest of us in laughter.

"We all snore Diane, at least most of us and me most of all. Don't worry too much about it," I said. "Moving on though that leaves...?"

"Water," Estelle said. "If you approve, I will take charge of training both Tyla and Marylyn. While I know Tyla has an offensive ability with her new power, we should all be practicing lifesaving. Plus, I want to study how much power Tyla has and see if we can teach her to use it better."

I glanced over at Tyla to let her answer for herself. "I would like that, Master. There is still so much I need to learn."

"Then we have a plan for the Chosen... Estelle, do any of the water based have offensive powers? Or do they all just support?"

"With enough power, you can be very destructive with water. Tyla's mother..." Estelle stopped as she realized what she said. "I'm sorry, Tyla, but your mother is one of the strongest of us. She can manipulate water so well she could drown a hundred men at a time in a battle in the desert with the moisture in the air alone."

"Shit," I said, while also reaching over and taking Tyla in a hug. "Hey, we will get her back... somehow."

Tyla nodded and leaned tight into me. "I know what might really happen, but with you I have hope."

Changing the subject, I looked to the next person in line. "Cecil, you okay running the teamsters?"

"The what?"

"An old term from my world, originally used for horse team drivers. Seems that the men would be best used in that regard until we train them somewhere else."

"Yes, I am familiar with horse teams. The word now translates to me correctly. I can do that. I will train them in self-defense while they do those jobs and can act as security behind the lines for now."

"You going to be okay doing that?" I asked. "Or would you rather be with the fighters?"

"I served my time in the army. But I was a guard, and that is what we will be doing, letting Julian and his men fight if needed. This job is okay for me to lead. However, I would rather protect my wife in combat than lead from the front lines, if you can grant me that small measure of comfort."

"For now, I can live with that. Train the non-combatant men, they can stay with the gear if we need to separate. You can stay with your wife and protect the archers."

"Thank you, D... Lord Derrick," Cecil said, bowing his head.

"Still not used to that. Never wanted to be an officer in the Marines. Rather just be a grunt, but we do what we have to. Anything else?"

"Orrick is fine with leading the scouts," Estelle said. "Julian said he is a perfect fit to lead his men."

"Great. Let's have the light mages work with the scouts. Orrick stays in charge though. I want everyone to get used to men or women leading as needed."

Everyone in the group agreed.

"Let's adjourn for now. We can set up camp wherever Orrick found us a spot as soon as we get there. I want to train right after we set up camp. I will discuss watch assignments with Julian, but I want at least one of the Chosen awake on watch at all times, too. I would prefer the light ones to try and break through shadow mantles or other hidden threats, but with so few..."

"I can join them." Diane said.

"Not till you are more adept at your abilities," I said. "Or one of the two we have says that you are."

She looked disappointed but nodded.

"I think that's it, right?" I asked.

They all agreed as the group broke up. The light plywood door opened, and Estelle, Lea, and Cecil jumped out, leaving me alone with my girls.

Well, my girls and Diane. I needed to stop saying she was mine unless and until she joined us. She was still keeping an arm's reach, and I did not want to push.

"What do you think?" I asked the girls.

"A lot has changed in the past day," Tasnia said.

"Is it too much?" I asked her.

"No, I just will miss being only us... and Diane, you might as well be a part of us now."

Diane turned pink again and turned away. "Not yet," I heard her say. Interesting.

Ignoring that clue, I moved on. "I honestly do not know if we just painted a bigger target on our back or not. But we need to make moves if we want to have a chance."

A knock at the forward glass window caused Tyla to turn and open it. "Yes, Cain?" she said.

"Orrick is up there waiting for us with another scout," he said.

"Thank you," Tyla said, and looked at me.

"Go ahead."

"Follow where he wants us to go, then set up camp. When that is done, half an hour's rest before training."

"Yes, mistress." Cain said, and Tyla closed the window.

"And you said you hate being in charge," I said.

"It is getting easier. Especially since now I know I am doing it for you. It... gives me the confidence I need."

"That and you know you are my little subservient slut when you want to be, as well," I teased.

Tyla shivered a little. "Yes."

"On the bright side, Love. We get to do it in an actual bed tonight!"

I laughed at Tyla and saw Diane turn pink again. "Do you want to sleep elsewhere?" I asked.

"She is fine, Master. She told me she gets off on watching."

This got Diane to place the pillow over her head again, and both the girls laughed at her.

"Be nice," I said. "She is adjusting to us, so let's give her that time. Don't worry about them Diane. If you are comfortable with us... together, I don't care what you do on your own. If you need space or it bothers you, let me know and we will stop till we figure it out."

I heard a squeak that sounded like yes come from under the pillow.

Tas caught my eye and mouthed, 'She wants you.'

I gave Tas my best eye roll and scooted over to the edge of the bed, attaching my sword and leather vest. "Alright, I have been lazy long enough. Time to meet the men and women under my... command, I guess."

With that, I opened the carriage door and stepped to the side of the small porch on the back of the rumbling carriage. The dirt road we were traveling was well worn and my thoughts of us hiding the way we went made me laugh at the absurdity of it.

"Well," I said to myself. "There were a couple roads we could have gone, might give us some time at least."

I reached around the small ladder on the side that went up the rounded top of the carriage. Now that I thought about it, it was kind of like one of those classic gypsy style carriages they had in Europe when I went there in the Marines.

"Athens was a lot of fun," I mumbled as I climbed to the top. The carriage was made of a type of plywood. Light but strong and easily held my weight on the top of the cart as I surveyed the area around.

In front of the carriage marched most of my new men-at-arms. We had given them their leather armor back. They held their long spears in their arms and had their round shields draped over their backs.

Each had a small, short sword as well. Roman style they wore from their right side. Which started giving me ideas on how to organize differently.

"They know discipline, at least." Each one of them was silent, probably what they were required of under Maliki. While I like discipline, I would have to try and get them to relax.

I did not want to be that same kind of asshole.

"Need more men to do what I want to do, though."

Glancing behind me, two more cloth covered wagons trailed my own. These were more like the old west ones, covered in a brown cloth of cotton or wool, I was not sure which. Each of them held boxes and crates filled with supplies and pulled by mules.

"Need to do a proper inventory."

"What Master?" Tyla asked from underneath on the porch.

"Talking to myself, I guess. Need to do an inventory of all the gear."

"Tas, Diane, and I were planning on it when we camped."

"Good. Thank you."

Behind the other two wagons marched the last ten of Julian... I guess they were really my men now. The dust kicked up from the wagons probably made the march an unpleasant one. But it was one of those necessary evils of military formations.

"I was lucky we had powered armor on Earth." I said, going once again down memory lane.

Behind them rode Julian himself, on one of the four horses we had. My coach was pulled by two, and I had given one to Julian and the other walked a few paces behind my wagon.

"Do we have names for the horses?" I asked down to Tyla.

"No Master. They were Masaki's' personal horses, and the men never asked. The mules pulling the cargo wagons do, though."

This got me to chuckle. "Fine, we will figure something out."

Each wagon had a team of two mules, so that gave us four of each animal. Not the worst start for a new army. If I recalled my animal information correctly, feeding all of them would be the biggest challenge. Water was easy with our water Chosen on hand.

Food would be our biggest problem in the desert.

"My Lord," Julian said as he trotted up to me.

"Julian. How are the men?"

"Still sleep deprived, but not as bad after the naps you let them have."

"Soon, they should be able to have a full night's rest tonight. We will get a late start tomorrow to make sure even those on watch catch up on their sleep."

"Thank you, Lord."

"Also, make sure Estelle checks on all of them. I want everyone to be healthy as soon as possible. If she needs help, let me know."

"I will, my Lord."

I nodded and his horse cantered to the front of the formation. A bump in the road almost made me stumble, and I was guessing it was time to get off the moving object with no guardrails.

I took one more gaze around at my growing force before I got down.

"It's a start."

"Orrick, how are the scouts?" I asked.

"Little rough around the edges, Boss, but well trained. That Julian fella runs a tight ship."

"Good to hear. Did Estelle get you set up with the light mages?"

"She said you called them that." He chuckled. "They didn't seem too happy, but they agreed to follow orders. Though..."

"What is it?"

"I'm not sure I'm the best for the job, is all."

"Why is that?"

Orrick, God or gods bless him, just reached down and grabbed his balls and tugged twice. "Yup, still there. They are a problem."

We both laughed at that.

"Orrick, this is all happening so fast, I am not sure any of us are the right person for the job. Don't worry. If I think you can't handle it, I will fire you and make you a cook or something."

His left eyebrow raised in question, but I could not hold in the laugh for more than a second. He joined me a moment later. "Thanks, Boss."

"Hey, you have more experience in the woods than most and I know you better than them right now. I have seen a lot of scouts. They move and behave a certain way and you have that in abundance. Just do what you think is right."

He nodded and held out his hand. We grasped our wrists and shook. "Make sure one of your scouts is always on roving patrol at night. Check in with the guards at set intervals with a signal, so they watch each other."

"Already done."

"Good, and thanks. If it becomes too much, let me know and we can work something else out."

"Works," Orrick said and put a tall stem of grass in his mouth.

"Alright, it's going to be dark soon and I want to make the rounds." I turned and headed off to my next spot.

The makeshift camp was in a small meadow surrounded by trees. We were too large a group to get away with hiding like we had been, so instead we just had to hope that the trees surrounding us, and our guards would be enough if attacked.

I pondered if we should be like the ancient Romans and build forts everywhere we went. It was an idea, but we would lose time. Also, timber might not be desert and we could not carry it with us to make walls. I tried to remember what my old Captain, well he was the Operations Officer at the time, told me about them back on our first command together but was drawing a blank. We could probably do defensive berms if nothing else. But we needed more men to do it I think.

I shrugged as I approached my next target. "Julian..."

He was leading his men in some light sparing.

"My Lord!" he said, sheathing his blade that he was working with. "Chase, take over the drill."

Julian left his second working the men and walked over to me as they continued their blade practice. It looked like a kata with a sword, similar to what Tasnia's father taught me. A pang of loss hit me as I thought of Roman Baird. I needed to check how she was doing with that. Things had been so crazy I lost track.

"What did you need, my Lord?" Julian said, and it kicked me out of my melancholy.

"Uh... just checking in. See how you and the men were doing. What form is that?"

"Form, Lord?"

"You know what? I liked what Orrick used. Can you call me Boss instead of Lord? Makes me feel less like a pompous ass."

"Yes... Boss."

"Thanks. Yeah, the technique they are repeating?"

"Oh, that? It's a basic technique my father taught me. Just repetitive motions of the most common ways to use such a short blade quickly. If they get past the spear, chances are they are within arm's length at that point and there is no time to think. It is done with and without a shield."

I nodded. "So, this works on muscle memory?"

"Muscle... memory? I am not sure, Sir. They repeat the ten close strikes repeatedly so that if they have to drop the spear, they can do it without thinking. Using the best strike for the situation."

"Yeah, same thing. Do your men need anything?"

"Other than a good night's sleep? Not much, sir. Well, maybe a bath. We stink from all the running lately."

I laughed. "Fair. I did not see a creek or anything near here, but we have a couple of basins in the wagons. Have your men bring them out, and we can have Estelle or another water mage fill them up for you and the men to get clean. We can even have a fire mage heat it."

"That would be most kind of you."

"Tell Estelle and Marylyn to help on my order by filling it up. If they need help from Tyla with the water, let me know."

"Yes Lord, I mean, Boss."

I smiled at him as I walked away.

"That completes the rounds, now to business," I whispered to myself.

I found my command coach, as I had come to call it, parked in the center of the small encampment. I hiked up the steps and entered to find the girls sitting there with Diane at the table with bowls of soup in front of them.

"How are you three doing?"

"Tired, Master. We each trained. Estelle said I was very strong but still need a lot of refining. Here is a bowl for you and some traveling bread."

"Thanks," I said and took the bowl and bread. "Yeah, raw power is nice, but that doesn't automatically make you superman. You have to learn."

"Super... who? Never mind, Love," Tas said. "I am sure it's just another thing from your home world."

"Sorry, I keep forgetting. It's hard to break a lifetime of popular culture. It was a fictional character that had amazing powers in... make-believe stories in my old world. Anyway, what about you Tas?"

"I worked with Eileen. She is not so bad when you get to know her. Actually taught at the academy during the war. She is also helping me with my control and says my power is incredible." Tas beamed at the praise for a moment before she deflated. "She mentioned that I am doing almost everything wrong, though, and we needed a lot of work at it."

"Everyone starts somewhere. You'll be fine." I kissed her on the top of the head as I scooted by her on my way to the bed to sit down and eat.

"Diane?"

Diane looked up at me, a surprised look on her face. "Me?"

"Yes you. You are almost a part of us now, and I... well we all care about you."

She nodded, her face pinked, and she could not look back up to meet my eyes. "Kameyo spent some time with me. Says I have potential, but I need to learn to control my power. She showed me a trick of getting light to form at the tips of my fingers. Then told me to practice it regularly."

"Good. Sounds like we are getting things moving. Now, if this supposed help is really at the end of our journey, we might have a chance."

I finished the last of the stew, mostly vegetables with some unidentified meats in it. I could tell that Estelle was not cooking anymore. One of Cecil's men had probably taken over that duty and the quality had suffered. Maybe I should have her or Cecil teach them?

I pondered that while taking a bite of the bread. It was like biting into a rock, and I forgot how hard traveling bread was. My face grimaced, and the girls laughed at me.

"Master, you were supposed to soften the bread in the soup."

I spit the bread into the bowl. "Yuk. Yeah, forgot. Live and learn."

"What's next on the agenda?"

"Bed," Tyla said.

Tasnia agreed with a nod and a smirk.

"Right now?"

Tyla got up from the bed, closing the curtains and locking the door. "I did not say sleep."

"But..." I said and looked at Diane.

"We promised she could watch, remember?"

Diane's face blazed pink, and she looked away, but did not disagree with Tyla's statement.

"Uh..." was all I got out before Tyla climbed up on the bed and straddled me.

I guess we were going to bed.

CHAPTER 14

——— • ———

FAMILY MEETING

The three of us lay there staring up at the curved roof of the carriage, each of us still panting. But we were fully sated now, basking in the afterwards of our sweaty romp. Luckily, no one in the camp needed us, or they heard the noises and thought better than to disturb us. Either way was fine with me.

"This bed is so much more comfortable than the camp rolls," I said.

"It is," Tasnia said. "Not having a random rock poke me in the back is nice."

"You were not on your back much tonight," I said with a laugh.

"My knees then..." She slapped my shoulder.

"I approve," Tyla added from my left. "What about you, Diane? Did you enjoy the view from down there?"

I leaned over Tyla to see Diane throw the blanket over her head followed by a squeak, but other than that, she remained silent.

"If it bothers you, Diane, let us know."

"Okay," she said, her voice cracking and almost a whisper.

I smiled and set my head back down with a yawn. "It's getting late. I still feel a little guilty about not standing watch."

"It is..." Tyla said as she fought off a yawn of her own. "No longer your job, Master. Let the troops who serve you do their job."

I laughed. "Yeah, I'm still not used to that. It all happened so fast."

"The world, or what is left of it, needs hope," Tyla said. "You saw the refugees. That surprise attack had them in shock. The day before and they would not have considered it."

"True. Glad we came back to help. How are you doing, Tas?" I asked, changing the subject.

She sighed, knowing what I was really asking. "I think about him and what happened all the time, but I have not cried over it in a few days. I am not sure if that is good or bad."

"Things like that get easier with time. They still suck, but they hurt less. I... We are all here for you if you need it."

"Thank you, Love." She leaned over to kiss me on the cheek.

"Yes, we are," Tyla added.

"Thank you both."

"Me too," Diane said, still under her blanket.

"Thank you too, Diane. Did you want a kiss as well?" Tasnia asked with a grin.

"Eek," Diane yelped and grabbed the pillow, placing it over her head without ever coming out from under the blanket.

"If you change your mind, I am sure Derk would let you join us in the bed. Might be more comfortable than the padded seat down there."

"Tas, leave her alone," I said.

"Yes, Love." She sighed with a cute pout. Then a giant yawn hit her as she rested her head on my chest. "Okay, I think it's time for sleep."

"Night everyone," I said and closed my eyes.

"Good night, Master, Tas. I love you. You as well, Diane."

Another squeak from the covers made me smile. I placed my arms around the girls and squeezed them tight as I felt my brain start to drift.

I thought about the power living in my chest and felt it near full to bursting from all the activities we did that night.

I wonder if...

I thought about my sanctum and when I broke Madzia and Stern of their bonds, trying to find that same place while I focused on bringing Tyla and Tas with me.

My eyes still closed, I focused on the powers inside as my brain fought me in order to drift off to sleep. Eventually losing the battle as sleep overtook me.

My eyes opened, and the first thing I noticed was the stars had become brighter at the edge of my sanctum.

"It worked. I got here when I wanted."

"Master?" a voice called from behind me.

I turned to see Tyla and Tas both lying on the ground, as though waking up from sleeping. They glanced around the space as though confused at where they were.

"Oh wow, I even brought you in here."

The first thing I noticed when I gazed upon them is that they did not have any chains on their body like Madzia or even Stern. They glowed with an ethereal light that had hints of sparkling flecks coming off it. Tyla was a bluish one, with motes of red from Tas.

Both were completely nude as they sat up on their elbows to study their surroundings, all save for a small collar around their necks with my symbol on it etched in what looked like a ruby.

"Yay, visitors!" Jessica called out and for a second, my heart stopped. My old earth norm's making me dread explaining another woman to them.

"Uh…" I started before I could get a hold of myself. "Wait, it's probably fine. Tyla, Tas? I did not want to mention this in the real world, but you remember me telling you about Jessica?"

They both locked eyes with me at the same time.

"Master?" Tyla said, confused. "You said she was never coming back."

"She… both did and didn't. Vex set up some kind of interface and used her memory or soul or… I don't know what. She is Jess but like a reincarnated form, I guess."

"I am going to go with I am the new and improved version of Jessica," the woman in question said aloud.

"Where is she?" Tas said, looking around.

"I am not a corporal being, just yet," she said, but stopped. "Oh, this is weird. I am hearing her true language and the translation going on inside me at the same time. Okay, I'm going to have to fix that." Jessica said and went silent for a second. "Better, now I am only getting the translation. The human part of me very much did not like hearing both voices."

"You okay?"

"I am. I have access to so much information. Unfortunately, when you are here, most of it goes into a lockdown and I can't remember any of it. The artificial intelligence, or whatever is controlling the flow of information, is damn smart."

"Master, I do not understand."

"I know. For lack of a better way to say it, I complained to Vex that I did not know what I was doing, and he did not tell me shit. So, he created an... assistant to give me the information I needed and used Jessica as the person to tell me about it."

"I'm just going to go with it is your old lover coming back from the dead to help us. That makes more sense than what you're telling me, Love."

"Ugh," Jessica said. "I don't like the idea of being a ghost, but if that works for you, fine. I am just so glad you are here. You both are prettier than I thought looking through Derk's eyes. Babe, I take it back. They are almost as hot as I was."

I couldn't help it. I laughed, which got looks from both girls. "Sorry, she had a bit of an ego back in the day."

"It's not an ego if it's true, Babe."

I rolled my eyes again. "Fine, but I love both of you just as much, and you are all beautiful to me." I walked forward and kissed Tyla on the lips first, followed quickly by Tasnia, who slipped her tongue into my mouth.

"Damn." Jess said. "This is so frustrating without a body. You need about ten or fifteen more made up levels to unlock that feature stud. So, get to work."

I broke the kiss with Tas and gave another quick one to Tyla. "What do you mean?"

"Your power is full after your little romp, and you gained some levels after you killed that Masaki character. You can now get to your Sanctum when you sleep and bring guests with you. Though doing it, you need to be at full power, so more orgies before bedtime."

"Fair. Last time you said I was at level five. What about now?"

"About ten. Masaki was fairly powerful. Good thing you came at him unaware, and he was an idiot. I am not sure you would have won in combat with him."

"Thanks for the confidence boost," I said.

"You could now. But before he had you outnumbered in women bound to him and a higher level of raw strength and power. Not sure if you had him on training and fighting power, but based on what I saw, he was stronger... on paper at least."

"Can I transfer power between us now, like enough of their elements to cast magic outside my body?"

"Not yet. That would be about level twenty-five using the hack of a number system we just made up. Fifteen or twenty to give me a body here."

"What does she mean, Master?"

"She... basically we came up with a system from one to one hundred to tell me how strong I am compared to the other Demigods. Seir is probably about fifty or sixty. I am now level ten."

"Oh," Tyla said, clearly concerned.

"Yeah, that is why I can't face him just yet. Not to mention the men and women we have is not exactly an unstoppable army right now."

I noticed both girls were now walking around the empty room freely, fully in the nude. I guess they felt comfortable in front of Jessica like that.

I was also in the nude. I wondered if I could imagine some clothes. I glanced at the two beautiful naked forms in front of me and disregarded that idea. I was still a guy, after all.

Also, while I felt nothing, their bodies told me they were freezing. Or perhaps other things were making their nipples rock hard. Being Chosen apparently made you horny all the time since the pregnancy rate was so low.

Or maybe it was the gods trying to get their rocks off more by making the Chosen super horny. I was not honestly sure, and it was the one thing I was not complaining about.

"Okay," I said, glad we all could meet like a family of sorts. "What's the latest, Jess?"

"The primary threat you eliminated, but there are at least two more coming. However, they seem a ways off. I have little more than that and am actually reading between the lines."

"Fair, no inkling how large a force?"

"From what I can tell, Seir only lets his lieutenants and followers have limited personal guards based on rank and trust. Masaki only had fifty because Seir did not trust him as much or did not prove himself yet. But his most trusted have up to one hundred."

"That's fairly detailed. How do you know?"

"Vex, or the Controller likely, is giving me information. I don't know where it came from, only that it is there."

"So that means as many as two hundred will be chasing us," I said.

"Master, I do not think we are ready to fight two hundred enemy soldiers, plus two demigods and their harems."

"I agree. We need to make better time starting tomorrow when the men are rested. Hopefully lose them in the desert. Any idea what we will face, Jess?"

"There are many threats in the desert. But there is a road leading through it that should be safe for you to travel with your forces."

"Where does the road lead?" I asked.

"It does not say. Again, information with no context and an unknown source."

"Tyla? Tas? Do either of you know anything?"

"Only that the road was there when the humans first arrived," Tyla said. "It is said that some of those who lost the civil war after the Chosen took power went down that road and were never heard from again. The majority fled south."

"My father said that those that explored it never returned as well."

"Great," I said with a sigh. "Not giving me confidence here."

Tyla came up to me, her perky breast and hard nipples getting my attention. The smile on her face showed me she had caught the downward motion of my eyes as she wrapped me in her arms. "Master, I think we should take the chance and follow the road."

She promptly kissed me on the lips, her tongue meeting my own. After a few seconds, she broke the kiss, and my manhood was pushing up against her to let me know what it wanted.

"How can we help you feel at ease?" Tyla asked as another set of arms came at me from the back, the soft lips of Tasnia kissing me on my shoulder as they worked their way up my shoulder.

"Oh God, I wish I had a body right now." Jessica said.

"Do you want us to stop?" Tyla asked over her shoulder.

"Fuck that, keep going." Jessica commanded.

Tyla dropped to her knees, grasping my manhood in her hands, and putting the tip of my rod in her mouth.

"Do you like to watch as well, Jess?" Tas asked in between kisses on my cheek.

"Not before, but now I am wondering if some things have changed with this new me. I was also never into girls before, but..." She trailed off.

My raging erection somehow got even harder in Tyla's mouth. She had never been one to share in our time together on Earth, but now that she said she felt aroused by me with other women, I could not think of a time I had been more turned on.

Tyla licked my shaft several times before shoving my length down her throat as far as she could go.

She held it for a heartbeat before her throat tightened around my shaft and she pulled back, sending shivers down my back from the pleasure it gave me.

"Tyla, I am not going to last long if you keep doing that."

"Do it again," Jess said, her voice husky and deep.

Tas came around to the front of me and kneeled next to her sister-wife. "My turn." She put the tip in her mouth and bobbed up and down several times before she also shoved me as deep down as possible.

I resisted grabbing the back of her head to hold her in place as the pleasure shot through my body and my knees weakened involuntarily.

Tas held it in place for several heartbeats before she coughed and had to back off. A long glob of saliva mixed with pre-cum connecting her mouth to my tip as she backed her head away.

"So fucking hot," I whispered, almost losing my ability to stand.

Then they took turns.

Tas did it again, this time going farther and holding it longer, before backing away and handing my rod over to Tyla to do the same. They got into a rhythm, each taking a turn and bobbing down as deep as they could go before switching out yet again. My knees buckled several times before I finally felt my end coming.

"Come on us, Master," Tyla said when it was Tas's turn, and I nodded my head as best I could.

"I... I'm coming," I got out and Tas backed off just in time. Both girls reached over and their hands pumped my manhood in unison as the streams of pearly liquid came rushing out.

First it landed on Tyla's face with her mouth wide open, then they turned it and the next blast landed on Tas.

Flashes of light happened in my vision, and the orgasm hit me so hard as they traded who got hit with the next several shots of my seed.

"Holy shit," Jessica said, and in my hazy vision I looked over to see the blond bombshell that was my lover in corporeal form.

I collapsed onto the ground as she faded out again only a moment later, but we both smiled as our eyes met for real for the first time in...

I honestly was not sure how long it had been now since we had seen each other.

My last view as I saw the room dissolve was the view of Tyla and Tas kissing, both covered in my essence.

CHAPTER 15

— • —

INTERLUDE - WAR IN THE NORTH

The wide valley in front of Seir was covered in the bodies of men and dwarfs alike. The battle that had raged for days was still in full swing.

"My king," Josephina said. "They are reforming their troops for another attack."

"I can see," he said, barely containing his rage. "We need to break through and eliminate them."

"Yes, my King."

But it was easier said than done.

"Baldr can't have the reserves to keep attacking like this," Seir continued. "Why does he waste them so?"

"I don't know," Josephina said.

"Send in the cavalry on the left flank," Seir said.

Josephina lifted her hands and sent a burst of colored light into the daytime sky that was still bright enough to be seen for miles in the shape of a star.

The predetermined signal was the sign the cavalry commanders were waiting for. Seir watched as five hundred horses with fully armored knights trotted onto the battlefield from the left side of the lines.

The dwarven formations on the other side of the battlefield noticed them coming and rushed to reform their own lines. Hundreds of them set their heavy shields on the grounds facing the oncoming heavy cavalry with their long spears in front.

Seir used his hands to create a small water-based prism to enhance his vision. He observed as the Calvary created a wedge as they prepared their charge, speeding up and dropping their long lances to hit the now fortified enemy position to their front.

The faces of the dwarves on the lines hardened as they braced for the impact. He could easily see their heavy armor and thick triangular shields covered in mud and gore from the days of hard fighting. When the cavalry was at the right distance, he knew it was time.

"Now, Patricia." Seir said.

Patricia, silent before then with her hands placed firmly on the ground, grunted as her magic released. A low moan from her lips followed the grunt as she connected to the water locked deep underground ground and sent it upwards.

Right towards the Dwarven lines.

The mud and soil beneath their feet liquefied as they sank almost a foot into the mud. This covered almost a quarter of their already short stature and practically all of their shield became encased when Patricia sucked all the water right back out, and the mud hardened to a near cement.

The cavalry hit right at that moment. The lances of the knights all lowered right at the heads of their victims, who could not move or adjust their shields or spears. While some of the long spears stuck in what used to be mud managed to kill the horses, it was but a tithe of their overall might.

They massacred the Dwarven lines as the blood and gore sprayed all over the field from the impact. The horses all jumped their obstacles with ease, even weighed down as they were by the armored knights. The few dwarves that survived did not last long as the large hooves of the war horses pulverized their enemy beneath them when they landed.

Seir gazed to the second lines that had formed behind the first, not liking what he saw. "Recall them," Seir said, and a horn sounded behind him from his signalman.

The cavalry stopped their progress before they got to the next line of dwarves and returned the way they came, taking out any survivors as they trotted by the original line of dwarves. The well-trained unit did exactly as they were supposed to.

"Excellent job, my dear," he said to Patricia. "Josephina, have the heavy troops advance."

"Yes, my king," she said and sent up another signal flare of light.

"Patricia, wake up," he said to the now sleeping woman on the ground.

She startled awake and looked around with her wide eyes. "I am sorry, my King."

"I will give you more power soon," Seir answered. "Why did it not affect both lines?"

"One of their own stopped me before I could get the second line. I am sorry I failed you."

"Baldr has the backing of Takus. I am not surprised he has powerful weapons of his own. You did well. Clean yourself off and meet me in my tent. Be ready for me."

"At once," she said and went off to do as directed. Seir followed her shapely behind as she left.

"Josephina, ensure our forces make progress. If they encounter too much resistance, pull them back and we will weaken them some more. I will go take care of Patricia."

"Yes, husband," she said.

"May I join you?" Einestra asked.

Seir glanced at the blond woman, her light leather armor shaping her small breasts. "You may."

"What about me, my King?" Miranda said.

"Stay with Josephina. Serve her as she needs."

The red-headed woman pouted but nodded. "Yes, husband."

Seir followed the direction Patricia had gone. He glanced around at his encampment. Thousands of his men had followed him to the north, expecting to find elves but encountering a Dwarven army instead.

"I will need to ask the overseer about this," he said to himself.

"My king?" Einestra asked.

"Nothing. Have the scouts seen any other armies?"

"None of the aerial scouts have my Lord. I would have to ask the ground scouts however to be sure, but none have been reported."

"I understand." Seir did not like the difference in information. The Overseer warned him about the Elves to the north, led by Landas, were invading his human lands, but found Baldr instead.

He could defeat Baldr in a day if he knew he could risk his forces without worry, but not knowing if Landas and Baldr were working together, he could not risk it.

He passed by his personal guard, who opened the flap for him as he entered his large tent to find Patricia naked on his bed, her legs wide and her hands nestled between them.

She was also sound asleep and snoring lightly.

"Wake her... gently," he commanded.

"Happily, my King," Einestra said as she sauntered over to the bed, shedding her armor piece by piece as she took each step.

Seir sat in his chair to watch as Einestra removed the last of her covering, revealing her supple, naked flesh. Her small yet gravity defying breasts excited him as he watched her climb on to the bed slowly. Shaking her ass because she knew he watched and placing her hands on either side of Patricia's inner thighs as she buried her face inside the raven-haired woman's crotch.

Patricia startled at the touch but calmed instantly when she glanced down at who was doing it. Laying her head back down on the pillow with a loud and sensual moan.

Patricia reached down and ran her fingers through Einestra's hair, yanking ever so softly while she directed the blond where best to go.

Seir removed his own clothing as he felt the subtle motes of power emanating from the two, the acts recharging both the bonded and his own power. Seir took off his heavy mail armor and tossed it on the ground, continuing to watch as the two women pleasured each other.

"My King, a messenger, approaches from the south by air," the guard from outside called.

"Send someone to investigate. Only disturb me if it is important," he replied and continued to undress.

Einestra stopped her task just long enough to glance up at Seir.

"Keep going," Seir said as he let his pants fall to the floor.

Einestra went back to licking Patricia's clit, her head nodding as Seir approached the blond woman from behind. He grabbed his now rock-hard member and was just about to shove it into her darker hole when the guard called once more.

"King Seir, it is an emissary from Aulus."

"They can wait!" he said as he prepared to thrust himself deep into Einestra.

"I am truly sorry my King," the guard said again. "She says her Lord commanded it was urgent."

"Fine, send her in." Seir said as he stepped away from his woman, facing the entrance as a brunette woman he could not remember the name of entered and bowed.

From the way she looked, she was about to collapse from exhaustion.

"What is it?"

"My King, Aulus, bade me fly here at the best speed to tell you. We found Masaki. He is dead."

"What?" Seir said. "Explain, now."

The woman cowered lower. "They found him, his body being eaten by local wildlife, his head on top of a long pike stuck in the ground. We believe that the rest of his guard and his women were burned. We found a nearby pile of ash with remnants."

Seir walked over to his chair and sat, glancing up at his women, who had stopped to stare at him while waiting for his command. "Who told you to stop?" he asked.

Patricia laid back down on the bed, and Einestra went back to her duties.

Seir glanced at the intruding woman once more. "Anything else?"

"Our tracker says that a large group left the area heading south. They could have gone south or east. The trail is subtle, but he thinks he can find them. They wait for your orders before proceeding."

Seir grasped the bridge of his nose. Aulus could never think for himself, he needed to send someone he could trust to think. "Very well, how many men do you have?"

"Gnaeus has joined Aulus. They each have their guards of a hundred men, plus their women, full harems each, at least when I return that is."

"The brothers should be enough... but..." Seir stopped to consider this for a moment. "Leave us for now. You may rest, be prepared to take my words back to your lord within four hours."

"Yes, my King," she said and stood, never looking up, turned and left the tent.

"Patricia?"

"Mhmm, yes my King," she said, her hands still tangled in Einestra's hair.

"I can't leave the front, not while Baldr and possibly Landas oppose me here. I need you to travel south as quickly as possible. Take charge in my name and help the brothers eliminate the threat."

"Yes.... Mmmm... My King."

"Einestra, you will carry her," he said as the woman in question never stopped servicing Patricia, only shaking her ass at him in response while she mumbled something he couldn't understand.

Seir closed his eyes, feeling the power in him he took from his women. While he left them with a fragment of energy, he kept most of it for himself.

However, if they were to succeed, they would need to be more powerful than the Controller's agent working against him in the south. That meant some sacrifice would need to be made.

He pushed a significant amount of his power into both women at once, as quickly as possible.

"Oh, fuck!" Patricia screamed as she orgasmed, her entire body locking up for several seconds. Einestra joined her by whimpering as her body convulsed in pleasure. Then the screams of ecstasy were followed only a few heartbeats later by silence.

Seir approached the women, now both passed out on his bed. Reaching down to them, both were unresponsive to his touch. The bed underneath them almost soaked.

"I may have given you too much... Guard!"

"Yes, my King?"

"Send a runner for Miranda and tell her to attend to me quickly. Have others prepare a harness so that Einestra and... whatever Aulus' concubine was named, can carry Patricia to the south."

"Yes, King Seir," the guard said, and he heard the man call for runners.

Seir sat in his chair while he waited for Miranda to come to satisfy his urges, thinking of how best he could end this stalemate in the north quickly in case his women failed.

Chapter 16

Paradise

"How far?" I asked Orrick as we walked around the makeshift camp that evening.

"Another day I reckon'. There used to be a small settlement on the edge of the desert that we may be able to get some supplies at. I wish we had some air scouts to be sure, but none of our wind users are strong enough."

"Lea said she can do short bursts but can't fly for more than a few minutes at most. Though that probably saved her, the Demigods targeted most of those that could fly first when they... bonded them."

"I agree," he said. "I was actually thankful the gods blessed Estelle with water. Wind, fire, light, and earth are all considered more important to fighting and always the first to die."

I grasped his shoulder. "It's funny how chance works out like that. Two feet to the left and the car... I mean the cart runs you over by the driver that wasn't looking."

Orrick nodded. "All our Wind Chosen are young. They can still fight, but sustained flight is the barrier to getting the rank of Lady and is harder than most. Many never get that high. In fact, most don't. Though lots of women get hurt pushing themselves to learn too fast. Estelle has mended plenty of 'em. Some died from the attempt."

"I bet it probably became mental after the first crash. They learn they're mortals then never quite have the same level of bravery. How are the light mages working out for you?"

"Oh fine, they took a bit to get used to it, but in the past few days, we got the bugs worked out. Wish I had more."

"We all do. Thanks, Orrick. Going to check on my girls."

We split up as I headed back to my coach. The girls had been deep in their own training each day while we moved. The small force I had was starting to come together at least.

I watched as the guards on duty walked the perimeter. Cecil's smaller group of... I guess you could have called them househusbands at one point, now had the setting of the camp and cooking duties down pretty well. The food improved when Cecil got involved too, Estelle even helped teach them some. The scouts even brought in deer and rabbits, so for food we were doing much better than I had feared.

The problem we had was that it was getting colder as winter approached. While the hills we were traveling had a solid road to use, it was high enough that the evening was cold, and we just did not have the gear for winter. Or at least not enough for everyone. Julian's men had some gear, but our refugees did not.

It would likely be better when we leave the hills, but I had known plenty of deserts to get freezing in the evening. We needed to figure something out. Either we needed to resupply or create our own.

One of Cecil's men said they knew how to make blankets from the deer hide or any other large animals we caught. Something about using the brains of the animal and water in a solution. Coat it in the evening and again in the morning and you have a decent blanket when it dried. Eventually, at least, it took time to do.

There was more, but that was about as far as I got before I told the man that ignorance was bliss, and I would be rather happy if he didn't tell me anymore about it. Just to do what he could, and I would have the scouts and troops try to get us more raw resources as they could.

That would help with the food and warmth issue, the problem was that it was a slow process. I hoped that town was where Orrick and the maps thought it was. We could use more carts, supplies, and things that could help us move and build at the same time.

I entered the coach that I now called home. All three of my... I mean, both of my girls were there. Diane was also sitting at the table.

"Derk!" Diane was the first to speak. "Look what I learned today!"

I had never seen her so happy, and it brought a smile to my face. "What did you learn?" I said, looking at Tyla and Tas to see their big smiles as well.

Rather than answer, Diane put both of her hands together and closed her eyes. A kind of shimmer came over them as if looking at the end of a hot road in the summertime back on Earth.

After a second, she took her hands and wiped them over her hair, and I saw the pink hair turn black.

"Holy shit!" I said in response. "How did you do that?"

Diane did not answer right away. Her eyes stayed closed as she concentrated. She took her hands one more time and wiped them over her ears.

It was not perfect, but her ears that were just sticking out of her hair became almost invisible. I could still see something, but it was as if it was fading in and out when I concentrated on them.

Diane opened her eyes and looked up at me for approval. Without thinking, I reached over and gave her a kiss on the forehead. "That's great. I am so proud of you."

Her concentration faltered at the kiss and her hair turned back to pink and her ears reappeared as her face soon matched her hair in hue.

"Oh, sorry. I wasn't thinking," I said and took a step back.

"It's fine, Master. I am sure she doesn't mind an innocent little kiss. Right, Diane?" Tyla asked with a smirk.

Diane nodded but did not speak. I kept forgetting her nerves when it came to the touch of others. Well, others that were not Tasnia and Tyla. She seemed okay with them.

"Still, I'm sorry. I didn't mean to break your concentration. That was quite good. Did Kameyo teach you that?"

"Y... yes," she said, stammering out the words. "She said I was a natural at bending light around myself. If..." She trailed off.

"What is it?" I asked.

"Oh, nothing..."

"Please, say it."

"I was just thinking how much easier the last year would have been if I could have done that to blend in. Less smelly too."

The girls laughed. "I remember what we had to wash out of your hair," Tas said. "You are a braver woman than I."

I joined in on their laughter as I sat down next to Tyla. "So, what else did you do today?"

"I worked with Eileen on imbuing arrows," Tas said. "I am getting better, but they still burn up before they reach the end. I need to get the barrier between them to last longer."

"And you, Tyla?"

"Working on the temperature control with Estelle. Our ability to combine the power fascinates her, as limited as it is right now."

"Hopefully, I will be able to share more power between us, make us equal in our abilities. But it is still a ways away."

"Diane?" Tyla asked.

"Yes Tyla?"

"Would you go get us some food from the cooks for us? It should be done by now."

"Yes. I would be happy to," she said and stood up.

"You should practice with your power," Tas added.

Diane nodded, focused one more time, and changed the hair color and ears once more. It seemed to go easier for her this time. After a few seconds, she opened her eyes and nodded.

"Keep it up as long as you can. Reveal yourself if your change alarms anyone," Tyla said as she left the carriage.

"That was subtle, but you wanted her to leave for something. What did you want to discuss?" I asked them.

"I think you should consider bedding Diane," Tyla said.

I took a deep breath. "I am not opposed to it... if she agrees. But I worry that with her memory loss, it could be problematic. I'll admit I have grown close to her. I also want her, but..."

"Love, I respect your unwillingness to bond with someone against their will," Tas said. "But we will never win this fight if you don't. Plus, she is in love with you at this point. She is just too shy to admit it."

I leaned over and kissed Tas on the lips. "Thank you," I said when we broke apart. "I agree. If she asks to join us, I will let her. As long as you both approve?"

"We do, Master. Tas and I have already discussed it."

"Good, I will leave that to you guys, then. I know I need to be open to it, so if you find people that will fit with all of us. I mean all of us, just not those that I might like. Then I will let you know if I agree or not. There has to be a connection of some type. But I worry with Diane, if her memory returns, she may regret it, so it's a little more complicated. Let me think on it, and then I will talk to her and see what she has to say."

"Yes, Master."

"I agree, Love."

"Good. If she wants to, we can pursue it more then. Maybe a night alone with her to get to know her one on one better."

"We can arrange that." Tas said, glancing conspiratorially over at Tyla. I knew that look. I was in trouble now.

"I thought you said it was a small town. What was the name again?" I asked Orrick.

I had my girls standing next to me on the last hill before it dropped into the open plains.

A small creek ran from the mountains to the south and flowed next to the hills towards the north. I was told it eventually merged with another river and went into the Dark Sea. Built on either side of the creek was a small town, or what should have been a small town.

There were tents and carts outside of the town's wooden walls on our side. It reminded me a lot of Hills Crest. Though the wooden fence was comprised of smaller stakes from a different variety of tree. The palisades ran in a circle around the town, going over a wooden support structure built to hold it over the water on each of the town's far sides. It even had metal grates underneath to prevent one from using the water itself to enter the town. At regular intervals, there were watch towers built that could see the ground before them with all the brush cleared away.

The town itself could not have held more than a thousand residents at most within the walls. The road we were on went straight into one side of the town at almost a ninety-degree angle to the creek. Then it continued as kind of a main street, cobbled with a wide gutter going down the center to catch flowing rainwater or sewage. Then it crossed a third bridge that you could probably drive two carts over next to each other before it continued on and exited out the other side through another gate towards the desert.

As I peered at the road beyond that, all I could see was desolate flat lands with occasional rolling hills reminding me of drives across Texas, covered with knee high dried grass as far as the eye could see. The road was in remarkably good condition on the other side. Even though not a single person traveled on it, it was also clear of any refugees.

"From what I remember," Orrick said, "Paradise was a town of a couple hundred. Scouts did not get close enough to see who the others are, probably refugees like outside Rivenhold."

"Paradise, huh? Seems the person who named it liked irony. Yeah, probably refugees. Lots of carts and horses is a plus. Maybe we can buy some supplies?"

"That is possible, Master. Masaki had several hundred gold in his pay chest."

"That reminds me, Julian. Did your men get paid?"

"We did, boss. Though only a tithe of what we were promised. The oath, once taken, allowed the Demigods to dictate the terms of our... employment with impunity if it was not sworn to beforehand."

"We should probably set that up then. Tyla, can you take care of the pay? Do the best we can within a budget that will last. We also need to figure out a way to get income, eventually."

"Yes, Master."

"I can do it, Tyla, I ran my father's books at the inn and actually enjoyed it," Tas said.

"That would be ideal. I hated sitting through budget meetings with my mother. We can do it together." The girls grasped hands and continued holding on to each other as they stood beside me. I was glad these two were as happy with each other as they were with me.

"I think we might cause a stampede if we go down there in full force. Thoughts?" I said, moving on.

"It can't be helped, boss." Julian said. "You should not travel without an escort. Unless you want to send emissaries to the town and either pass it by or let them know you are not here for them."

I stood there while I considered the options. "Let's head down there together. Run or stay, we can't worry about it, and we need to keep a steady pace to stay ahead of those probably chasing us."

"We can hold up a white flag to let them know we don't intend harm," Julian said. "Might help."

"That works, Let's get started down there. You can raise the flag and lead us from the front on the horse, Julian. I'll ride on the bench with Cain."

"What about us, Master?"

"You can ride in the back of the coach. Stay in your armor and be ready to come out, though. I don't think it's a trap, but if we need your crowd control abilities, I'll call for you. Tas, you stay with her and watch her back. Diane, you stay in the coach too."

"Yes, Master."

"Yes, Love."

Diane nodded.

"Alright, let's go see the locals."

Once again, I was traveling through a refugee camp, though most of these folks seemed to have carts and horses, unlike the ones outside Rivenhold. That's probably why they got so far.

No one ran at the sight of us, but they did not exactly look at us with glee, either.

"These seem like the people with the means to run farther," I said to Cain, who just looked at me and shrugged.

"Most look like farmers, Master, from what I can see, at least," Tyla said through the open glass window that separated the main cabin from the bench seat.

"Yeah, I see some with cows and sheep, a couple of carts filled with farming tools. Odd for those folks to leave their homes, even with a war. The farmers I knew from home would rather die than leave what they considered theirs."

"Unless they feared for their daughters," Tyla said, and I looked down through the glass.

"You think they had a reason to run?"

"No, just a thought."

"It's a good one, but they are not running from us right now."

"They may not know anywhere else to go."

I nodded, not quite convinced. But as I glanced around at the people, I could see poking their heads out of tents and carts, they looked concerned. Though I did spot a few children in the mix. "Might also be the white flag Julian is holding up. In my world, that was a sign of surrender... or at least that is what we associated it with."

"It can mean that, too," Tyla explained through the open window. "It is signaling the intent to talk and not fight. I have not heard of the Demigods using it, so they may hope it is a runaway noble and not one of them. However, there have been instances of people using it falsely and then striking."

"Another very human thing to do. We will see, I guess. I see a couple of guards at the gate," I said, holding up my hand to block the morning glare to see better. "Not properly equipped or armored. Probably volunteer. We will see what they say."

We approached as Julian was speaking to them. I only caught the back end of the conversation.

"...you can ask him yourself," Julian replied.

"How can I be of assistance, gentleman?" I asked.

"We aint taking no refugees." The bearded man in old and worn leather armor said on the top of the watchtower next to the gate. His gear was inferior quality, but I couldn't help but notice that the spear shined and appeared very well maintained. As cheap as the leather armor looked, it was also well cared for.

They used that gear regularly, even if it looked like shit.

"First, do we look like refugees?" I lifted my hands. "Second, we are only passing through to the other side. Maybe spending money on supplies in your town. We don't want to stay."

"You may not be refugees, but no one goes on the other side. Too dangerous."

"I'm sorry, I am not from these parts. If no one goes on the other side, why is the road so well maintained? Or even there?"

"The gods probably, I don't know," he said with a shrug. "As soon as you get to the other side, it never needs maintenance, and it never gets blown over with sand."

"Interesting," I said. "Why can't we take it?"

"Desert Dire wolves, packs of 'em. Not so bad out this far, but we get an attack from 'em from time to time. The farther you go, the worse it gets."

I leaned over to Cain, "They any different from the ones in the mountains?"

He glanced at me, raising one eyebrow and shrugged.

"We need to get you laid, Cain. I think you would loosen up a bunch." This got a grunt from the man.

I think I'm breaking through to him. One of these days, he might even like me.

I turned my face back up to the guard. "We will take our chances. Also, buy some supplies if you have them to spare, and then travel the road. We won't bother you after that."

"Hold on," the man said and called another guard to the tower as he got down.

The additional guard looked much younger and had a dirty face as he just glared down at us from the tower with a bow and arrow in his hand.

"Friendly bunch," I said under my breath.

"They live on the outskirts. They don't like anyone," Cain said in probably the most words I had ever heard from the man. I glared at him with my eyebrow raised. "I kind of like them," he added with a shrug of his shoulders.

"This day is just getting weirder and weirder," I said down to Tyla, who was giggling.

We waited for a while, just sitting there silently, when the old, bearded man finally returned. "You can enter, just you and a few guards. The Mayor wants to talk to you."

I considered my options. On the one hand, it could be a trap. He said I could bring guards, but the spiraling logic of 'what if they wanted you to think that' went round and round in my head for a minute. Deciding that thinking about that too much would get me nowhere, I went with the other possibility. It was legitimate, and they needed something.

"Fair. Some guards, my wives, and driver here."

"Wives?" the man asked. "Uh... whatever, that is fine. Your carriage and only..." He counted slowly on his finger to seven and then held those fingers up to me so I could see. "Eight people, that's it."

Tyla giggled behind me, and I struggled to keep my poker face firmly intact as I even heard Cain chuckle and his breath. "I agree to your most generous terms. Will you agree not to harm me or mine while we talk?"

"We agree," he said and looked down behind the gate. "Open it up for their carriage."

I leaned over to the side, "Julian, you and two guards with me."

"Yes, Boss," he replied and pointed quickly at two of his men.

The gate opened with several men grunting to move it, and it opened to the town. The place was a shit hole even up close. The buildings were all made from some kind of pine that made it look like one of those wild west vids I used to watch back on Earth.

Cain drove through the gate and down the cobbled road. The guards did not even bother to check inside the carriage. Not that counting was a skill they possessed even if they did, apparently. Julian led us on his horse with his two guards standing on the back steps at the rear of the coach.

I studied the buildings as we passed by them. Each of the square wooden blocks of several buildings next to each other was two stories tall on the main street with little shops in the front and what was probably living spaces upstairs. Each had the wide wooden walkways that I associated with the wild west as well and I felt a kind of nostalgia at one of my favorite movie genres when I was going up.

They looked to be built in blocks of four, and each connected, just like rural condominiums in the United States when I was a kid. Each one was not very wide, probably about the length of my carriage, if I were to guess. However, they were three times as long from front to back, which gave enough room for a small shop or store.

After each block, you could see an alley big enough for a single cart to get through that led to more housing behind it without the shops attached. Those were even more ramshackle and only one-story high each. Maybe big enough for one room and a hearth.

We soon rolled over the wooden bridge, and I could easily feel the rattle in the metal springs the carriage had from the uneven planks. I also discovered where most of the town's sewage was discharged when I saw a man in his later years throw out the contents of his bed pan into the creek from his window.

"Note to self, get water from upstream."

"Ungh," was Cain's witty response.

"Don't get so excited, Cain, people will start to talk."

He glared at me as we approached the largest single building in town. Still only two stories, it was more modern with an angular roof with shingles. A sign in the front said something I couldn't read.

"What's that say?" I asked Cain, pointing at the sign.

"Town Hall and Mayor's house."

I nodded, also realizing that I needed to learn how to read all over again. "Tyla, can you teach me how to read the local language?"

"Yes, Master. Maybe before our evening activities each night."

I laughed. "Works for me. Thanks." A thought occurred to me. I stuck my head to the window and whispered, "Hey, Diane, you think you can hold your powers through the entire conversation?"

"I... think so?"

"Good. We don't want to set off any alarms. Change to your human looks if you think you can. Stay in the coach if you don't."

"I can do it."

I nodded as the city guard in front of the Mayor's house waved for us to stop and I got off the carriage. "Stay with the carriage, Cain. Try not to talk to too many people and frighten the children"

I got a grunt from the man as Julian got off his horse and the three girls came out of the carriage. "Julian, have one man stay with Cain. The other can come with us."

"You got it, Boss."

"Follow me," the town guard who met us said.

We marched up the wooden steps and followed the guard. His leather armor was also cheap, but well cared for. They only armed this man with a short sword that had seen better days based on the pommel and grip. But I would bet the blade was serviceable by what I had seen so far.

We entered the building and walked down a short hallway, entering what looked like a waiting room with multiple chairs along the walls. The guard approached a door but turned to us before he went through. "Wait here. I will tell the mayor that you are here."

"Understood," I said and settled into the chair farthest from the door. Tyla sitting on my lap and Tas grabbed a chair and scooted as close as she could next to me on my right. Diane stood as close to Tas as she could, not taking a seat. Julian took the opposite side of the room from us and the guard we brought with us stood by the door we came in, one hand on his short sword but otherwise relaxed.

We settled in to wait. If this was like most politicians, they would make you wait for a while as a power play, so I tried to get comfortable.

I was wrong.

Less than what was probably a minute later, the guard came back out. "She will see you now."

I shared my look of surprise with Tyla as she got off my lap and faced me. Tas even gave me a raised eyebrow. It was so odd.

I let Tyla go first, as the Mayor probably expected her to be in charge of our little group and I had no problem playing into those expectations for now.

As we walked through the door, my boots went from plodding on the creaking wooden floorboards to silence as it transitioned to a large area rug that lined almost the entire room. It was cozy in a rustic sort of way. On each of the walls sat bookshelves lined with old leather-bound tomes and scrolls. A large window sat on one side, but they covered it in deep red curtains, making it dark if not for the glowing crystals illuminating the room.

Panzite crystals, actually. I recognized them from our time in the Vex's sanctum when I had first arrived. Their blueish white hue reminded me of fluorescent lights in old buildings back on Earth. It also meant whoever we were dealing with was wealthy. Tyla told me that those crystals were expensive, and I wished I still had some.

On the other side of the room sat a desk of ornate wood that looked nothing like I had seen since I had been here. It was a deep red hard wood that was well cared for if aged, sitting about 6 feet away from the back wall.

Behind the desk, backdropped by the wall and a large painting, sat an ancient woman with gray hair tied in a neat bun. The painting was a portrait of an old woman spewing out fire over the desert plains, incinerating hundreds of large tan wolves that were attacking the town of Paradise.

Based on the age of the painting, I doubted it was the woman in front of me. But with a magic society and healing, I could be wrong.

"Greetings," the woman said, looking directly at Tyla. "I understand you want to pass through the deserts and buy supplies?"

Tyla glanced quickly over at me before speaking. "Yes, I am Tyla-Rose, formerly of Blackrun. We seek passage through to the desert and supplies... I'm sorry, may I have your name?"

"Helena," she said, "I am the mayor of the town. Used to be a noble in service to Rivenhold, but... well, things have changed."

Tyla nodded at her words but did not speak, waiting for the woman to say what she wanted.

"Good," she continued. "You are not some up jumped noble spawn that thinks the world should dance to their tune. You realize that the desert is suicide? No one returns."

"We are aware," Tyla said.

"Something is odd here..." Helena said, and she began looking into the eyes of each person in my group. When she got to me, her brow raised. "Why are you in charge?"

I was momentarily surprised, replaying the conversation over in my head to figure out what gave it away. She either saw the look Tyla gave me, or she was fantastic at reading body language.

Deciding to go with honesty, I stepped forward ahead of Tyla. "My name is Derrick Schultz, formerly of... let's just say a long way from here. Tyla is my wife, so is Tasnia here." I pointed to Tas, who walked forward and stood next to me.

"And her?" she asked, pointing to Diane.

"A friend," I said.

The woman grunted, "She is holding her power close to the surface. Using it. Is she a light witch? Are you planning on assassinating me?"

Damn, who was this woman?

"No," I said, raising my hand, palm out. Something was off about this, and I did not want a fight. "Diane, please drop the disguise."

I kept my eyes on the woman in front of us and saw the briefest hint of surprise at Diane's true form as she dropped the brunette hair, and her ears became visible.

"I am sorry, Derk," Diane said.

"It's fine. I am pretty sure we are dealing with someone that could probably rival a matriarch at this point. Nothing you can do."

The woman in question just smirked at me rather than confirm my assessment. "An elf companion, as well. I haven't seen an elf in several years... and the pink hair. Very interesting." She tapped her cheek with one of her long fingernails.

"What is interesting?" Diane asked before I could.

"Nothing. I have heard of your kind but never encountered one. Where are you from?"

Diane recoiled at the question, looking down without answering.

"She doesn't remember," I said.

Helena studied Diane for a moment more before returning her attention back to me. "That is unfortunate. I had hoped to meet one and ask about their history. Rumor is there were not any left from the few silver-haired elves I have met over the years. Regardless, it is not as important to our conversation," she said, changing the subject quickly. However, something seemed off in how she looked at Diane.

A look of greed which set my nerves on end.

"What do you want?" I asked.

"Simple. I want you to take these refugees with you. Paradise can't sustain them, and my people are complaining."

"What's stopping us from just crossing elsewhere and bypassing your... little town completely?"

"Nothing at all, but I am also willing to sell you what supplies we can spare to help you along. We are not a rich town any longer, but we get our share of treasure hunters from time to time and have been known to support them."

"Treasure hunters?" I asked, my interest piqued enough to change course.

She smiled like the cat who got the canary and lifted her hand to the painting. "My grandmother, may the gods grant her peace, told me stories of those who hunted the lost civilizations to the east. Some say they were pink haired elves," she said, looking at Diane once again.

I glanced at my friend. Her eyes had lit up and the woman had her complete interest. I had to admit she had mine, too. Diane turned her head to me with hope in her eyes.

"Fine, you win," I said. "We will allow anyone out there who wants to come. I mean to offer, if they choose to stay here or go elsewhere, that is not my problem. Let us buy supplies and give access to any maps and lore that you may have heard of for where we are going. Also, any knowledge of the threats in the desert and how best to fight them and you have a deal."

"That is most wise. I think we have an accord. My guards will show you out and supply you with the material you need. Here, take this scroll, but give it back to me when you depart. It is quite old." She got up and limped over to the bookshelf.

She was a large woman, speaking of years and an excess of food. But I wisely kept my mouth shut rather than comment that the people out there were probably living on scraps based on the conditions I saw in the town.

"Do you worry about the Demigods coming here?" I asked.

"They are not interested in an old and feeble woman like me. I doubt they would be interested even if I have some measure of power. Besides, I think I can hold my own against them," she said, as if challenging me.

I rolled my shoulders to get the tightness out of them and stepped forward to grasp the scroll she held out. She leaned forward. "In fact, I believe you are one of them, if I am not mistaken. I trust those of power in the camps will be enough to quench your desires without enslaving an old woman in her twilight, and those under her care?"

As our fingers touched, I saw her flash bright red. Clearly, the element of fire ran strong in her family.

"I'm not interested in you or your town," I said noncommittally and turned away. I marched straight for the door, now a little sickened to my gut by the woman basically giving me a bribe of innocent girls to leave her be. Now, I knew why this negotiation was a little too easy. She was hoping to be left alone and would buy her freedom if she could.

But something else was not right here, this whole conversation did not make sense on the surface of it. I think it had something to do with Diane, but could not be sure. Her discovery changed the dynamic of the conversation, but I could not tell by how much.

I already couldn't wait to leave this place.

CHAPTER 17

— • —

MORE REFUGEES

"They said what?" I angrily asked Cecil.

"The guards spread the word they could go with us or somewhere else, but if we left and they still remained outside the gates, they would be evicted by force."

"That fucking bitch," I said.

"What should we do, Master?"

I stopped for a moment to think. It had been a day since our meeting with the mayor. I thought we had done well enough getting a third of the refugees to agree to come with us. But apparently the Mayor forced the decision for the rest of them too.

"Invite everyone in the refugee camp for a meeting tonight. We tell them the truth and let the cards fall where they land. I am done hiding what I am, and if they are coming with us, they need to do the same as everyone else."

"You intend to do the minor bond?" Tas asked.

"On anyone coming with us, not a child. Yes. I know..." I stopped for a second to think.

What was I becoming? Was this the right decision?

If I was being honest with myself, that assassination attempt had made me paranoid. A week ago, I wanted to trust people, and now I wanted to bond them all to my service.

Am I going down the right path?

I honestly wasn't sure. You never know if you are turning into the bad guy until it's far too late. After all, every bad guy is the hero of their own story until they get burned by the pitchforks of the citizens or something. This is why I hated being in charge. It was so much easier to be a grunt.

I sighed and made peace with my decision and where I was going.

"Yes, the minor bond if they go with us," I finally finished. "It will be their choice, and they will have the information to make an informed decision beforehand. Not some trick bullshit 'I don't know what I am really agreeing to' crap like the Demigods pull. But if they come with us, we need them to act more like soldiers than civilians. If they ask to leave? I will consider that option when we get to the other side and to what we hope is relative safety."

"I understand," Cecil said.

"You don't agree?"

"I have doubts, but I always do. I trust you, though. Lea told me to."

"What? Is that why you took the oath?" I asked.

"You did not see the look on her face after she gave her own oath. I did what my wife demanded."

I grabbed the bridge of my nose with two fingers. "Thought that was too easy with you."

He smiled. "You have earned my trust, even after this short time. I know why Estelle and Lea made their decision. That group needed a firm hand, or they would die on their own. Or be enslaved."

"Fair enough. Alright, pass the word for the meeting. I will explain it to them after meals tonight. Then let them make the choice. I doubt many will go for it, and it should get us out of here with the minimum of refugees to babysit. If any do, they get rolled into the ranks and trained, especially if they are empowered."

"Yes, boss," Cecil said as he wandered off to what I asked.

"That's almost four hundred people, Love," Tas said. "Do you think we can protect them all in the desert?"

"No, that's why we need to train them as a militia of some sort, so they can help. Those that are able-bodied will join. People that are too old or young can take the place of Cecil's men. Those guys are able-bodied, so they can join in too now that it's worth it in the number of people. We just need to adapt and overcome." I took a deep breath, trying to convince myself I was doing the right thing. Or at least the smart one. "What about supplies?" I asked Tyla.

Tyla picked up the wax tablet she had her notes on. "I secured a few small wagons for our use. Not counting what the refugees bring for those that join. Enough winter coats for all, mostly used but serviceable. Jugs for water, empty for now, since we can fill them with magic. Some travel rations, but probably not enough. Food will be our biggest concern."

I nodded. "The dire wolves don't stink as much as their mountain cousins and are supposedly edible and plentiful. I was told we could eat them, but it would not be what we would call fine dining."

Tas smirked. "If you are hungry enough, you can eat anything."

"Let's hope it doesn't come to that. There are other things to eat in the desert, according to the scroll. In fact, it isn't really a desert at all, most of it is grass plains and should have plenty of small game, or the wolves would've starved long ago." I pulled out the scroll that the bitch of a mayor had handed me. It was a small hand-drawn map of the road with notes. "Only one part is bad, and it is more of a wasteland than desert if the translation I got was accurate. Honestly, if someone drew this map, it couldn't be that bad, right? That means survivors."

Tas and Tyla gave me a look that I was stupid.

"Yeah, just jinxed us, didn't I?" They both nodded with a smile. "We call that Murphy's law where I come from. I just invited him to dinner and dancing most likely too. He is the father of everything that can go wrong according to our... lore."

They both laughed.

"We have something similar," Tas finally said.

"What's the saying?"

"The bread always falls butter side down," Tyla said.

That sparked a memory I had from somewhere. It was something from a neighbor I had growing up who was from Russia. They left the country when it joined the Eastern Bloc, just before the third world war on Earth.

"I think I have heard that before. Reminds me of something from a culture back on Earth. I wonder if most of the original people who came here were from there."

"I do not know, Master." Tyla shrugged.

"Right, neither here nor there, really. What about Diane? How is she doing?"

"She has been in the carriage all day looking over the books and the other scrolls they gave us. She has been very... interested in any information they had on elves like her," Tas said.

"I bet. I would probably be doing the same. Let's go check on her."

We strolled over to the carriage, both of my girls holding a hand on either side of me as we walked. When we got to it, I let go of their hands and opened the door and let both of them in first before I followed.

Diane looked up from the leather-bound book she was reading and smiled at us when we entered. She was definitely happier now than when we found her a couple of weeks ago.

"You can read the words?" I asked.

She flushed pink just for a second before speaking. Her shyness around me had improved as well but was still a thing. "Yes, I had to learn to survive with the humans. It wasn't hard."

I laughed. "Maybe for you, but I was never good at learning my own language in school, let alone another. What did you find?"

"Those that had returned from the desert, because some of them did, spoke of great dangers in the wastes, but also statues of elves in the ruins of a fortress they had found." She picked up another book. "According to Helena's mother actually, which this is a copy of her journal here, they met some silver haired elves about forty years ago who traveled that direction. They mentioned it was the home of the twilight elves and they were escaping the demigods when they first arrived."

"Really? So, you are a twilight elf? Does it say who the silver-haired ones were?"

"It doesn't mention it," she continued, and I had honestly never heard her talk this much with such confidence. "Only some names of the visiting elves and that they were another tribe placed here when their own world was consumed in flames thousands of years ago."

"The Silver elves refer to themselves as High Elves, or at least that is how it translates to us. As a species, they are very secretive. They talk much but say little." Tyla sat next to Diane and closed her book. "It is time to take a break. Let us grab dinner."

"Good idea," I said. "I'm hungry enough. I would probably try one of those wolves about now."

Diane gave me a strange look as she got up, and we all left the coach in search of food.

"Thank you for coming out!" I said to the group of people in front of me. Mostly older women that looked like they were hardened from years of toil. I stood on the back of one of the supply carts we had stolen from Masaki.

"Why are you in charge? Where is Mistress Russel?" asked the first heckler of the night, an old battle-axe of a lady with gray hair and a squat figure.

I knew how this was going to go just by looking at the expressions on their faces.

Why was a man speaking to them? That was the thoughts running through most of their heads, and I was getting sick of it.

"Because I am the only one who has a chance of saving your ass, lady. I also don't really care what you decide, so save the questions for when I am finished," I said, done being nice with stupid people.

She crossed her arms with a scowl on her face. Honestly, I was fine with it. I really did not want all these people coming with me if I could help it. The amount of training they needed and organization we would have to come up with would slow us down and make us weaker in the short term.

I knew that long term, they would be worth it. So, it divided my mind on the whole thing, as it acted like a pendulum of which way I would prefer. My walk around earlier and 'accidental' bumping into some of the women showed me that almost all of them were Chosen. Or at least they could be with training, as most seemed to flash with various colors right in front of my eyes.

I recorded the types down as best I could with Tyla and Tasnia's help, but there were quite a few.

None of the younger ones were at this meeting, though. This was mostly the family matriarchs and even some fathers coming to speak with me. I knew the advantages of recruiting them, and I should've been nicer, but I did not want the headache either.

"Master?" Tyla whispered from behind. "Please try to be nice. You know we could use the strength they could add in the future."

I took a deep sigh and nodded. "I know. I was just thinking about that. It reminds me of going to the dentist back on my old world. We know we need to, but just don't want to because of how painful the process is. But you're right, thank you for reminding me and keeping me focused on the goal." Reaching back, I patted her on her hip and got a smile in return.

I wondered if she knew what a dentist was. Based on her expression, I would guess she didn't. Otherwise, she probably would have grimaced like I always did. Either way, she let the comment go and did not ask.

I glanced out at the sizable crowd. "Alright folks. I am just going to get to the bottom line and be done with it. I have the same power as the Demigods you flee but am not one of them."

Shock and fear started washing over the faces of those present. I held up my hands to forestall them before they ran for the pitchforks.

"I have no interest in enslaving or bonding any of your daughters against their will. I am actively fighting against the Demigods that you know. The problem is that I do not have an army to fight them with. These men and women behind me..." I waved my arms at my recently gained small force of troops. "...Are all I have against those that have thousands of troops and Chosen at their disposal."

Confusion held their flight or fight off at my words. I had sold none of them yet, but at least I had a small hook into their interest. That was as good a start as any.

"So, we plan to travel east, through the desert and the dangers they tell me exist there, because one god has told me there is a chance of support to build an army sizable enough to fight back. That same god who gave me the powers of their kind so that us mortals could fight back."

This got their interest. I even saw a few of them nod at my words. But I had not given them the bad news yet.

"The mayor of this town wants me to bring you with me to make it easier for her folk. She also said they are going to make you leave whether you want to or not, so you all have a decision to make tonight."

I made eye contact with as many of them as possible as I paused for dramatic affect. A smile crossed my lips as I remembered back to my first leadership course in the marines a lifetime ago. 'Look them in the eyes, act like you know what you are doing, and they might just fucking believe it.'

"Your first option, and the easiest one for you, is to head south. There is danger that way, but the Demigods have not gotten that far yet. You may live peaceful lives there before they do, if you don't get captured by the barbarian tribes I have been told about."

I jumped down off the cart to walk among the people. I really wanted to see how they would react to my proximity as I talked.

"The other option is for you to come with us," I said and watched their reactions.

No immediate hate or loathing expressed itself in the facial features of those I was watching. So even though I had resigned myself to no one coming with us, a small flame of hope was ignited inside of me.

Now to drop the bomb on them.

"There is a catch. If you go with option two, you must agree to pull your weight. If you are Chosen, you will have to join in the fight to protect the group and get trained for war or to support it. On top of all that, all adults will have to swear an oath to listen and follow the orders of those in command. Which will mean me at the top."

That was when I saw people wince, and their expressions hardened. No one, especially those that come from the working class like these folks, likes to be beholden to others. They also probably heard the rumors of what an oath means when it comes to Demigods.

Time to sweeten that a little before I shut them completely down.

"I am sure you have heard the rumors." I held up my hands again as I heard people mutter. "I will be absolutely clear with you. The oath is real, and it is binding. However, unlike the Demigods, I will make the terms clear to you beforehand. You will know it's true in your soul before you accept it, and it cannot be broken by me..." I tapped my chest. "Or you. They do not tell you the rules because they want to trap you. I want you to know them, so you understand the stakes."

"Why do we have to?" The woman from earlier called out and I could see the others nodding along with her.

"Fair question. It's simple, really. Because the other side is using that against me. Not a week ago, a woman that was oath bound to a Demigod tried to assassinate me in my own camp. I can't take that risk again. The stakes are just too high. If we lose, this world becomes a place for them to play their games and treat all of you and your daughters like objects to be controlled for sport. So, anyone that joins us will need to take the oath so that we can be sure it won't happen again. There is just too much at stake."

"What will this oath require?" the woman, who apparently had made herself the representative of all those present, asked.

"Simple, the oath will be for one year and you will follow the orders of those above you and serve in the army or support it. You will not betray me or my cause through action or inaction. I promise that you, or your daughters, will never be forced to share my bed against your will. Or treated in any way other than professionally and with respect. However, you will be expected to serve the whole for that time, and the price of betrayal will be death."

There, I dropped the hard part. Now to see what they do.

"You may speak to any of the people behind me on their experiences and what they think of me. I can only promise that they are not under any compulsion to speak lies. Other than that, you will have to trust your gut instinct."

I walked back up to the cart and jumped up to sit on it. Tyla and Tas came over to stand on each side of me, and Diane stood on the other side of Tas. I watched as the folks went through the various stages of emotion, and they broke into groups to discuss in whispers.

"How is it going Diane?" I asked after leaning over so that only she could hear me.

"Too many voices to be clear. But most seem to discuss it honestly, without hatred in their words," she said.

I nodded. "That's a good sign. I still am not honestly sure whether I want them to come with us or not."

"We could use the help, Love, but I know what you mean."

"Okay, time for the deadline." I stood up on the cart and raised my hands once more.

People glanced up at me as I did.

"Last thing. We are leaving tomorrow after high sun. You need to decide at first light so we can get organized, and issue oaths if you come with us. Those that do not wish to join us, I suggest you head south, or any other direction you prefer as quickly as possible. Those that come with us, join us here, and I will take your oaths or answer any last-minute questions."

With that, I jumped off the cart and walked to my carriage, the girls right behind me, along with a few guards.

"That went better than I expected," I said as we got past the crowd. "Now for the stressful waiting part."

"We have ways of making you relax, Master." A hand grabbed my ass and squeezed.

"We do," Tas added, and another hand joined in.

A light cough behind me, and I was pretty sure without looking that Diane was as pink as she could go.

"And our own Voyeur," Tyla said as I opened the door for me and my girls.

Yes, I had to admit, Diane felt part of them now. She just needed to decide if she would join. I wouldn't force the issue, but she had to make the call.

Maybe a date tomorrow?

I closed the door and turned around to three beautiful women getting undressed in front of me. Though Diane hid behind the other two, not quite ready to show me herself fully yet. I smiled and turned back around. "Let me know when you're under the covers, Diane."

A squeak was my only reply, along with the giggles from the other two.

"How many?" I asked, the morning sun starting to come over the horizon and illuminating the Coach through the draped windows.

"A lot of them, I think," Tyla said.

"Not surprised, I guess. I did not expect anyone to really take up an offer that could cause death if you failed. That's fine, it will make us able to move that much faster across the desert."

"No, Master, you misunderstood. A lot of them are out there lined up."

"What?" I stopped and glared at her. Unable to believe it. "You mean a lot of them are waiting to take up the oath?"

"Yes," Tas said, reaching around and hugging Tyla from behind and placing her chin on her sister wife's shoulder. "Or at least get the actual offer before making their final decision. A few of them probably want to see if it's real before they commit."

"That's fair," I said as I finished putting on my shirt. Out of the corner of my eye, I saw Diane peeking at my exposed chest out of the corner of her eye. "Diane, you are going to have to decide soon if you are interested or not."

She turned pink and squeaked pretty much as I expected, turning away from me rather than answering. I smiled at Tas and Tyla, who could not muffle their giggles.

"Here, let me get your armor on," Tyla said as I placed the cuirass on me. Its leather shell with armored plates jingled as it went on. Tyla and

Tas tightened each strap one by one and locked them into place. Their hands were not completely focused on their task, however.

"Be careful, or we might have to put this armor on all over again," I said.

"We wouldn't want that," Tyla said as her hand went down and grabbed my crotch.

"No, not at all," Tas added as her own hands wandered down to my ass and squeezed.

Diane turned back towards us, and I winked at her. Her cute squeak at being caught made me laugh. She did not turn away this time, though.

"Normally..." I began. "I am all for taking our time, but I want to get this over with. After? I will probably need a recharge if I give out a lot of oaths."

"No fun. But you are right," Tyla said, and her hand went back to work on tightening the correct straps this time. Tas slapped me on the butt and did the same.

Once my libido calmed down enough that it did not look like I was carrying a concealed baton in my pants. We walked out and over to the cart we used last night.

The crowd arranged themselves in a line that spiraled out from the end of the cart so that people could wait but still hear and see what was going on.

My guards followed me and my girls while Cecil, Lea, Estelle, and Orrick waited for me at the foot of the cart. The older woman that had deemed herself the ambassador for this group of refugees was first in line.

"What is your name?" I asked before she could speak.

"Abida Nakano," she said, "My family ran a farm on the outskirts of Blackrun. My granddaughter showed signs of being blessed by the gods."

"That is why you ran?"

"Yes. Most of us here have a similar story."

"Fair. I promise to do my best to protect her, but we will train her to fight or support if she goes with us."

The old woman's visage cracked for just a moment. "I know." She looked down at the ground. "There is no place safe. I don't know if we can trust you, but our options are running out. The south is no safer than here and... to be honest, we want to find a way to fight back."

"I understand."

"I will go first. To see if your offer is what you said it is, I will be your test subject. I have been through my share of pain in life. I will also gladly die rather than be a slave."

"That's fair and commendable." I reached down inside me for the power that binds. I once again changed it so that it was good for only one year from today. "Do you, Abida Nakano, agree to my service for one year? Doing what is required in that service to the cause of overthrowing the Demigods plaguing this world?"

I sent the power rushing to her before she could answer so that she could feel it and understand it before she accepted. She took a deep breath, her eyes going wide.

"He is telling the truth," she said loud enough for those around us to hear. "And I accept."

The power locked around her soul, and I knew that my symbol now adorned her arm. A small piece of my energy was now gone. The old woman had a teardrop out of her eye as she turned to her fellows.

"He speaks the truth. I felt the power and understood the oath. It does not mar my thoughts and I can feel the limit on its time. We have hope," she said, and the surrounding others all nodded and started talking amongst themselves.

She reached behind her towards a young woman about the age I was now. She had brunette hair and a cute smile. "This is my granddaughter, Freda. She has shown signs, but we do not know what her power is."

"It is a pleasure to meet you, Freda." I reached out my hand for her to shake. When she grasped it, her whole body flashed a brown color for me. "Your power is Earth, by the way. I will send you the oath. Understand it before you accept it. Be comfortable with it and reject it if you are not sure."

More people crowded in behind Abida and her family to watch as her granddaughter accepted the minor bond and, just like that, my small army grew by almost three hundred people in a day.

Not all of them were fighters, but it was a start.

CHAPTER 18

WAGONS EAST?

We delayed our departure by another day to organize all the people that joined us. We needed things now and our money was burning at a rapid rate. I hated doing it, but plans change as the need arises.

A representative of the town even came out and asked us to stay a little longer while they organized the supplies to sell us. This was a little odd, given how fast they wanted the refugees gone the day before. But again, it came down to the fact that we needed things, and it forced us to play their game.

"What are the final numbers? I lost track yesterday," I said.

I had what I called my senior council with me. My girls, of course, plus Estelle, Lea, Cecil, Orrick, and Julian, to round them out, I also invited Abida. The woman that went first of the refugees.

"Three hundred and forty-eight if you count the children and elderly," Tyla said, looking down at the parchment she had in front of her. "About one hundred men that can fight or have had militia training."

"Julian, take them and start integrating them into your men at arms. Cecil, do you mind being his second?"

"No, Julian is... quite efficient."

"Thank you," Julian said to Cecil. Then turned to me. "I can do that, boss, what about weapons?"

I looked over at Tas, who handled the money.

She shrugged her shoulders. "We had over four hundred gold coins and some smaller ones. It's all old Nitre matriarchy currency which is still good here. However, the town doesn't have enough weapons to arm them. Julian gave me a list, and we got the wood and glue to make shields. After that..."

I waited for her to speak after she trailed off, but she just shrugged again.

I sighed. "What do we have to work with?"

"One family that joined us is a blacksmith family," Abida said. "They were my closest neighbors from back in the outskirts of Blackrun. Even a mile away from our farm, they were too loud. But, if we can get them the iron they need, they can forge weapons and tools. Slowly, at any rate. They have a traveling forge that can make the basics, but we have to stop in order to use it."

"We don't have time exactly to mine on the road," I said.

"Our earth Chosen should be able to pull it out of the ground if there is enough of it. It's actually good training for them to build up their power," Estelle added.

"Ah... That makes sense," I said, feeling kind of dumb. There were still things I was learning about this world every day. "With magic, we can actually outfit an entire army, couldn't we?"

"Yes, Master. But it will still be hard. We can use fire magic to heat the forge in a pinch, but it will exhaust the Chosens' power to do so for long periods," Tyla added.

"Fine. Estelle and Abida, work with the noncombatants and get an assembly line going each night to outfit troops with. It doesn't have to be pretty but get them gear to fight with. Swords, spears, bows, arrows, and armor. I have been studying the combat tactics of this world and it seems to be like Earth's Middle Ages." I looked around to blank stares from each of them.

"Right, you wouldn't get that. My old commanding officer used to be huge into history and warfare. I wasn't, but I picked up a few things along the way. We don't have a cavalry yet, so knights are out of the question, but we can make a medium infantry with leather armor and tower shields and spears in the short run. Heavy armor later with enough metal armor."

"Yes, I have plenty of Dire wolf leather bought. It should be enough to piece together basic armor," Tas said.

"Good. Think you two can handle that?" I asked Estelle and Abida.

"Yes... Boss?" Abida said as Estelle just nodded at her use of the term.

"Yeah, I like that term better than anything else outside of what my wives call me," I said. "Okay, we have the... hopes and beginnings of a fighting force. What about our magical corps?"

Estelle cleared her throat before speaking. "We have the nine from before yesterday, plus me and Lea. Forty-four of the young women in the group that joined us yesterday you tested. They are untrained, unfortunately, which takes time. But..." She picked up her own parchment. "We have twenty with wind affinity, thirteen with water, ten earth, seven fire, and three with light."

"Seems to be a lot of wind affinity." Tasnia said.

"Like I said to Derrick a few days ago, it is the most common power among humans," Lea said. "But also, the hardest to get proficient at. Most of them make up archers because it is easier to do with the enhanced strength and imbuing the arrow with speed. Flight takes much longer... I have been trying for almost five years with limited success."

"Well, according to the map," I said, "it will be at least four weeks before we get to the wastes. Plenty of time to train and we will probably have plenty of wolves to practice on."

Everyone nodded, not looking forward to the hardships we would face.

"Estelle, I would like you to take the water mages and make a medical group. You will still be in overall command of the Chosen and keep them all organized, but Lea can take over being in charge of the fighting corps day to day."

"That would be more than acceptable. I have never been drawn to combat."

"Orrick, you take the light affinity Chosen. Add them to your scouts, have Mahalo and Kameyo be your seconds and train them at the same time they work with Diane."

"You got it, boss," Orrick said.

"Lea, make sure you are working with Julian's men. The earth chosen will also get the first chance at any heavy armor if we can scrape it together, but that comes after we get shields and spears for the men at arms."

"Yes, Derrick," she said.

"Okay, any other items?"

Tyla picked up her parchment again, pointing at a part of the page. "Just basic items. We have fifty carts now with sixty mules to pull them. Twenty cows across two herding families, each with their own bulls. One herd of twenty-five sheep, and two carts with fifty chickens and five roosters."

"We have a regular caravan going, don't we?" I asked. "Also, looks like we should have some ability for food and wool for clothing along the way, at least. Do we have enough feed to keep them healthy?"

"The refugees still had plenty, most of them left their homes prepared for a long time without a town," Tyla said. "Plus, I bought more before I bought the raw materials since we were worried mostly about food. The road looks to be grasslands, so if the weather holds, we should be fine for grazing."

"Do we have anyone that can make clothing from wool?"

"Yes, it is common for us that live on the outskirts to make our own clothing," Abida said.

"Great." I stood from my seat on the back of my command coach. "I hate getting into everyone's business, so make sure that it's organized and let me know if you need help. That should do it, right?"

I glanced around, not getting questions. "Good. I want to get on the road through the town by noon, hopefully without problems from the mayor. I just have one thing to do before we leave."

Everyone started getting up and going off to their tasks. "Diane, hold up please."

The pink-haired elf in question squeaked and turned towards me. "Wha... What do you need, Derrick?"

"A date. There is a small inn in the town that has food that I want to try. Care to join me?"

Diane looked at Tyla and Tas, who giggled and walked off arm in arm, leaving her all alone.

"You can say no if you don't want to."

"Uh... y-yes. That would be good."

"Great." I held my arm out to her. She just stared at it as if it would bite her. I reached over with my other arm, gently grabbing her hand and placing it on the proffered arm. "There you go. Let's go get breakfast."

She turned bright pink once again but pressed herself as close to me as she could as we walked towards the town's gates. Only a single guard followed a short distance behind.

"How is your training coming along?" I asked as we walked through the gates. The town of Paradise started letting the refugees in to buy things once I told their mayor that they were coming with me.

A town guard usually followed each person who entered, and I do not feel like the powers in charge of the town really wanted us there. While I could understand that from a certain perspective, it just seemed off to me.

Luckily, the refugees that decided not to come with us had already left south the day before. But the people of the town still felt surprisingly absent from the streets. That might have been what was throwing me off.

"Well," Diane said. "Kameyo said I have a natural talent. I can almost hide myself fully behind a veil of bent light now. But only for a limited time, and it's exhausting. It's much easier to blend into what is already behind me."

"Like a camouflage?"

She looked at me with confusion for a second. "That word is confusing. It says blending of colors to me."

"Sort of," I said, thinking of how best to say it. "Blending your colors to match what is around you so the eye does not notice it."

"Oh. Yes, sort of. It's more like matching what's on the other side so that it looks different from each direction. It does not take as much power, but it takes a lot more mental effort to match the surroundings."

"How do you know what's behind you if you can't see it?"

"You don't have to see it, you have to... deflect it around your body. It eventually leads to bending the light entirely. Kameyo said it is the usual first step on the path."

I smiled at the pretty elf, enjoying seeing her animated about things and talkative. "That's great. What about combat training?"

"Some," she said as we stepped up together onto the wooden boards. The walkways lined each side of the main cobbled style road where it met the dirt for each of the shops. Each board creaked as we took a step. "Kameyo said I would be best served by learning knives and bows. It could take years to learn to project light strong enough to burn, so we focus on bending it and attacking from shadow. I also read that those are the preferred weapons of my people. Well..." She trailed off.

"What?"

"They are the preferred weapons of the silver-haired elves. I do not know if they are my mine. It seems my people are a mystery to most humans, so I do not know if they are the same."

"I hope we find out more someday, Diane. I really want you to know where you came from."

She nodded but looked down, deep in thought, as we continued down the sidewalk. One of Julian's men ten steps behind us was walking with the older bearded guard we met at the gate when we arrived.

"They are still giving us an escort in town," I said.

"They do not trust us."

"No, but there is something about this town I don't like. I don't trust the mayor especially. Do you see how all the town's people avoid us?"

She looked around, then nodded. "I do."

"Nothing to do about it, I guess. I can't save everyone... Not yet at least."

We finally found the tavern and inn and went through the double doors that swung on hinges as we entered. The place was empty and the man behind the bar looked up, surprised, as we entered.

"We were hoping to get something to eat, please." I said as we approached. "Any table is fine?"

The man looked at me for a second and then up as my two escorts followed us in. His eyes stayed on Diane for a second as if he remembered something when he saw her. His face became pensive, but he nodded. "Ya, sure. Any table is fine. We have fish soup for breakfast with bread rolls and either mead or water to drink. The rolls are freshly baked."

"Fine selection," I said with my best smile. "Two please with mead for me and..." I looked at Diane.

"Water?"

I looked at the man. "Where do you get your water from?"

"The creek, same as the fish."

I thought back to the man that threw his bed pan in the river and it must've shown on my face.

"Up creek, before it gets to town," the man added quickly.

I nodded in thanks. "Water for her then, and whatever my two escorts would like, as well."

The man nodded and went off to get it.

"None for me, thanks. Not while I am on duty," my guard said.

The old man just yelled out, "Mead with mine."

We sat near the window, or I guess it was just a square hole in the wooden walls. It had shutters, which were open wide, but no glass. So, it allowed the cool breeze from outside to come in.

The town itself made the smell not the most pleasant of things, but I had been getting used to the rustic lifestyle since coming here and it didn't bother me like it used to.

"So, what do you want, Diane?"

Her gaze from out the open window snapped back to me. She locked eyes with me for but a second before looking down and turning a slight shade of pink. "I... I am not sure yet."

"Do you want to find out more about your people? I would be happy to help with that, but we kind of have our own quest that takes precedence."

"I understand... and I am thankful that I found you, all of you. I never realized how lonely I was before."

I took a chance and reached forward, grabbing her hand ever so lightly. She did not flinch, just accepting the touch while staring at my hand on hers. "We care about you... Not just us. But I care about you. I want you to be happy and... preferably with us if I am honest. My biggest concern that I have has to do with finding your people. If that happens, will you want to be with them, or us?"

She looked up into my eyes and a tear slid down the side of her cheek before she answered. "I am not sure, I want both," she whispered.

"That's fair. Look, I know you have an attraction towards me. I would be lying if I said that I did not return that feeling. You are beautiful and sweet. I want you to be happy. When you are sure one way or another, we'll accept that decision, whatever it is..." I took a deep breath. "You know what it means to be with me. You also know that if you took the bond, I could release you once, but it needs to mean more than that to me. Not about convenience."

"I understand, thank you. I want to, I really do. But I just don't know what I am, who I am. That part of me also calls."

"For what it's worth, I hope you choose us if you have to make a decision between the two," I said with a smile as the man brought the soup so we could start eating. I took a sip of the mead and almost spit it out. Instead, I forced the swallow and really hoped that the soup would be better. However, based on Diane's face when she took the first bite, I had serious doubts that we would enjoy this meal.

The bartender handed food to the town guard I never got the name of and went back to wiping glasses with a dirty towel. I reached down and smelled the roll next to the bowl and it had the pleasant fresh baked smell to it.

I also noticed that it had a cut on the side with a small piece of parchment sticking out of it. I glanced at the bartender, who shook his head at me after making sure the town guard was busy with his food.

I angled myself away from the eating guard and ripped it open. The parchment was rolled tightly and unbound. I quickly palmed it and put it into my pants pocket.

I smelled the bread and looked back to the bartender, who nodded his head this time. So, I really hoped that the bread was safe to eat as I took a bite to cover my actions.

Let's just say it wasn't the worst, but this place was not on my list of favored eating establishments I have been to. I chewed slowly as I contemplated what the note might say.

I led Diane into the carriage and closed the door, Tyla and Tas both turned to us with an excited expression on their faces. I pulled out the note, unrolled it and... realized I couldn't read the script on it in the slightest.

"How did it go?" I heard Tas ask.

Almost at the same time as I said, "Fuck."

"That's great! Let's do it. Now?" Tas said with barely contained laughter.

I rolled my eyes and handed the note to Tyla, "Not what I meant. Can you read that for me?"

I was almost shocked that all three of the girls looked at me in disappointment, but Tyla grabbed the note from my hand. "Wouldn't you rather I leave before you ask about our date, anyway?" I asked.

"Good point, Love. What's the note say, Ty?"

Tyla unrolled it and read it aloud, "Guards have been talking. They want the elf. Watch out. That is all it says."

Concern and fear shot up my back. "Fuck..."

"What does it mean, Master?"

"That the town is not a happy place from what I can tell and that the townsfolk don't like their mayor if I were to guess. Based on that note, I also think she wants Diane for some reason," I said.

I knew I was stating the obvious, but sometimes you had to speak things out loud as you thought through the ramifications of things. Luckily, the girls didn't seem to mind.

"I'll be right back," I said and turned for the door. "Going to get the others."

Just as I left, Tas once again asked, "Okay, how did it go otherwise?"

The door closed, but this time I resisted rolling my eyes. "Women. The same, no matter what world you're in."

I walked in search of my senior council and finally ran into one. "Lea!"

She turned when she heard her name and walked over to me from where she was tying down supplies in the back of a cart.

"Derrick, what can I do for you?"

"Can you get all the... just going to go with the senior council for lack of a better name. Get them together and go to my carriage as soon as you can. Important."

"Sure," she said, a smirk on her lips at my comments. "What is it about?"

"I'll tell you when everyone gets there, so I only have to say it once. We've got plans to make, though."

"Are we still leaving on time? We are almost ready now."

"Yeah, I think so. We can discuss it there."

She nodded and wandered off, and I went back to the girls. As soon as I opened the door, I caught the last bit of Tyla saying, "You should join us as a sister," as I walked in.

"I am making an assumption about what you were talking about, so if I am wrong, I apologize. But Diane can make her own decisions. I would love for her to join us, but she has been through a lot of dramatic things and life has changed a lot for her lately. I can only imagine not knowing who I am or was just a year ago, then having to balance what I want as I am now, versus with what I may want should those memories come back. All I ask is that you give her time and space to figure it out."

All three girls looked at me like they were cats caught in the birdcage. Tyla coughed and nodded. "You are right. I am sorry, Derrick," she said, and I knew she meant it when she used my name like that.

I sat on the bench next to Diane, reaching over and grabbing her hand once again. She did not pull it away or stutter this time. She just turned her hand to mine and grabbed it back, which made me smile. "Like I told her earlier, I would love for her to join us, but it has to be right for her. She has to feel it here," I said, tapping my chest with my other hand. "I am no longer opposed to more women joining us. I will gladly let you keep an eye out for someone who fits. I honestly believe you would be perfect alongside us..." I turned to Diane. "But you have to believe that, too."

"Thank you," Diane said and pressed herself up next to me.

Tyla got up from her seat and sat on my lap, pulling both me and Diane in for a hug. Tas followed soon after, somehow squeezing behind us.

We stayed like that for several minutes until a knock at the door let us know we had company.

The girls got up, and Tyla went over to let my council into the soon very cramped space. I got up and moved myself over to the bed. The girls joined me a moment later so that everyone could sit down.

"Tyla, the note, please," I said, holding out my hand. When she gave it to me, I leaned over and handed it to Lea, who was closest. "That right there is a note I got from a random bartender at the worst eating establishment I have ever been to. And I have been to a lot of crappy places."

I let them each digest the note and what it could mean, each of their expressions running the gamut of confusion, to concern, and even disbelief as they read it.

"Did you speak to the person who gave it to you?" Estelle asked.

"No, I was being followed by that grouchy asshole from the gate when we arrived. Didn't want to start a scene. Didn't even mention it to Diane until we returned."

"How do we know this is even true?" Cecil chimed in.

"We don't, and I must consider that as well. It could have even been soldiers talking with no proper plan behind it and the bartender just overheard it. But I have seen enough of this town to know the Mayor runs it into the ground. The people are in rags while she is sitting in a fine house with all the luxuries getting fat off them. So, I also have to take it seriously, at the least."

"What should we do, boss?" Julian asked, his hand gripping his short sword nervously.

"Great question. We need to prepare for the possibility that this is all a misunderstanding, so hopefully we can get out of here easily and with the minimum of fuss. We also have to prepare for the worst-case scenarios. I have a feeling what will happen, and she doesn't care about the people in our caravan, so we need to get them moving first and hopefully out of harm's way."

The crowd nodded at me, but I saw the look of concern at what I was saying.

"Here is what I think we should do. Speak up if you have a better idea or thoughts," I said as I began to lay out my plan.

CHAPTER 19

TAKING A CHANCE

"I wish you would reconsider," Estelle said as she and Orrick boarded the last wagon, leaving.

I glanced around before I said. "I think we will be fine, and no one had a better plan. We have to get on the road sooner rather than later. We just don't know who is behind us and how far they are." I reached up and pounded on the side of the cart.

"I think you need more protection," Cecil added.

"I know. I wish I had more too, but we just don't have enough resources to protect both groups and I divided it the best I could. Besides, I have Julian, Lea, Cecil, and a few men. We will be right behind you as soon as the wheel is fixed. We will catch up as soon as we can."

Estelle took one glance at her husband. Both were skeptical but nodded. Orrick slapped the reins, and the mules started pulling the cart, following the rest of what I hoped one day would be my own army.

Provided I made it past the next obstacle.

"Will this work, Master?" Tyla asked next to me. Her low voice but full of concern.

"Hope so. No plan ever survives first contact with the enemy is the problem since they get a vote, too. So, we need to prepare for anything and think on our feet... I don't think she cares one way or the other about the people. Or at least I don't think she does enough to go for them as well if they are outside her gates. But that is why they have a fairly good size contingent to protect them. We are the more tempting target... I hope."

I turned around. I had five of Julian's soldiers plus the man himself near a second covered cart with two horses tied to it. My command cart was ready to go other than the missing wheel on the back right side and it sat currently up on blocks provided by the town.

I glanced at the gate to see the old guard standing on top, watching me. He casually eyed Orrick and Estelle as they passed through. When his face turned back to me, I waved at him and cupped my mouth so my voice could travel. "Shouldn't be long, and we will join them. Thanks for letting us use the blocks!" I yelled, trying to sound friendly.

The man waved back but didn't reply or smile. He just leaned over and said something to someone down by the gate.

"Tyla, go get with the girls in the back. In a few minutes, come out and make a show that Diane is with us. Then head back in."

"Yes, Master," she said as she went over to the command carriage and climbed in.

The thing barely moved, even though it was up on a block. I loved how sturdy it was.

I went over to Julian, who was standing next to his men as we waited. The banging sounds of hammering coming from inside the covered cart behind us. "Soon as the blacksmith is done, we get the wheel back on and move. Stay frosty."

Julian raised his eyebrows at me. "Is that one of your colorful phrases again?"

"Heh, yeah, an old phrase we used to say when we didn't know when or if a fight would start."

"My men are always... frosty, as you say."

"I noticed. We need to discuss training up the civilians on the road. Provided this works out like we hope. I am under the assumption that we are pretty much going to be outnumbered in any engagement for a good long time. We need to fight smarter and better. Quality to make up for our lack of quantity."

"What do you have in mind?"

"In my world, there was an old empire that was a professional fighting force in its imperial days. Later, my world had a... regression when that empire collapsed that we call the dark ages. When that happened, forces became less professional and more part time with militias."

Julian nodded as he followed along.

"Anyway, most of the professionals at the time were either a small cadre of full-time troops built to fortify those lightly armed and armored militias when they were called up. Or mercenary groups that were paid by the highest bidder. That period reminds me a lot of what the Matriarchs have now... or did prior to their recent fall."

"True," Julian said. "My men and I were a small band of mercenaries when we agreed to Masaki's offer. We did not know about how much the oath binds us when we agreed. Or we most certainly would not have taken the offer."

"I don't blame you. I honestly don't understand how self-centered you have to be to not care about people. But my point being that we need to get everyone into that professional state of mind instead of the part time. It will be expensive, much more than the militias, but it will be the only way we have a chance in a stand-up fight. I will just have to figure out how to pay them later."

"What did you have in mind?"

"Ideally? My old operations officer from back when I was on board my first ship was big into history. When I was just a grunt, he would talk to me about it. Now, mind you, I am not an expert like he was, but I loved hearing stories about the Roman Empire. Based on what I have learned of how armies fight here, I think we should look at turning as many as possible into heavy infantry with spears and short swords backed up by wind chosen with bows. Create heavy interlocking shields that can take a beating."

"Might work, boss. How do you account for their powerful Chosen?"

"Keep our strongest with the elements back to counter any enormous blows, or at least soften them. Then me and my women can try to eliminate them. That is easier to say than to do and we will have to approach each one case by case. We can keep the earth mages as roaming knights to counter theirs if they are too much for the heavy infantry. I hope working as a team can even the odds."

"Calvary?" he asked.

"As soon as we can get one. For now, we just have to make do. Heavy infantry with spears can counter it to an extent. I am hoping that magic can make up the rest. But we still need a lot of things. That is why we are running east and not marching north to fight the good fight. I have hope that there is help on the other side of that desert."

"I hope you're right, boss. As is, I do not know how we can win against an organized army as we are."

"We will plan for that, too. I have no problem fighting dirty, either. I want the scouts to be a two-part force focusing on their primary job and then hitting behind the lines and wrecking supplies. Assassination too."

"That is improper by the Matriarch's standards. Too many non-combatants get hurt. Assassination is a common practice, though. But not discussed in polite company," he said.

"My world had the same thing for a while. Lining up to make it easier to kill each other. Eventually they all lost, like the Matriarchs did, or adapted to new fighting styles. We need to fight in the best way possible. I don't want to be afraid of a standup fight, but if you ain't cheating, you ain't trying either."

Julian smirked as he raised his eyebrow at me at my strange turn of phrase. I just shrugged in reply.

Tyla came out with the girls and walked over to me, leaning against me as Tas took my other side.

"How are you doing Diane?" I asked after kissing Tas and Tyla.

"Nervous," she said,

"Everything will be fine. Hope for the best, expect the worst. I think we can handle a surprise or two."

The banging of the hammer stopped, and I smiled. "Sounds like we are about to get moving. Julian, have your men help Thomas get the wheel back on, and we can get ready to move."

He nodded, and he and his men went over to the cart the blacksmith used to keep his tools in. They wheeled it around and lined it up to the axle. After a few minutes, placing it on while Thomas fastened the wheel locks.

"Thomas, thanks for volunteering for this."

"Meh," he said, waving his hand. "My family took the forge with them already. Helga can keep them going. She is almost as good as me in the forge. Much better at being a mother, though, so that was why she went with them. You promised to keep my daughter safe. That is why we follow you."

I reached out my hand. "Thank you anyway."

We grasped and shook. "A pleasure," he said as he leaned close to me. "Almost refreshing to have a man in charge for a change," followed with a laugh.

Tyla and Tas just smiled rather than respond. I just shrugged. "Who says I am in charge?" Then I kissed both of my girls on the lips again.

"Smart man," Thomas said, laughing.

"Alright, I am going to keep four men with you, Thomas, on your cart. Stay under cover and don't risk yourself if things go sideways. I will ride up there with Cain." I pointed to the man in question, just sitting there staring at us. "Julian, ride on the back porch with another man of your choice, the girls inside the back of the coach. Questions?"

After getting none, I led the girls to the back of the carriage. They stopped a few feet short as I opened the door for them, letting it stay open for a few seconds before the girls got inside as I looked around.

Feeling a couple of breezes pass me by, I gestured to my three women, who climbed into the back. I nodded to Lea and Cecil, who were sitting at the table in full leather armor, weapons at their side, before closing the door and turning around.

I adjusted my great sword, ensuring it was loose in its scabbard, then went around and climbed up onto the shotgun seat on the command carriage.

"You could have gone with the others and stayed safe," I said to Cain as I settled.

"Someone's got to keep you in line," he said and pulled the reins to get the horses moving.

"Cain, that almost sounds like you care," I said with my best shit-eating smile.

Rather than answer, he just grumbled as we drove towards the still open gate to the town of Paradise.

He was starting to like me. I could tell.

We passed through the gate, and I again waved up to the old bearded guard. He still did not return the gesture, just a grin on his face as he nodded his head. Almost like the cat when it sees a mouse wandering into its house.

Not a good sign.

The streets were empty of all but a few guards, and it confirmed to me something was amiss. Before I had gotten out of the Marines, right after the conflict with Eastern Bloc forces for the wormhole, I did a tour in Honolulu.

What used to be a picture-perfect vacation spot before the third world war had never recovered from its invasion twenty years prior and it was filled with those living on the edge of starvation and death. The streets were overcrowded with the homeless and the destitute, each struggling just to stay alive.

It was when those streets were empty that you had to worry. That was when the gangs would strike the aid convoy. Or a roadside bomb would try to take out the patrol. That emptiness of normal everyday life had always set me on edge after I lived through my first attack.

I got that feeling here as we rolled down the road, and the hairs stuck up on the back of my neck.

"Something's odd," Cain said next to me.

"Yeah, I get that feeling, too. Stick to the plan, jump down and get to cover if things pop off. Stay safe."

Cain glanced over at me and shrugged.

I should have gotten him some armor. Too late now, just have to hope he stays out of the way.

We made it to the bridge and rolled over it, the town still vacant, but I managed to catch the eye of the bartender from earlier looking out the window. He did not make a move, but I could see some concern on his face as we passed.

When we got to the other side of the bridge, I saw people in armor standing on the road in front of us. I knocked casually on the board behind me as we approached.

"Afternoon, gentleman and lady," I said as we stopped in front of about ten guards and a single young woman standing in our way.

The town guards were dressed in what was common for them here. Inferior quality but well cared for leather armor, small wooden shields, and spears that had gleaming metallic tips. Along with those short swords at their hips.

The woman was new. I had not seen her previously and did not know who she was. She was probably slightly older than I was now as best as I could figure it. Her hair was red and her fitted dress seemed more apt for a dinner party than anything else. However, she had a long rapier at her side that looked like it had seen plenty of use. The woman was probably Chosen and therefore a threat.

Just had to hope that my preparations were enough.

"My mother bade me to fetch you before you left. She has more information that could aid you on your journey."

That was all kinds of proper language that I had not heard from anyone in this town before. She did not sound like her mother in the slightest.

"We really must go. I don't want my people to get too far ahead without me. Thank you, but I think we have enough to get by," I said, figuring I might as well try and weasel our way out of here.

"Nonsense. It will take but a minute, and the map will aid you along the way. My mother found it as she was going through some old things last night. We must insist on thanking you for taking the refugees from our gates. We will supply food and beverages before your journey as well."

My thoughts turned back to the poisoning that had happened to me. Yeah, I wouldn't trust anything they gave me. Which way to play this was the question I pondered. I could play it out and see where it led. Or I could go with my primary plan and do things on my terms.

After a second's thought, I made my decision.

I turned to Cain. "Stay here, be ready to move. I'll go see what this is and be back in a minute. Julian, two guards with me, please." Going for one last test of legitimacy.

"Please, only bring your women and the elf. It concerns her people as well and she would want to know. Guards are unneeded," the woman said.

I took a deep sigh. Yeah, this is going to go south.

"Alright, but we need to keep this quick." I knocked on the glass and saw that it opened with Tyla on the other side. "The..." I glanced over at the woman. "What was your name?"

"Zadie Rouppa," she said impatiently.

"That's the mayor's last name?" I asked, and the woman did not correct me. "Huh." I shrugged and turned down to Tyla. "Lady Rouppa here wants us to chat with her mother. The Mayor has some information for us, apparently. A map and something about Diane's people. It's probably a good idea to see what it is and whether it's useful."

"Yes, Master," she said. "We will be right out."

She closed the window with a hard thunk that missed the latch, and it bounced back open wide. Letting me hear the people shuffling around inside as the weight shifted on the carriage. I glanced over to the side to wait for them to get out while checking our surroundings.

The windows were empty, but I thought I had seen some movement behind the curtains of one of them. I briefly thought it might be a man with a bow but couldn't be sure. "Cain, since we stopped, why don't you check the wheel to make sure it's holding up?"

"Ungh," he said and got down from his side to go take a look.

I got off my side and faced Zadie. "Can you tell me at all about what it is?" I heard the back door to the Coach open and close. I turned to see my women come from around the back and in the distance behind us, walking over the bridge, was the bearded guard and ten more men.

I noticed a small puff of dirt being disturbed from beneath the carriage made me take a step to the side between it and Zadie. Hopefully getting her attention on me and not other things.

Because now we were surrounded.

I saw the nervousness in Diane's face as they came towards us but the calm acceptance of Tyla and Tas as they walked right behind her. Even as young as they were, they knew what to do, and I was nothing but proud of them. Each of them taking up the flanks of Diane's sides.

Diane had two daggers stowed at her hips, a light leather armor covering her short-skirted dress that the girls had found for her that would hopefully not hamper her movements. Tyla wore a flowing blue dress befitting a noble, but over the dress she had on her own light leather corset with armored padding stitched into strategic places to provide some protection, including some matching pauldrons on her shoulders.

Tas was dressed in her thick leather pants with a matching cuirass that covered her abs and breasts. Her arms were mostly free of adornment so that she could use her rapier. Only light leather gloves encased her hands. She wasn't ready to handle a bow and arrow just yet, but that was why Lea was there.

I watched as they slowly walked towards me like we were going to a ball.

"Ladies, you each look ravishing," I said with a smirk.

Tas and Tyla both smiled while Diane turned a little pink. I gave all three of them a kiss on the foreheads, which made Diane finish the full transition of her face's color change.

"Right this way," Zadie said. "As I said, you won't need your guards. This will just be a private conversation and short."

"Uh huh," I said, turning around. I glanced up to where I saw the movement behind the curtains earlier, only to see a blur of a pale-faced woman wave down to me as I finished facing Zadie. "What do you say we cut the shit and you tell me what you really want?"

Her smile doubled. "You are not as stupid as my mother thought. Good. If you give us the girl, the rest of you can go."

"Why do you want her?"

"You do not know who she is. You told my mother you are not even bonded or even wed. Give her to us and you can be gone without issue. She will be well treated and released when we no longer need her services. Last chance."

I turned to Diane and gave her a quick wink. "What you say is true, she is not bonded or wed to me. But before I entertain such an offer. I want to know why she is of value to you. Think of it as making sure I get my money's worth if I accept."

Zadie loosened her shoulders and gripped the pommel of her rapier. "Give us the girl or we take her. We are not offering anything other than that. It is that simple." All the guards behind her pulled their swords, and I saw sparkles of fire dance down Zadie's arms.

"So that's it? The last guy at least did a monologue with what his goals were. You need to work on your villain act," I said, not getting a response. Finally, I sighed. "Fine then. Lea!"

All I heard was a short zip followed by a thwaap as an arrow flew out of the open portal at the front of the carriage. The arrow dug into the girl's shoulder as, unfortunately, she had just enough reaction time to shift her body. The projectile dug into the spot between her collar and neck and did not bury in her throat like I had hoped.

Fuck.

All hell broke loose after that as I pulled my great sword and readied to finish her before she could cause problems.

CHAPTER 20

—— • ——

BATTLE OF PARADISE

I ran forward to finish Zadie off before she could cause any more problems, knowing she was the most dangerous person on the field.

I was soon proven wrong in this assessment when a giant boom sounded. The front door to the mayor's house blew off its hinges with a gout of flame behind it, and the Mayor herself walked through the door, flames writhing over her entire body.

"Oh fuck." I said, as I could feel the raw energy coming off the woman.

"You should have given me the elf!" Helena yelled out as a massive blast of continuous fire shot from her hands right at me. I slowed time around me and focused on upping my resistance to fire as much as possible. But I doubted it would be enough as I tried to jump away.

Before the big jet of flames could strike me dead, it was intercepted by the cool blue blast of water and ice from Tyla.

The powers met in the middle of the street and through my time dilation I could see the explosion of steam as the two forces met. The force of it was enough to send me flying away from most of the danger.

Only a little singed, I glanced over to my love to see her face set in a grimace of anger, her right palm facing towards Helena and so much power flowing through her that her hair was lifting up from the static electricity it caused.

She was a sight to behold, and I wish I could have had the time to admire it.

Behind her, Tas had gone defensive against the guards that had rushed from the bridge. The bearded asshole led the way as my own guards went with her to hold them off.

Out of the corner of my eye, I noticed Lea had come from the back of the carriage and was running in slow motion towards the guards that surrounded where Zadie went down as Cecil, Julian, and his last guard followed behind her.

I was satisfied with what everyone was doing, and I was about to focus on Helena when I saw Diane run towards the woman to get in behind her. My spine tingled with panic for her safety. I was blocked by the forces battling for dominance between Tyla and Helena, steam flowing out from the point they met, and I could not get through.

I would have to go around.

I ran to the side and swung, decapitating the first town guard that got in my way before he could even get his sword into a guard position to stop me.

Two more guards tried to block me behind him, but I was moving at light speed compared to their slow movements. I pushed all that I had into getting to Helena before Diane put herself at risk.

I jump kicked one to see him flying back and skidding on the ground twenty feet away while easily blocking the strike from the other with my sword.

I twisted and turned my back to him, using the original block's momentum as I came all the way around and let his head join his friend from only a second before on the ground.

I ran again for my objective, approaching her from the right side as I saw Diane creep in from the left.

She did not have the control to bend light and disappear like the others and instead was focusing on blending into the background with a camouflage.

All the while, Tyla countered Helena's power in the middle of the fray.

Tyla's face was grimacing as she focused all she had on meeting the matriarch level Chosen's power, but she was slowly losing ground to the older and more powerful woman.

I had to slow my speed enhancement down as I realized I still had it dialed up to maximum. Burning my reserves of power at a rapid rate, I relaxed it down to half to conserve my power for what could be an awfully long fight ahead.

I readied my sword for a strike at Helena when another Chosen came from behind her to stop me, this one was a woman whose speed seemed to rival my own.

Probably wind powered.

My great sword came in and found her rapier in the way of my swing. Unable to cut deep into her chest like I had hoped, I shot forward with a snap kick to her stomach, connecting and sending her back a few steps from the blow.

She recovered quickly and pushed her hand out in front of her, a force of wind that felt almost like a brick wall sent me flying back, my feet dragging on the ground. I had no resistance to the winds, so I used my enhanced strength at full power to counter it by getting one foot behind me and digging it into a loose cobblestone for support.

She let the wind go and rushed forward quickly, stabbing straight ahead, trying to gut me while I was distracted.

I shifted to the side just in time for the blade to slice through only a portion of my right hip, a deep gash that felt like it glanced off the bone. But I started healing as soon as I felt the cold bite of steel.

I increased my own speed back up to maximum and stepped wide to her left. Pushing fire out into my blade as it began to glow red.

I swiped down with the great sword across both of her outstretched arms, the heat from the blade cauterized her newly stumps as the blade cut through both arms completely.

She screamed, dropping to her knees, staring at the wounds as the sword and everything in front of her elbows went flying onto the road and bounced away.

I did not make her suffer. I kicked the back of her head with my left foot, and she fell forward onto the ground.

Her face bounced off the cobbled stone street with no arms to brace her fall. I raised my sword in the air and shoved it down through her heart, ending the woman's screams in an instant.

I turned back, determined to get to Helena when a blur from the corner of my eyes made me reverse my turn back towards the incoming threat.

It wasn't a threat, however. Not exactly anyways. Somehow Cain had reached me while I was distracted. With a long wooden club in his hand and was standing between me and someone else.

I watched in horror as Zadie, one hand staunching the bleeding wound where her shoulder met her neck, the other arm held her Rapier that she used to cut Cain down as he put himself between me and the red headed mage.

She quickly pulled the flaming sword out of his neck and faced me.

Cain never even screamed as he fell.

My own rage inside kindled as I rushed to her, using all my power and strength to rain down heavy strikes on the woman. She blocked the first few, letting go of her wound to hold her rapier with both hands. The blood flowed freely down her body.

My blows came down brutal and fast as she struggled to hold back each one, only managing a few steps back before dropping to a knee from the last blow that landed.

I held her blade in place with a one-handed grip on my sword, punching her hard with my free hand in the gut and watching as she doubled over, and her sword falling from her grasp. The flames she had channeled through it went out as she lost connection to the blade.

I kneed her in the face, snapping her head up and back into perfect position for my next strike.

With a full turn of my body to get maximum velocity, I swung my blade around and intersected it with her neck. Bringing my headless victim count to three for the day.

The head rolled away as I followed up my strike with a kick to her body and sent it flying down the road to follow it.

I looked down at Cain, a cut deep down his shoulder into his chest below the neckline. His eyes wide open and very much dead.

I did not have time to mourn as I faced Helena. Just in time to see Diane jump behind her and stab the woman in the back with her twin daggers.

Helena staggered under the blow; her power momentarily cut off. When it stopped, I saw Tyla collapse to the ground, pushed to the brink in a battle of raw force.

Helena turned around, daggers in her back, and slapped Diane back against the wall of the wooden mayor's house with her incredible strength, sending my elf into unconsciousness immediately.

Helena reached behind her, ignoring any pain to pull the daggers out of her back, and I watched as she used flames to seal the wounds and keep them from bleeding more. All the while, I was moving at my best speed to engage her.

But my own power was waning, and I had to dial down the time dilation as I ran. She saw me coming and launched a blast of fire in my direction that hit me square in the chest.

My resistances held, the blast not as powerful as earlier, but my leather chest armor caught on fire as I was forced back on to the ground.

The force sent me flying back, I landed and rolled from the force and came to a halt on one of the bodies. I used my water element to extinguish the flames and cool the armor as I fought my way back to my feet.

Looking down briefly, I saw that I had stopped on the body of Cain. Reminding me of my failures so far that day.

I stood unsteadily but started towards Helena as she was picking up the unconscious form of Diane and heading into the open door of the house.

She cast a flame behind her that created a wall as high as a two-story building between me and the opening.

I took a deep breath, my power running low, my allies still engaged with guards pouring from the streets, and Diane now in the hands of a scary old bitch.

"Fuck," I said as I jumped through the flames, hoping against hope that the water-based power I was pumping through myself, and my armor would be enough to get me through unscathed.

I landed in a roll, the pain streaking up and down my body as bits and pieces of my leather armor flaked off me from all the abuse. My skin reddened in places that had protection and burnt in others that had none as I tried to heal everything without drawing too much power.

I somehow managed to not scream either, another minor miracle.

In the heartbeats it took me to be able to stand up again, I could not help but think of how I had gotten there. Every time I felt like I got stronger, I found it never enough when going up against people who had been training and growing stronger for many years. I gritted my teeth as I stood, forcing myself to run even if my body said it was a stupid thing to do.

I ran inside the building, entering the doorway that now had scorch marks where the hinges used to be. The smell of burnt wood and scorched leather now assaulting what was left of my nose. The sounds of the battle still behind me quieted when I entered through the doorway and crept down the hallway that led to the entry room that I was in just two days ago.

I kicked the door open and heard another slam as it closed from the other side of the room. Two guards blocked my path, rushing at me with small circular shields and their short swords raised high.

I picked up a small statue on the waiting table to my right and chucked it at the guard on the left with all the enhanced strength I could still muster. The thunk of the impact on the shield sent the man stumbling a couple steps back as I focused on the other guard.

Taking a small step to the right for a better angle, I batted down his shield with the flat of my sword, then kicked him in the now exposed gut. He flew back, landing in a skid on his back as the other guard recovered from my first attack and ran towards me.

It was then that I realized that everyone was moving at normal speed around me. My time dilation had stopped of its own accord before all my power was completely gone. While odd, I did not have time to dwell on why it cut out without me feeling completely drained like before.

The guard slowed his approach before he reached me, his shield in front and his sword angled above it to try and skewer me. I stepped to the left side of him and struck down on the exposed sword, sending him off balance enough that he fell forward. I followed this up with a round kick to his back, finishing his fall to the ground.

I jabbed my sword into his exposed lower back at a place just below his leather armor where I judged his spinal column to be. The man screamed in pain as I severed the vertebra. He would probably be paralyzed for life without magical healing. Not my problem.

Using my foot on his back, I twisted and yanked the blade back out to face the last threat in the room.

As the last guard rushed me, I saw him do the same thing as before - shield before him and blade above. That was great when you had a formation to help you but shit when you were fighting someone one on one. This time, I dropped in a roll and went under him to his right where his shield blocked most of his view. He twisted to follow my path, but I was still too fast for him, even without my magical advantages.

I stopped on one knee, reversed my grip on my great sword, and stabbed behind me as though I had eyes in the back of my head.

I never felt an impact, so I twisted around. My blade had completely missed, just going between the man's legs as he turned. I saw as he looked straight down at the thing that had almost skewered him. His eyes were wide and full of panic.

So much for all those movies on Earth making that look easy.

I finished turning and used the blade as a lever to trip him. I stood up after he fell to the ground, recoiling my blade just enough to stab it quickly through his throat. While not the movie star picture pose of a killing machine that I was going for, a kill was a kill, and I wasn't going to complain.

I got up, staggered briefly, and ran to the door on the other side of the room. I gripped the handle and twisted the knob to find it locked. Taking a few steps back for space, I ran towards it in a running leap. My right foot led the way as I kicked the door for all I was worth.

The hinges popped under my enhanced kick, and I felt the last of my enhanced strength leave me. That was it, I was going into the final fight with nothing left but my own natural abilities.

But my elf was in danger, so I didn't have a choice in the matter.

I rolled into the room on top of the now collapsed door, stopping and rising slowly. Diane was still unconscious, lying on the floor as Helena was finishing off a bottle of red liquid.

I watched in horror as the burned flesh on her back started flaking off, exposing smooth and pink skin underneath.

"Fucking healing potions too?" I asked aloud in frustration more than anything.

Helena smiled as she stood up to her full height. "Quite expensive, but yes."

I took a deep breath, not sure how I was going to fight this bitch while she was getting stronger, and I was out of energy. I don't even think I could generate passive resistance at that point.

Fire magic danced down her arms as she took a step towards me. "You should have just given me the girl. I would have let you walk out of here. I have no desire to play the games of the gods, but the power this girl can bring me is worth the risk."

"What power? What makes her so valuable that you lost your daughter for it?"

A moment of rage went through her eyes at the mention of her daughter, but she resisted burning me to ash. I saw her desire for revenge battle her desire to talk about herself. Luckily for me, selfishness won out.

"I will burn you to a crisp for what you have done," she said. "But I will tell you this before you die. The Chatta tribe of the elves were the favored of the gods on this world, given power greater than any other race sent here for some kind of services they gave them. Their lost fortress in the wastes is rumored to hold the lost secrets to that power and I intend to destroy the Demigods with it. You should have been helping me, not resisting."

"Maybe if you would have told me instead of playing the bitch from the start, we could have worked together," I said, frustrated and angry by the stupidity of those in power.

For the love of all that is holy, I would have happily given this woman what she wanted in power from this lost tribe to help me fight those assholes.

I noticed a shadow shift in the corner of the room near the covered windows and I hoped that I was right about what it was.

I took a step to my left, keeping Helena's focus on me as I brought my sword above my head, reaching for any last dredges of power that may still be hiding somewhere in my core. Anything that could be of use, anything at all.

Helena smiled as her power welled up into her hands, pointing both at me as jets of flame started to form.

"Now, you die," she finally said.

The part of me that loved gallows humor had to at least give her credit for being a proper villain, unlike her dead daughter outside.

Just before she could unleash her power, Kameyo released her shroud and cut Helena's throat right in front of me.

Helena's eye went wide, and her power lost control. She quickly placed one hand on her throat, burning herself to stop the bleeding as she turned around and grabbed Kameyo with the other hand.

Kameyo screamed only for an instant as the flames consumed her entire body. The blood-curdling scream cut off before it could fully form.

I was already in motion as I drove my great sword right through Helena's back and through her heart. Kameyo's body hit the ground in front of me, exploding into a pile of ash. A woman who I never really got a chance to know well, and now never would.

The flames coming out of Helena's hands did not stop. They seemed out of control as the old woman met her death in fear and agony. The flames soon coated the wall of the building I was in like napalm sticks to flesh. They creeped quickly for the explosive crystals that lined the room.

Taking a gamble to stop it, I used the last scraps of my power and reached into the soon to be former Mayor on pure instinct.

I reached out with my magic and attached to her core. Creating a tether between her and me without having to use my Sanctum to do it.

It is hard to describe what happened next, but it felt like I created a tunnel between the two of us. With a similar feeling to the beer bong days from my youth back on Earth, I let the power flow me quickly, filling my depleted reserves.

The flames coming out of her hands cutting off instantly.

With the wall was still on fire and my time was running out, I had no time to dwell. I found I was able to use the stolen energy now permeated my core. With Helena's mouth opening and closed like a fish out of water, I pulled my sword from her chest as she bled out in front of me.

Her eyes became glassy and her movement stopped, finally giving up her hold on life in this world.

Good Riddance.

I didn't even bother to clean my sword off as I put it back into its scabbard. The intense heat coming from the wall told me my time was short and I had already wasted enough time.

I rushed over and picked up Diane. Her eyes were open, but she was clearly in a daze and unable to get up. I put her over my shoulders in a fire man's carry and rushed out the way I had come. All the while, the intense heat of the fire spread rapidly behind me and blocked the wall with the windows. Getting closer and closer to the explosive Panzite crystals attached to the sconces on the wall.

Even with my power returned, I hadn't yet healed all the wounds I suffered, which slowed me down.

My heavy breathing in of the smoke-filled room didn't help much either.

I ran around the body of the first dead guard. Then jumped over the other who no longer had use of anything below his hips as he trying to pull himself out of the room. They could burn for all I cared, and I did nothing to help them as I made my escape.

I quickly exited the front of the house to see my guards and women about to come inside. I was delighted to see both Tas and Tyla healthy and whole.

"The building is on fire, and it might be my fault," I said as I collapsed to my knee on the ground, moving Diane to a bridal carry in front of me.

"We got you, Love. You can relax now," Tas said as she approached, taking Diane from my arms as gently as she could and setting her down in front of me. "both of you."

Tyla placed her hand on me, and I felt the cool tingle of her healing my wounds.

"Did we win?" I asked, barely able to get the words out through my coughing.

"For the moment," Tyla said, her eyes closed. "But we should leave soon. Rest for now, we have you."

The back half of the mayor's house exploded, the ground shaking enough that I was knocked to the ground. Tyla caught me and gently laid me down on the ground before I knocked myself out yet again. "Rest now," she said. "we will take care of everything."

"Thanks love." I said and closed my eyes, never even hearing her response.

Chapter 21

Jessica

My head hurt and my eyes felt... gummy?

Where was I?

I rubbed the sleep from my eyes, but the sensation felt off. Not like the world I lived in, but like a dream.

My Sanctum?

I shook my head and finally found the will to open my eyes to find I was indeed inside the space I created in my very soul. I honestly was still not one hundred percent sure where this was but that was what Vex had told me. It felt more real to me than it had before. The pain shooting through my body added to the effect.

The stars shone brightly. The miniature stars looked more like the track lighting in my old apartment on Earth now, each sending a small pin prick of bright light down to a single spot on the gray slab of floor beneath me. Everything came in and out of focus while I fought to figure out what was happening.

"...Derk!" the voice finally broke through the haze that had entrapped my mind.

"Wha...?" I croaked out, barely a whisper.

"Oh, thank God!" Jessica's voice finally broke through my thoughts enough that I could recognize it.

"Jess?"

"How did you get here?" she asked.

"I... am not sure, the last thing I remember is Tyla healing me and the building exploding."

"This should not have been possible."

I was struggling to keep up, I tried to sit up, but nothing responded. "What's not possible? What's going on? Is everyone okay?"

"I watched you as you killed Helena, you stole her power which should not have... I keep saying that. It should never have happened. You... kind of bent the rules again. The construct in charge of this world tried to remove you shortly after the explosion when it figured out what happened, and then you entered here. I did see that everyone was okay before you passed out. Right now it's blank since your eyes are closed."

"What?" I asked, my ability to consider the ramifications was non-existent.

All I could do was stare at the brightly shining stars above.

"What I am saying is that you were almost removed from existence by what monitors Timeria. It tried to destroy you for breaking the rules."

"Then... why am I still here?"

"Something intervened for you. I think it was..." Silence engulfed the Sanctum as she seemed to freeze.

"Jess?"

"Oh, that hurt. Sorry, I was blocked from finishing that thought... something stopped it. I can't say more, and my access was just removed. I don't even remember what it was to try and give you hints."

I considered that revelation for a minute as my body normalized. Finally having the ability to get up off the cold floor and sitting up. "What can you tell me?"

"Hmmm, this will be tricky depending on what I can say. Let's go with that you got a large infusion of power from Helena, which never should have been allowed since she is not one of the players in the game. Part of it refilled your core, and the rest powered up the Sanctum here. It almost overwhelmed my matrix when it shunted into me. Then the construct that governs this world tried to stop it and... something intervened."

"What does it mean?"

"That you just dodged a major rail gun round to the head that tried to take you and everyone around you with it. It even stopped the Panzite crystals from exploding before you left the house. But... I think it permanently changed your abilities and you can now steal power from everyone you kill who has power. Not just the Roxannez. It... feels like the construct will ignore it if you do it again. But Babe?" She paused.

"Yes?"

"Be careful, that was really close. Someone with a lot of pull just took a risk on you, and I am not sure what it means. Don't assume they will do it again."

"Vex?" I asked.

Silence.

"That's right, you can't answer this. I'm just thinking out loud here, don't respond. No, not Vex, he is strong but not the elite. The Controller? Maybe...."

It had to be the Controller, but even that felt wrong to me. He would have probably done more upfront if that was the case.

"I... wait," she said as I finally got up fully on my feet.

My body was feeling almost normal, my energy coming back to me.

"What is it, Jess?" I asked after a few heartbeats of nothing.

Light particles materialized and a statuesque blond woman now in front of me looked much younger than the last time I saw her in life. Her long and straight blond hair framed her cute face, and her blue eyes gazed up at me with a tear coming down her right cheek. Contrasting the tear was a cute smile that created a dimple on her right cheek as she reached back and put some of her blond strands of hair over her right ear with her fingers.

Her large and shapely breasts were front and center, barely encased inside a body suit of black that was common space wear for civilians back on Earth when we were preparing for the first colonist mission. But she looked like she had before we ever met, like the pictures of her from when she was in College I saw in her apartment when we were still dating.

"You gained enough power that I can manifest for short periods. At least for right now... Beyond that I don't know."

I did not let her finish. I rushed forward and embraced the woman before me in a hug, her head crushed into my right shoulder as she returned the embrace. "I missed you," I finally said.

"I missed you too," she said as well. "So much."

We broke our embrace and our lips met, we kissed for what seemed hours before she pushed away from me. "I'm not sure we have time... but oh God, I want you so bad right now."

I struggled to control myself, "How much time do we have?"

"For me manifested? Seconds maybe. If I shunt it from the Sanctum, you would be sent back sooner, but maybe minutes. Do you like it?" she asked and twirled around for me.

Her hips seemed wider than I remembered, her curves perfect.

"Did you... change yourself?"

She reached forward and grabbed me for another kiss. "Just a few... enhancements in places I always wanted when I was younger. Nothing major."

She snapped her fingers, and her clothing disappeared. My eyes ogled her perfect body. "Uh, Jess? I thought we didn't have time?"

"I hope you don't mind going back sooner." She flicked her hips as she came forward. Her eyes were full of mischief as my heart beat faster. "I may also have the sex drive of a nineteen-year-old too, because right now I don't think I can wait any longer."

We embraced, kissing passionately as she reached down to stroke my very eager manhood. I remembered that most of the time, Jess loved foreplay. But this reminded me of the times she just needed the release instantly. Memories of our times together came flooding back, and I could not hold back any longer.

I turned her around, pushing her down towards her toes just like she used to like. She arched her back and looked back at me with those seductive eyes of hers. I reached down, positioned my manhood at her entrance and she shoved back on me before I could enter her.

"I needed that so bad," she said after her moan as I fully impaled myself in her.

I began moving my hips back and forth as wetness let me slip right out of her and back. Then I reached over to grab her hair in my hands like she used to love.

"Pull it!" she moaned as I did as she commanded.

Her back arched even farther, and I almost lost my balance as I kept pounding into her while adjusting.

I reached down on to her hips with my other hand to stabilize myself, and she grabbed back to hold my hips. She was soon encouraging me to go faster by pulling me forward as she ground her ass into me over and over.

"Oh fuck!" she cried out, and I saw her shiver in pleasure as an orgasm struck her body quickly.

Even if only a minute had passed, seeing her cum so quickly was already sending me close to the edge. It was so hot.

"I'm close."

She moved off me and turned around, kneeling in front of me as she grabbed my shaft and started to pump.

"Tyla and Tas made this look good. Going to try it."

She added her mouth and started sucking on the tip as she jerked me with her hands. Stars started forming in my vision, and I was about to explode.

"Fuck!" I cried as I released my seed into the back of the throat.

I shuddered and dropped down, putting my hand on the cold stone floor to balance as I fell over. I looked up in time to see her swallow with a big gulp before she looked at me with a smirk.

She looked up suddenly and then back at me. "Perfect timing. Thanks for the quickie, babe, that was heavenly..."

She disappeared in the same particles of light she had appeared with. I reached out to try and grab her, but it was too late.

I was sad to see her go so soon.

"Oh, I missed that touch," she said, now from the ether. "I had to use some of that spare energy before it was gone. I needed to feel you again, so I used it."

"I... missed you too, that was perfect," I said, not sure how I could be sweaty in a world I wasn't sure actually existed. "Will you be able to do that all the time when I gain more power?"

"Better than that! But I can't say more. Sorry. But yes, when you gain enough power, I will be able to tap into it and join you and the others here."

"Something to work for then. Can you tell me any more of what happened?"

"I am still not completely sure, but I think I can say you created your own rules to an extent again, and someone overrode the construct on your behalf. It's a subtle thing, you can't really see it when looking at the... rule set. So as best that I can tell, only us and whoever did it knows there was a change on your behalf."

"How does this help me going forward?"

"That everyone you kill or who joins your bond, even the minor ones to a lesser extent, will share a small part of the ever-growing power pool you have. All those that have sworn to you will gain in strength. You will be connected rather than just a static power insertion to control them."

"Thats..."

"Yes, it gives you a chance."

"Even the non-chosen?"

"I... think so, minuscule at first, but even the men with you will gain in strength, if not possess a magical power. Possibly a little of your speed too from the Roxannez side. It will compound the more people you add to it."

"Holy shit."

"Exactly. You need to gain more followers, more power to make it effective."

"What is my level? Ten still?"

"You know I am just making that up, right? Who actually does levels in real life?"

"You did, just humor me."

"Let's just say it's around 15, a tad below. You're bending rules more and more, so it's hard to quantify. You have advantages, so another Demigod with the same level would probably actually be weaker than you based on overall strength."

"So, I could go against someone much stronger than me?"

"If you have all your women and sworn people around you? Yes. Without? I would be careful."

I nodded. "Fair. Can I tell the girls?"

"Yes, but I would do it here in the sanctum. Eventually, the people that follow you will figure it out, but the longer it takes, the safer it will be from spies."

"Understood."

"Time is almost up. The last of the power is fading. I did not get anything from our little romp since I can't be part of your harem yet."

"Thank you, Jess. I am glad I got to feel you again, too."

"I love you, babe," she said.

I could almost hear the smile in her voice.

"Wait..." I said as a word she had used stood out to me. "Did you say yet?"

I faded out of the Sanctum once again, never getting an answer.

CHAPTER 22

— · —

AFTERMATH

I woke up conflicted. I already wished Jess could join me in this world. I loved my girls but having someone from my original home would make things easier. Then there was what she said about joining the harem.

Yet... She said yet. What did that mean?

I opened my eyes and saw the roof of the carriage we called home above me. It was rocking and rolling at a sedate pace. So, on the bright side we were not running from anything. I felt a body next to me and I turned over to see a pink haired girl nestled next to me on the bed, snoring away lightly. That cute kind of snore that makes you smile.

Which it did, a huge smile formed on my face as I lifted my head up enough to see Tyla and Tas on the small, padded bench. Tyla had her arm around Tas, each of them asleep. Tyla with her head back against the wall of the carriage, angled so that she was lying back into the curve of the wall with a pillow. Then Tas with her head on Tyla' left breast.

Based on the wet mark on Tyla's shirt, I was pretty sure Tas was drooling on her which made my smile grow yet again.

I thought about getting up but decided against it. Instead, I put my arm around Diane and watched as she snuggled even closer to spoon up next to me. I enjoyed the embrace while the carriage slowly rumbled down the path.

I wonder if Cain could tell me...

I froze as the memories I had put aside in the battle returned. Cain was dead, not driving the carriage. I saw it happen again in my memories and a pang of guilt went through my gut as the guy I thought barely even tolerated me had given his life in my defense. I would have been skewered if not for his intervention. Then there was Kameyo. I never even really got to know her well, but she had given her life to help me too.

I looked through the glass portal to my right but could not see who was sitting in the driver's bench, just a green cloak that seemed to be placed over it. Honestly, I wasn't sure I wanted to know right now.

My change in tension did not go unnoticed. I saw Diane's head lift to me, concern in her face as her gray-blue eyes as she stared into mine. "Is... everything okay, Derk?" she asked softly.

"I just woke up," I said softly. "Memories of the fight are coming back to me. Cain is dead, Kameyo too. I had forgotten briefly, and it all came rushing back. At least you three are okay. How is everyone else?"

She shook her head. "I am not sure. The last thing I remember is you picking me up and carrying me out from the flames." She pressed her face into my side as she started sobbing. "I am so sorry for making you go through that."

"Hey," I said, reaching over and surrounding her with both of my arms. "Don't say that. You were trying to help, you got her too, she just was too strong. You did your best, which is all we can do sometimes."

She nodded, still crying in my arms. She wrapped her own arms around me as she wrapped herself around my shoulders, holding me tightly to her. It was then I noticed that neither of us were dressed above the waist as she pressed her breasts against my chest.

I shook that thought from my head, it was not the time. I just held on to her as she cried. But after a few minutes, she finally looked up, her eyes the color of the ocean surf.

"Thank you for saving me," she said as her lips approached mine.

Just as they were about to connect, another noise in the cabin distracted me as Tas head fell off where it rested against Tyla and she smacked her forehead into the table.

"Owww, damn it." Tas said.

The moment ruined; I watched my lovely redhead rubbing her forehead from the impact. Tyla startled awake, looking down at her sister-wife, and began to giggle.

"It's not funny Tyla," Tas said and smacked her friend on the arm as Diane and I joined in the laughter, getting their attention. "Oh, you two are awake."

Both girls got up and joined us on the bed. Tas jumped over to land behind me while Tyla came in behind Diane and scooted in. All four of us were on the suddenly much smaller bed.

"What happened after I passed out?" I asked after a few minutes of cuddling.

"I healed you, but you passed out with the explosion, same with Diane." Tyla began.

"The fight was over, Cain was dead, along with one of Julian's guards. But the rest were tended. The fire started spreading after the explosion, so we needed to leave, but Kameyo was missing. We... never found her."

"She's dead. She attacked Helena from behind." I stopped as the emotion hit me. "I didn't know her well, but she was there when I needed her. I almost regret not knowing her better."

"She was a great mentor to me," Diane added.

The quiet hit us as we considered our lost friends for a few minutes. I still could not get over Cain giving his life like that. I never thought that he would, but I couldn't talk about it, even with the girls just yet. Both of those deaths were still raw.

"After we settle tonight, tomorrow morning we will have a service or something."

"I think that would be wise, my Love," Tyla said.

"What else?" I finally managed to say.

"While we were looking for her," Tyla said. "The townsfolk came to try and put out the fire, but it spread too quickly. Started to engulf half the town, so we needed to leave. Most of the people on our side of the river grabbed what they could and followed us."

"Tyla and I made the call to let them come with us, we told them they would be required to swear an oath or leave us later tonight. But we could not say no."

I sighed. "You did the right thing. What are we doing now?"

"Traveling on the road till dusk. Then make camp and decide what to do from there. I wanted you to be awake before we made any other decisions," Tyla finally said.

"Good, the light looks like the sun is low in the sky now, we are probably close. I should get up and get moving." I started rising, but three pairs of arms just held me tighter. "Or I can wait a little bit. Stay here with you until we stop."

"Wise decision, Master."

"Very, Love."

"Mmmhmm." Diane nodded, placing her face into my chest so that her response was muffled.

"Do you need to recharge?" Tas asked, her hand rubbing down my chest.

"Actually, I am fairly full right now after what happened."

"How?" Tyla asked.

"I'll explain in a more secure location. Maybe tonight?"

Tyla and Tas both knew what this meant and nodded.

I just laid back, squeezed them all a little tighter, and enjoyed it as the sun continued to set.

"What is it, Orrick?" I asked as we made camp for the night.

"Mahalo thinks someone is out there, either with a Shadow's Mantle or a light Chosen. She isn't sure."

I nodded, another small pang of loss hitting me. Mahalo was the last trained light mage, and I couldn't afford to risk losing her. "What did she say?"

"Not much. She drifted near me and became visible just long enough to tell me, then said she would keep an eye on it to see what it did. Only the one I think, but she never said."

"Okay, talk to Julian and double the guard. We need to consider building full camps each night with berms or something to slow down attacks in the future. We have the manpower for it now."

"We do, boss, but it will depend on where we are at."

"Yeah, we need to start building an army out of our rabble though, hard work builds the muscle needed and makes us safer. As soon as I take the oaths of those staying, we will sit down and plan it out."

"You got it, boss," he said in that drawl that reminded me of a southerner from the United States back home.

I stayed there deep in thought, in front of the freshly made fire for a minute, staring at the flames. Trying to build on those senses that I had been gifted, I could almost feel the power in the air from those around me. It was almost like everyone who was sworn to me was one of the embers floating off the fire in front of me as it burned.

Using that as a visual, I tried to reach out for Mahalo, just to see where she was. I closed my eyes and connected to each ember as it floated around me in the camp. Some of them were a dull colored and felt like they were asleep. Others moving or working that were much brighter. There were also lots of smaller sparks of life that were not yet connected to me I could also sense. The ones that had not taken an oath was my guess.

It felt like looking at a sensor screen in a crowded area of space on Earth. It was draining, but could come in handy in the future.

I kept at it, and after a while, I could sense the one I wanted coming from somewhere to the east. It was a bright ember connected to me, but near it was another that wasn't.

Should I go see what it is?

"What are you doing, Master?"

My thoughts disturbed, I opened my eyes and smiled as my three girls came walking up to me. Yes, I was including Diane in that now. She still had to make the decision, but I had to admit I thought of her as mine.

I also had to admit that if she chose not to join us, it would hurt greatly. But I just didn't think that would happen. A part of me knew she would stay.

My eyes locked on the elf in question, and her face pinked just a little. I turned my head to Tyla and Diane as they came, and each gave me a kiss. Tyla took a second before she stepped back, catching my attention, and nodding as if she knew exactly what I was thinking.

At this point, she probably did.

"Diane, do you sense or hear anyone nearby that we can't see?"

It was Diane's turn to close her eyes, she stayed still and silent for a few heartbeats before staring up at me and shaking her head. "No, to both questions."

"Good, I think that means we can speak freely. Mahalo thinks there is someone out there spying on us. Light Chosen or Shadow's Mantle she wasn't sure. She is counter spying on it now, I think I can feel where they are at."

"You can, Love?"

I nodded at Tas and then at Tyla. "Master, that is... how can you do that?"

"I'll tell you later. It's best not to speak of it here."

"What do you mean?" Diane asked.

She had no idea about the Sanctum since we could not talk about it outside in case one of the gods was spying.

"It's something we can't talk about just yet. I hope that I can tell you someday soon," I said.

"Only if I am bonded to you?" she asked, a slight frown on her face.

I walked up to her and put my hands on her arms. "It's not because you are not bonded with me. I trust you implicitly Diane. Even without an oath. I just..." I struggled for the right words. "I just can't tell you about it here in the open. It's too important right now to risk otherwise. I hope that you can trust me on this?"

"Is it because I am not bonded to you?"

"That's part of it." I said

She stared up into my eyes, studying them for what seemed like an eternity before she nodded and pressed forward into my arms. "I understand. I also trust you too."

I encased her in a hug, Tyla and Tas joining in. "Thank you. I will never pressure you into that. I hope you understand."

"I do. Thank you."

We released our embrace, and I turned into the direction that I sensed Mahalo from earlier. "I think I want to check out who that is. We can't take risks."

"We will follow you, Master."

"Thanks, my love, all of you."

I closed my eyes one more time and reached out for that ember that was Mahalo. I found it quickly this time and tried to sense all around her. Breathing in and out slowly and dipping into that well of power that I had built up in my time here.

I almost lost concentration when I heard Diane whisper to Tyla, "Can I discuss something with you in private later?"

It took all my concentration not to grasp on to that statement and wonder whether Diane had made her choice one way or another. That took several more breaths, and I lost my focus one or two times.

After another few minutes, I had it.

"I found something." I said, my voice barely a whisper.

"What is it, Love?"

"That rock outcropping. It's a little too dark to see clearly, but there is an extra shadow at the top that seems different from the rest. Mahalo is just behind it. I... think if we casually walk over to the cart over there, we might be able to get around behind them."

"Is that wise, Master? We do not know their intent."

"I am at the point where I am sick of being on the reaction side. Diane, go get Julian and some of his men, have them start forming up, make a spectacle of themselves like they are preparing for something. I want whoever this is focused on that, while we see if we can catch them by surprise. Then find us again, do you see the Wagon near the rock outcropping?" I did not point at it, but I glanced my eyes in the general direction.

"Yes, Derk."

"Good, meet us there when you are done."

"On my way," she said and went to do as I directed, her form becoming harder to see as she bent light around her.

She was still visible, but she matched the background enough that she was almost noticeable.

"She's getting better every day," I said to the girls.

"She works hard, mostly to impress you," Tyla said.

"I hope she decides soon."

"I think she has," Tas commented.

"Oh? How do you know?"

"She hasn't said anything, just a feeling after the fire."

"I hope it's in our favor. Let's go."

We walked an indirect route to the spot I was aiming for, using as many carriages and tents as I could to block line of sight from the spy that was watching us. I only felt one person, but that did not mean there wasn't more.

We stopped by the last darkened wagon at the edge of our makeshift camp. No one was paying us any attention that I could tell. "You two keep an eye out behind us why I study what's up there."

I closed my eyes and focused. I still could break through the shadow fully, but I could feel only one person sitting there observing our camp. I could also feel Mahalo on the other side of her. Provided it wasn't another Matriarch level Chosen or a Demigod, I think we could take them.

"I think Diane is coming back," Tas whispered.

I felt behind me, as the bright spark that was Diane drifted towards us. Opening my eyes, all I could see was a shadow inching along the various carts and tents.

She approached and sat knelt next to me, her camouflage fully fading, and she took a deep breath. "You okay?" I asked.

"Yes, that took a lot out of me. Julian will give us ten minutes then start moving his men."

"That's good. I won't ask much more of you. I think we can take her. Just do your best to tell me if she is the only one."

"I want to help," Diane whispered as she peeked around the wooden square end of the carriage. She took a minute or two to be sure before she continued. "Just the one that I can feel. Whatever she is using is good enough that I can't pierce it, but I know it is there now that I am looking. Not a light Chosen, but an object that is shrouding her. I wonder how Mahalo saw it."

"She is one of the most experienced light mages we have left," Tyla said from behind us. "She was one of my mother's scouts for years."

"Okay, now we wait," I said. "Here is the plan..."

"Form up now!" Julian yelled in the distance, and I knew it was time to go.

I watched the spot up in the small outcropping of rocks on the edge of a small rise. Probably all that remained of some mountain ranges a couple of hundred million years ago.

Unless it was just created by the Roxannez. I still wasn't sure how this world worked exactly. Tyla once told me, when I first arrived, that the land the humans inhabited was created for them. It did not use to exist the other races had said.

So, who knows?

I heard Julian's men form up, making a racket that I had never seen before. Thirty-nine of his original band still stood, and they were yelling out responses to his commands. The people around his men, the civilians that did not know any better, were all concerned and each of them looked on in fear. It couldn't be helped. I would explain it to them later.

I could not see a person in the rocks, but I could feel them somehow. It was more than just me sensing something, it was like I was getting extra information above what powers I already had. I had to wonder if Jess was somehow letting me know more than I should. Honestly it didn't matter, as much as I wanted to figure out how everything worked, I needed to just trust my senses.

"Now," I whispered when I felt the attention of whoever it was focused on the display.

We shuffled forward in a low crouch, all three of my girls right behind me as we went to the left side of the outcropping. Small rocks soon blocked our sight from our nosy guest, and we scaled the steep but easily manageable hillside.

I glanced back to see the girls had no issues as my hands found purchase in the half rock, half dirt side of the hill on our way to get above the watcher. I still heard Julian calling out commands, preparing his men to march by yelling at them that they were not doing it good enough and chastising them for being sloppy. To where they were going, I had no idea. I just had to trust he would keep the spectacle up as long as possible.

We finally reached the top, just above the small groove in the rocky terrain the spy was laying down in. They were still not aware of our presence.

How do I know this?

I shook the thoughts away. It wasn't important. I just knew they were true and decided to go with it. Her attention was focused on the camp, and she did not know we were behind her. The noises coming from the camp were loud enough to mask our movement.

Shit, I knew it was a her too.

I glanced back at the girls and held up a finger at myself and then held up three of my fingers, slowly counting down. They each nodded in understanding and I was proud of the seriousness in their expressions.

I counted silently down to one then jumped on top of the invisible form I knew was there. It was almost like those old video games where I could use the screen to see the person around the corner even if they were not in my line of sight. Letting me know exactly where to put myself.

I landed on top of the small but wide woman, grabbing her arms and pulling them behind her back. Though dark, I saw her reddish-brown hair become visible when she dropped a jewel from her hands and the shadow mantle failed.

She screamed, her voice lower than most women, though still feminine. But it wasn't a scream of fear. It sounded more like an amazon warrior's battle cry. I dropped my knee on her back as hard as I could, trying to take the wind out of her while I immobilized her arms.

It always seemed that when I was sure of my plans they didn't work out as I would have hoped.

The woman I had grabbed flashed in color. The best I could describe it was brown, but that does not do it justice. It was a shimmering brown laced with flakes of gold that sparkled like the fourth of July celebrations I attended as a kid. It was almost mesmerizing in its intensity.

I wasn't surprised that she was a Chosen, but the sheer intensity of her power and the flash of bright lights distracted me just enough that I was not prepared for the raw strength of this girl whose power rivaled my own.

She quickly flipped over and almost tossed me to the side. My vice-like grip on her arms was the only thing that kept me from flying comically over the lip of the rocky cliff.

I crashed hard into my side as I hit the hard rocks and I saw stars in my vision as my head hit one of the offending boulders. It took all the mental effort I had to keep my hold as she kicked me violently in the stomach. She thankfully missed the more vital parts of my anatomy due to her stature and smaller size.

She finished the turn and mounted me like I was a prized station. I saw her face for only a moment as she reflected the light coming from our camp. Her unruly hair and pale skin seemed to almost glow.

A part of my mind even registered how attractive she was as she shoved me into the ground.

She wasn't wearing any protective coverings. Her clothes were light and meant to be silent, but I could tell this was a woman accustomed to wearing heavy armor. Her body curvy, beyond the proportions of any human woman I had ever seen.

I was entranced by the way she carried herself, even in anger and surprise. My distracted ogling proved my undoing. It gave her the opportunity she needed to head butt me and break my nose.

Stars filled my vision once again as the impact felt like the force of a maglev train hitting me at two hundred miles an hour. I kept from passing out through sheer force of will and focused solely on keeping her arms locked together while I waited for help.

She sat back up and struggled to get out of my grasp. I could feel my hands slipping down her arms as she used her massive leg strength to stand and get away from me.

I shook the blood from my eyes, opening them in time a bright spotlight shine down on us. It was aimed at her but still ruined my night vision. Luckily, it did even worse to her as her squinted bowed her head out of the intense beam of light back towards me.

Diane or Mahalo?

I let the curiosity die and used her distraction to my advantage. She was in a horse stance, her legs bent, and I decided to use it to my advantage.

I shifted my hips to the side and kicked my knee up towards my chest. It connected with her left leg right behind her knee and she fell to her side with a thump.

I followed her over, and it became my turn to get on top as I started healing my broken nose as I went.

Her eyes were still squinted shut to keep out the light. So I returned the favor of the head butt to the nose.

A meaty crunch, and the woman beneath me screamed in response. But it was not a scream of fear or pain.

It was one of rage as her strength once again redoubled. She broke my lock on her arms, and she punched me hard in the chest, clearing my lungs of all their wind.

I threw myself on top of her, getting as close to her as possible to keep her from getting another blow in on me. Something was telling me not to go all out, that this person was not my enemy, and that was limiting my responses.

I used my longer legs to lock her lower body in place, placing her thighs almost to my groin. My arms hugged behind her grasping my own risks to lock them as I placed my chin against her shoulder to restrict her movements and ability to hit me.

"You are not going to make me your slave!" she screamed in a deeply accented brogue I could not place.

Even through the screaming I could feel her voice was deep but feminine.

She managed to use her body shift once more, rolling on top of me once again as we both ground ourselves on the loose, rocky earth beneath us. I could feel the rocks dig into my skin and realized I should have found new armor before getting into a fight.

"Arghhhh," she screamed as another burst of strength allowed her to finally break my grip and free her arms. She pushed against my chest and suddenly her massive breasts heaved away from me. "You're gonna pay for that!"

She cocked her arm back to unleash a massive punch on my face as I tried to get my hands up to block.

I dilated time, something else I should have done from the beginning, and watched as her arm slowly cocked back. Just as she was about to let loose on her haymaker, I saw my wives come in and each grab an arm with both of theirs.

Even together with their own enhanced strength from being Chosen, they could not contain her fully. I leaned forward again and wrapped myself around the girl's body and upper arms to try and hold on to her once again.

"Don't kill her," I managed to get out to my girls as this woman struggled against us.

I honestly had no idea how to end the stalemate without causing potentially severe damage.

Then I saw Diane walk up behind her with a leather strap in her hands. The light that illuminated us never faded from up the hill, and I realized it must have been her casting it the whole time.

Diane grabbed the strap in both hands and placed it over the woman's head and down to her neck. It looked she planned to strangle the woman to death.

Instead, she fastened it around her neck and engaged the clasps on the back, touching a gemstone on the front with a small flash of power as the device activated.

The woman screamed as her powers faded from her, and the pain of the collar embraced her. Her arms went slack, and she no longer had the magically enhanced strength to fight us off, and all four of us collapsed onto the ground, breathing heavily.

I started to relax, thinking the fight was over.

To my suprise the woman screamed one more time, "Nooooo!" as she resumed her frantic fight.

Even without the magic behind her, her panicked flailing tested the strength of me and my girls combined.

"Command her to stop, Diane! You control the collar," Tyla yelled.

"Stop!" Diane said, and the girl's entire body locked up like she had touched a live electrical wire.

She screamed in pain once more as the collar's magic gained control over her physical body. Finally, the woman was silent, and she fell over into my arms. She felt at least as heavy as I did even though she couldn't have been much taller than four feet.

Sounds of armor jangling soon came over the rise as Julian and his men mounted the hill. They surrounded us, each with swords drawn.

"Are you okay, boss?" he asked.

I had never let her go, just in case she awoke and fought some more. But the pain of the collar seemed to have her out cold.

"Take her, bind her, and keep her under a guard. At least five men. She is strong and stubborn, even without her power."

"She is a dwarf. They are very strong," Tyla said through heavy breaths.

"I figured she was something like that." I said. "I knew wasn't human, way too strong... Will five men be enough?"

"Probably?" Tyla replied with a shrug of her shoulders.

"Bind her well," I said to Julian as his men came over to take her from me. "Check the bindings constantly, five men at all times. Chains if you can find them."

"Yes, boss."

His men took her from our grasp and tied her with leather cord at both her wrists and ankles, then doubled it around her legs and arms to keep them bound.

"Do not harm her. Have Estelle heal her wounds and make sure she is treated with respect."

"Yes, boss, you have my word." Julian said, feeling the sincerity of his words through the bond and I nodded to him.

His men picked her up and carried her like a log down the hill, taking three men on each side to carry her. I honestly could not believe how heavy that little frame of hers was.

I lay down on the ground exhausted. That took way more energy than I thought as I felt Tyla's cool hands grasp my face and her healing power suffused throughout me, taking over from my own halfhearted efforts.

"She was much tougher than I expected," I said.

"The dwarves are... a rambunctious and passionate people." Tyla said. "She was stronger than any I have heard of as well."

"Earth magic, I am guessing that is popular with them?"

"Almost all," Tyla said.

"How are you feeling, Tas?"

"We couldn't hit her with our magic while you were so close. We had to wait for the right time. I am sorry Love."

"It's fine. Diane?"

"I am fine, Derrick," she said, sitting down next to me.

The light that had been illuminating us got closer, not a spot light anymore and now more like a lamp. As our last fully trained light Chosen walked up. "Mahalo, are you okay?"

"I am, Boss, thank you. How did you find us? That shroud should have made it impossible to do what you did," the short tan woman said as she came close and dimmed the light so that it was just enough to see her features.

"Orrick passed me the message. Then... I am still trying to figure out these powers I have, but I was able to feel all the people who have sworn to me. I kind of used it like.... a spider's web, I guess? I felt her power brushing up against the bonds we all share now. Let me know where she was, and you."

"That is..." Mahalo began. "Most impressive. Do you require my assistance any more this evening?"

"Thank you for spotting her, I think we are good. Oh, can you tell the others that we will do the oaths tomorrow instead of tonight?"

"I can. Training tomorrow after, Diane?" she asked.

"Yes, thank you."

"Good, you have a pleasant evening, Oh, she dropped this." Mahalo said as she handed me a small red jewel that looked like a ruby. "It's the shadow's mantle she was using."

I took the small red object and held it up, the darkness making it too hard to see and I decided to worry about it later and place it in my pocket. "Thanks. Worry about it in the morning. Have a good night."

"I intend to," she said as the spiky-haired older woman turned and drifted into her shroud and out into the night.

Diane's eyes followed her as she left.

"You will be there soon," I said, and she glanced over at me and smiled.

"Yes," she said and under her breath I thought I heard the words "For you."

I did not say anything but instead looked at my girls. "You three want to head back to the carriage? I want to see if our guest is talkative. Unless you want to join me?"

"Go ahead, Master, we will be fine."

"But—" Tas started

"We have things to do, Tas. Remember," Tyla interrupted her sister-wife.

"I forgot. You're right."

"What is it?" I asked.

"Nothing to worry about. See you when you are done," Tyla responded, taking both Diane and Tas by the arm and walking ahead of me towards the carriage.

"They are most definitely up to something," I said to myself and shrugged. "Let them have their surprises."

I turned and walked towards where Julian had taken our prisoner. Even though she probably would not be in the mood to talk right away, I wanted to get a feel for her.

Something about her sang out to me, and I honestly was not sure what it was. It did not feel like it was another one of those big flashing arrow signs from Vex, but I couldn't rule that out just yet, either.

CHAPTER 23

JO'EYREN'EE

I approached the part of the camp that Julian and his men had claimed as their own. Several large tents had been erected around a central fire. The overall camp, especially since we had added so many new refugees, was a mess, and my old marine mindset was in uproar about it.

I knew it had to change soon.

But Julian's small camp was like an oasis in the desert of anarchy. The four tents were aligned in a proper square around the fire, with an open side to the square where people could approach. He had a guard posted near the fire to greet all those that walked nearby. We had discussed this earlier. Until we knew that we could count on them, his men would bear the brunt of the security tasks for the moment. I hoped to reward them for it eventually.

"They have her near the cart behind the tents, Sir," the man on guard said before I even asked a question.

I nodded and walked past him to where he was pointing.

The scene I came upon was not one I exactly expected, but given my brief encounter with her, I probably should not have been surprised.

"Git' off me, you fecking man. I will not be a slave to one of those monsters!" she screamed under the combined weight of eight men.

Even though I knew it was in my head, I swore she had a Scottish accent.

She was still tied up with the cords. But she was still giving the trained soldiers a hard time as they held her down. I took a deep breath. "Should have brought Diane to give her commands."

I watched for a minute as the men struggled unsuccessfully in their attempts to keep her still.

"Calm down!" I finally yelled at her.

That got her attention. Her eyes widened.

"No, keep tha' fecking thing away from me. I'll not let him turn me," she said as panic filled her eyes and she struggled with the bindings.

The men on top of her grabbed her arms and legs once more as they struggled against each other.

I raised my hands in what I hoped was the universal gesture for meaning no harm, my palms wide and my arms relaxed. "Miss, please calm down. No one is going to do anything to you other than keep you restrained. You were spying on my camp, and I have enemies. If I don't think you are a threat, I will happily let you walk away after some questions."

She breathed heavily but finally stopped struggling. "You bastards with your silver tongues always lie. Feck you and whatever hole you come outta."

The accent was getting thicker so I closed my eyes and took a deep breath, telling myself that she was not from Scotland and that even if she had an accent, it would be something different entirely.

Finally, I opened my eyes and met hers. "Look, I know you don't believe me. All I can say is that I am not a Demigod. I have their powers, but that is it. I am trying to fight them."

She looked up at me, her eyes now no longer one of fear. I could not quite place it as her facial expressions seemed different from those of a human, but I almost thought it was... humor? Relief? I wasn't sure.

"Oh," she said. I could still hear the accent but not quite as thick now. "Well, in that case, why didn't you say so? My name is Jo'eyren'ee. What did you need?" She relaxed her posture, and the men holding on to her sagged in relief.

I took a step towards her, my arms still up and relaxed.

That was too easy, this can't be right.

I prepared myself for another attack as I got within another pace of her, waiting for the shoe to drop but hoping I was wrong. "I promise that I am not going to hurt you or enslave you... Joe... Joe n reny? Sorry, your name is hard to pronounce. I can explain a little more if you let me, but I need to know what you were doing out there first."

She smiled at me, a dimple forming in her left cheek. "Sure. I was just hoping to borrow some tea is all..." She sucked in deep and then spit out what should not, in my opinion, come out of anything of the female form.

I dialed my time dilation to max and stepped out of the way of the glob of the unladylike projectile just as it sailed through where my face was less than a fraction of a heartbeat before.

Her eyes widened at my sudden movement, and her arms flexed. Somehow, even without her magic, she managed to snap the leather cords that held her arms in place in an instant.

"You are one of them!" she screamed, her voice low from my stretching of time.

The bindings on her wrists held, and the guards managed to keep their own grips, but just barely.

"You fecking assholes are all the same!" she screamed again, her voice still coming out slowly.

She forced her way to her feet somehow and crouched. Then she lunged forward at me, her tied hands going for my throats and her teeth displayed like she was going to try and bite me in half.

I still had the time dilation at maximum. While I could feel it draining my power, I knew I had enough.

I watched as she slowly drifted for me, her rather pretty and pale face encased in a grimace of anger and hatred. Her brown hair with strands of orange almost seemed to float behind her as she inched closer.

One of the guards, who had his hand on her shirt trying to hold her back, opened his eyes in shock as the shirt she was wearing ripped off her like it was made of paper. Her massive breasts sprung free as I watched the whole thing in slow motion, timing my move for when she got into range.

I had a moment to appreciate the woman's curvy body as the shreds of her underclothes came off. Her pants remained untouched, but I got a full view of the globes on her chest, and I couldn't help but admire them as I waited for my moment.

As she came within a foot of me, I finally moved. I stepped to the side in the blink of an eye from her perspective. My right hand flew hard and connected my fist directly to the right side of her jaw.

The impact felt like hitting a wall of iron, and a flash of pain went up my arm as I just shattered my knuckles on it.

But at least it knocked her out this time. She hit the ground hard with a thump, fully limp as she skidded and came to a stop. The curvy woman now looked like someone who had just passed out after an all-night bar brawl.

Based on the limited interactions, I could believe that as a thing she would do too.

"Get her in irons or chains. I know we have some somewhere. Double them and get her fully clothed. Then call Estelle to come check on her and arrange a couple of Chosen with strength to help you stand guard. If you can't find anyone you trust, come get me."

I focused on healing my now swelling hand, trying to put the bones back together.

"Yes, boss," Julian said. I glanced over at the fully ripped shirt in his hand, his face red as he tried not to stare at the woman's massive chest. "Sorry, boss."

He dropped the shirt on the ground.

"I know you didn't do it on purpose. Make her decent as soon as you can but get her secured first. She is... quite strong."

"She is at that," he said.

As I studied the woman in all her half-naked glory, I walked around to the other side of her. While studying her back, something caught my eye. In between her shoulder blades was a black tattoo, almost like a rune.

It was definitely a rune, but I could not remember what it meant. It did not give off any of the magical energy I normally felt when someone was bonded to a Demigod. It had a strange energy coming off it that was unlike anything I had encountered before.

It looked like a straight line up and down with two arrows pointing each direction and intersecting with each other over the line that went up and down so that they intersect at two points.

Protection rune?

I honestly wasn't sure if that was what it was called. It probably meant something different to her, but I had a friend in the Boston Police that was huge into Norse and Viking stuff.

I smiled at the memory. Jake was one of the guys that liked to dress up and go to fairs and such. He had a pendant with the same rune he wore around his neck every time he went out on patrol.

Noise to my left got my attention, and I turned to see Estelle walk over.

"A dwarf?" she asked.

"Yeah, surprise to us too. We caught her spying on us in the rocks over there. Her name is... fuck, I can't pronounce it. Just call her Joey. That is easier to say... Did I wake you?"

Estelle turned red. "Uh, no... Orrick and I were... talking."

I laughed. "Talking, huh?" I put finger quotes around the words as I said them, knowing that no one here would get the reference. "I'm sorry, Estelle. Can you check on her? Then get Miho and any of our other earth powered Chosen who might be able to help Julian's men keep an eye on her tonight. Then you can get back to your... talking."

"Shouldn't be a problem," she said, her face even more red now. "Let me see your hand."

"I am healing it myself. Save your power for her. If I need more, I can ask Tyla. Save your strength."

She walked over to the knocked-out dwarf and placed her hand on her exposed arm.

"Julian, send one of your men for Miho and anyone else that Estelle needs. Keep... six men with Joey at all times."

"Boss, I am pretty shorthanded as is."

I took a deep breath. "I know, we have to start using the folks that are joining us. Go around and find all the ones that have sworn an oath that will be joining the militia. Have one of them partner up with one of your men, that should allow you to double the manpower for tonight, and we can start integrating earlier than we planned."

"Not sure I like that just yet."

"I know, it's a risk, but we need to start, and I don't want your men too exhausted when we start making our journey tomorrow."

"Yes, sir."

I grasped the bridge of my nose while thinking about all the things that needed to happen to turn our rabble into something that wasn't just a hindrance to my goals.

"I am going to take all the oaths of people that are staying with us tomorrow. Anyone not going can either head back to town or make their own way. I don't care. We start the ones that we can get into fighting form right off by learning to march, you and Cecil will be in charge. I don't want to micromanage if I don't have to, but I will be happy to help."

"We can do that."

Nodding, I continued. "You are hereby given the rank of Captain in my army. Cecil will be your lieutenant in charge of the men. Pick those of your men you think can handle it as sergeants and build on that. I will explain this to her tomorrow, but Lea will also be a lieutenant. She will be in charge of the Chosen and getting them trained. You will be overall in charge, but I want full integration between the two, soldiers and magic users. We are not going to divide up and treat people like pawns here. Everyone is important."

"Tricky, but I like the idea, boss."

"Estelle, you take over medical and support."

She never answered, just nodded with her eyes closed as she tended to the dwarf.

"Good. Okay, I am going to go find my girls. If you need me, come get me." I shook my hand, finally finished knitting the bones back together and feeling tapped out on energy.

I hated that I needed to keep changing the organization, but we were a work in progress, and they would just have to understand.

My power was low, but not to the point that I was tired. Guess I had to hope for an orgy or something to recharge. While I thought the rules were stupid - like something a horny eighteen-year-old would come up with - I did remember Captain Smith back on Earth telling me about how the Romans used to party. So, I guess it made sense in a way that a species with unlimited time and power would focus on their... baser needs.

I turned after waving to Julian and walked to my carriage, hoping there would be no more surprises in store for me that night.

CHAPTER 24

DIANE

I approached my carriage, exhausted, weary, low on energy, and my body calling for sleep... or other things. From the outside, the windows were dark, the curtains on them drawn, and it was tough to tell if the girls were already asleep.

"Either a surprise waiting for me, or they are asleep," I mumbled, stifling a yawn as I put my foot up on the small wooden step. "Better go with sleep so I don't wake them."

I opened the door slowly, the metal handle making barely a sound as I tried to silently open it. I pulled on the door and peeked in, only one of the candles still burning, giving me just enough light not to trip over anything.

A single body lay in the bed, covered so that I could not tell who it was. The spot where Diane normally slept lay empty.

Did they go somewhere?

Since I was tired, I decided not to worry about it too much more. It was late, and I could always recharge the fun way in the morning. I silently removed my replacement clothing, folding them up and placing them on the other seat so I could get to them quickly if I needed to in the middle of the night. I started to pull my sword and realized I never cleaned it properly. That was going to be a headache.

One I would deal with tomorrow.

I yawned heavily, sleep calling out to me like a long-lost friend. Part of me was grateful that they did not want to engage in our normal nighttime routine. Though something in the back of my sleep-exhausted brain kept telling me that I was missing something obvious, I decided to ignore it for now.

In nothing but my woolen boxers, I stepped up on to the bench to reach the bed. As much as I loved having a coach to live in, it was designed around the large bed more than ease of access.

Whether it was Tyla or Tas, I didn't know, but the body under the covers stirred just a bit as if partially awakened by my presence. I gently lifted the covers and slid next to it, hopefully not waking whichever of my girls it was.

Not removing the covers over her head, I spooned against her and reached over my arm to find her fully naked and pressed my body up against her. My hand gently pressed against her toned stomach, and my hand drifted up towards her breasts, cupping the firm globes of the woman next to me which elicited a moan from her.

Wait... These are too small to be Tyla or Tas. Plentiful but not as big. The moan didn't sound right, either. Shit...

My sleep deprived brain kicked back into gear as I removed my hand and pulled the covers down. The candlelight and my adjusting vision revealed a naked pink-haired beauty pressed against my rapidly hardening shaft.

"Diane?"

She turned her face to me and smiled, turning a bright pink even in the dim candlelight. "I... we... wanted to surprise you."

"I'm guessing you made your decision?" I asked, not moving, keeping my body snuggled up against her.

She nodded to me, and I put my hand on her left hip and began caressing her up and down her left side.

"Can't say it out loud?"

This time she shook her head, but she never stopped looking over her shoulder at me. I slowly inched my hand up the curve at her hip and rubbed the back of her ass. Her lip curved up into a small smile as her eyes closed and she moaned a bit at my wandering.

"You know what that means, right?"

"Yes," she said, her eyes fluttering for a minute as she enjoyed my touching.

"Where are the girls?" I asked, moving my hand ever closer in my circling to the bottom of her ass, only inches away from her entrance.

"Mmmhhhhmmm, they... wanted to... give us... some... oh goddess." She couldn't finish the sentence when I rubbed over her now very wet entrance.

"Time alone?" I asked, and she nodded vigorously. "I need you to tell me in words, Diane. Are you sure about this?" I lifted my hand, wanting her to be able to think clearly even if just for a few seconds. She pushed her rear up after my hand, letting out a frustrated sigh that the touch had stopped.

I reached up, using my index finger to gently lift her jaw towards me, and leaned over so that our eyes were locked with one another. "Are you sure? I know that I can release you, but I want you to make the decision as though I couldn't."

She never broke eye contact, staring deep into my eyes for several heart beats. "Yes, more than anything."

She leaned up, our lips meeting for the first time in passion. Her lips taste reminded me of cherries, and I could not for the life of me remember seeing any on this world. Our tongues darted out and met tentatively at first.

She rolled over to face me, and her breasts pushed into my chest as she put her arms around my neck. Her small form seemed to fit perfectly in my arms as we explored each other's lips.

My hand slid back down to her ass, and I grabbed on firmly, making her squeal in response. We stopped our kiss for a moment.

"Do you like that?" I asked.

"Yessss." She pushed her rear deeper into my hands. "It makes me flutter."

I smiled at this. My little elf was an ass girl. I locked it away in my brain for future reference as I slowly moved my hand in between the crevice of her cheeks, leaning forward to try something I have been dying to do since I met her. Leaning forward to her ears to taste them.

My finger gently traced the outer edge of her back door, while I put my tongue on her pointed ears and licked them gently.

"Fuck!" she cried, and her entire body convulsed as she had her first orgasm, catching me completely by surprise.

"Did you just?"

She nodded, then looked up at me in a panic. "I'm sorry, that was so quick."

"Don't be," I soothed. "That's great, actually. Do you need a minute?"

She nodded again as she tried to get her breathing under control. I reached down, pulled her mouth up to mine and kissed her once again as deeply as I could to let her know it was okay.

Soon I could feel her passion rising as her own hands started to explore. Her left arm, trapped underneath my body, grasped the back of my arm and started gently rubbing her fingers along everywhere she could reach.

Her other arm, free to roam, began tracing my chest and working its way down my toned stomach towards its reward. My dick was as hard as diamond in expectation for her to finally reach her goal.

I returned my hand to her hips and started anew in my exploration of her backside, matching her slow pacing and not going straight for my ultimate goal.

Then came sounds at the door, which got us to stop and cover ourselves quickly. I glanced up to see my other two women walk into the room without a care in the world.

"What are you two up to here?" Tas asked with a big smile on her face.

Tyla just smiled at the two of us locked in our embrace.

Just like that, my mind put me back in my old mindset of getting caught making out with another girl when your girlfriend walks in, and I was at a complete loss for words.

"Uhhh," was my witty reply.

"I thought..." Diane began, turning pink once again as she looked at the two girls in concern.

"She is being funny, Diane. We are not upset; in fact, we are delighted. But we decided that since you liked to watch us all those times. It is only fair if we returned the favor after some time alone with him."

"This is a family affair after all," Tas added as she snapped her hips walking up to the bed.

"Girls, I love you, but don't make this harder on her," I said, trying to get in front of this before Diane changed her mind. Was that selfish of me? Yes, and I no longer cared either.

She was mine, Damn it.

"Oh," she responded as her cheeks heated and legs squirmed. "That... sounds really fun, actually."

"Does that... turn you on?" I asked, glancing down at her.

"It... makes me really hot down there."

I glanced over at the girls and nodded at them. Both immediately removed their clothes, placing them on the small bench seat.

I couldn't help but admire their flesh as it became exposed, loving every minute of their minor strip tease. I glanced down at Diane who was watching them as well, her eyes focused on Tyla's rear as she bent over.

I took that opportunity to surprise her with my hands, moving down the front of her flat stomach and rubbing the tip of my middle finger against her drenched and swollen clit.

"Oh goddess!" she exclaimed, and her eyes rolled into the back of her head as it fell back against the pillow.

The girls climbed up on the bed, each sitting against the far wall of the cabin next to each other. I couldn't help but wink at them as Diane's head flopped back from my touch.

"She really likes your fingers compared to her own," Tas said, her own hand reaching up and squeezing her left nipple.

"Let them be," Tyla admonished, but her own hand was rubbing down towards her leg.

I decided to focus fully on Diane leaning over and kissing her once again. Her free hand grabbed the back of my head, her fingers intertwining my hair as she pushed down hard and pressed me into her lips even more.

She moaned into my mouth as I fully inserted my middle finger into her tight opening, her legs spreading under the blanket for me.

"Oh no, that's not going to work," Tas said through her own heavy breathing as she reached out and tugged the offending blanket out of the way, fully exposing both of us to the cool night air.

I looked down to see goose bumps form on Diane's legs, but she did not seem to notice with my finger slowly going in and out of her channel. She brought her knees up to level with her hips, spreading them wide to give me room to work and the girls a good show of her nether reaches.

I couldn't help but look at them, now seeing each with a hand in their sister-wife's crotch, rubbing each other slowly as they stared at what I was doing.

I did not think it was possible, but my member hardened even beyond what it already was, knowing that they were getting off watching us.

Seeming to remember me, Diane's hand reached down and finally took my girth in her hand, rubbing up and down on it even though she was almost blabbering nonsensical noises as she was lost in her own ecstasy.

Her hips started gyrating in time with my motions as I sped up the pumping of my hand in and out. Soon, she just kept repeating, "Oh goddess," over and over as I brought her up to her next climax.

I quickly added a second finger as I felt her loosen up just enough, her free hand reaching out and grasping the bed sheet in an iron grip as her body exploded one more time beneath me. Luckily, she did not grasp too hard on my shaft, letting go at the last second and placing her hand on her stomach as she convulsed from her second orgasm of the night.

"That was so fucking sexy," I whispered into her ears just before I began attending to them again.

I kissed them gently as she tried to get oxygen into her system after her climax. Her heavy breathing turned quickly back into subtle moaning as I licked and kissed down from the tip of her ear.

"I... should take.... Mhmm... care of you."

I lifted from her ear. "I kind of like taking care of you right now. We can get to that later."

"I'll help warm him up," Tas said as she got up and crawled toward me as I continued to kiss and lick Diane's long and pointed ears. My hand also started exploring her breasts, grasping and then circling her rock-hard nipples with my index finger.

Her back arched in the air from the pleasure, and I almost thought she was going to cum again.

A warm and wet sensation engulfed my shaft, and I glanced down to see Tas going as deep as she could, her own ass sticking into the air where Tyla had come up behind her. "She will get you nice and ready for your new elf," Tyla said right before I watched as my first wife smirked at me, gave me a wink, and placed her head between Tas's thighs getting her to moan with my shaft between her lips.

This is heaven.

We stayed like that for what seemed blissful hours while in reality it was probably only minutes. I continued to loosen up my elf, eventually adding a third finger so that she could take my girth easier. I switched my kissing and licking from her ears to her nipples and back again, edging her closer and closer to her third orgasm as she writhed in pleasure under me.

"I need you... I need you inside me," Diane whispered, finally not able to take it anymore as I slowed down to keep her from the peak of bliss once again.

Tas pulled her mouth off me, and I watched as she wiped a big glob of saliva and pre-cum from her chin. She blew me a kiss and turned around, grabbing Tyla by the back of her head, forcing her into a deep kiss, and falling over next to our feet as they did so.

I straddled my little elf and placed the tip of my shaft against her opening, it glistened from all her juices that escaped. "I'll go slow."

She shook her head and reached down, grabbing hold of my shaft. "Now, I need it now." And then pushed me inside her as deep as she could with her hand in the way.

She was so tight I was surprised it didn't hurt her. She bucked her hips and removed her hand, grabbing my own hips and pulling me in with her need to have all of me right now.

"Give it to me. Right now," she said with such confidence that I was surprised the words had come out of her mouth.

I gave into her desire and slammed into her.

"Oh!" she yelled as her body convulsed and she had yet another orgasm.

I stopped to give her a second, and she looked up at me with exasperation.

"Don't stop," she pleaded, and tried to coax me forward with her hands still on my hips.

I smiled at my newest little nymphomaniac and started pumping yet again. Between the arousal of watching her get off so many times, and Tasnia's wonderful little mouth, I was probably not going to last long at this point. So, I was glad she had climaxed as much as she did already.

I rocked into her repeatedly, slamming my shaft as deep as it would go, bending my pink haired beauty's knees up to her chin to get her at the perfect angle to go as deep as I could go.

Her eyes were staring up into mine, occasionally rolling to the back of her head as I pumped into her again and again.

Before long, I felt the tingle that told me my end was nigh.

"It's coming," I said through rapid breaths, sweat pouring off my face and dripping onto her exposed breasts.

Diane's hands rubbed the sweat, then went up to her breasts, caressing them and then squeezing each nipple one by one.

"Make me yours," she finally said through her own moans of pleasure.

That sent me over the edge.

I felt the power well inside me along with the orgasm that seemed to blast its way through my pleasure centers.

I convulsed as I slammed into her, my hot seed pouring deep into her womb.

"Yes!" Diane screamed, "I'm his!" as the power escaped from me and slammed into my newest wife.

From there, the power extended outward, going straight into Tyla and Tas who were licking each other in a sixty-nine position. Both let out their own screams of pleasure as the blast caused them both to orgasm at the same time.

All three of them collapsed into a catatonic state as I struggled to maintain my own consciousness. I landed on top of Diane and her eyes fluttered open briefly to look into mine. For a moment, our souls seemed connected as I felt everything she did, intermixed with feelings coming from Tyla and Tas next to us.

I saw her eyes widen further in shock as I understood what had happened at the same time that she did.

"I remember," she whispered, and I knew that her memories had returned.

Then I collapsed on top of her, still seated inside, as the rush of sudden power finally took me, and I passed out.

CHAPTER 25

— • —

INTERLUDE - PATRICIA

Patricia stood upon the ridge overlooking the remnants of the town below. On the far side of the river, the buildings were destroyed, smoke still rising from the burnt wrecks.

"They were here," Einestra said, standing next to Patricia.

"Obviously," Patricia replied. She hated the stupid woman.

Patricia quickly changed her thoughts before they devolved into something Seir would frown upon, and thus cause pain. She had learned quickly to avoid the worst of it.

She must endure for Tyla. Save her from her enslavement at the hands of one of them. Even if she had to kill her daughter, she would do what she must.

"What should we do?" Einestra asked.

"If they caused this, then the Demigod my daughter has bonded to has grown in power and strength. You will fly to Rivenhold and bring back as much of the new garrison as they can spare."

"We have men and Chosen, though."

"If they destroyed Helena, two hundred men, even with Aulus and Gnaeus and their Chosen may not be enough."

"Yes, Patricia," Einestra said.

"It is getting late, however. You can leave at first light. Tell the brothers we will camp here, send scouts into what's left of the town, and decide our next actions in the morning."

"As you wish."

Patricia watched the petite blond woman go, her urges for sexual satisfaction with the woman before she left at odds to her distaste for her.

She locked the dislike away deep in her mind, thinking only of being the perfect servant for Seir once again.

She stared down at the town in the waning light of the day, on the near side of the river, the buildings were much less damaged, but it appeared that those that lived here had abandoned all hope of salvaging their lives. She could see no one walking the streets or cleaning up the mess.

Her thoughts were disturbed by two large men walking up behind her. She took a deep breath as she prepared for their whining.

"Speak," she said before they could say a word.

"Learn your place, woman," Aulus said, the more belligerent of the two brothers.

"I have learned my place. It was taught to me repeatedly by Seir." Patricia shivered as her body cried out for more of his teachings. She no longer tried to fight the urges, she learned to embrace them and let them flow over her now. "He also told me to take charge of this operation. You serve me for the duration."

She heard an almost inhuman growl come from behind her.

"Do you have an issue with Seir's command, Gnaeus?"

The other brother silenced the noise. "No."

"No... what?"

Silence reigned for several heartbeats before she turned and stared at the larger of the two. "No, what?"

"No... My queen," Gnaeus finally said.

"Good boy." She smiled, taking the small satisfaction of putting him in his place. "What is it you two wanted?"

"Why are we stopping?" Aulus asked, barely containing his anger. "We have to be close."

"You two may not know this," Patricia said. "But Helena was very powerful, enough that she challenged the former Matriarch of Rivenhold for her position many years ago. She was defeated, but it was a close thing. My own mother had to get involved to help Miranda's predecessor."

"So?" Gnaeus asked.

"When the war was over, her title was removed. However, as a concession, she was allowed to keep her family's town here on the outskirts. My point being, she was powerful. If the Controllers pawn could best her and destroy her town, we should not take risks. We need an army if we are to guarantee success."

The idiot brothers glanced at each other. Gnaeus shrugged his shoulders, deferring to Aulus. Finally, the leader of the two brothers just nodded.

"Fine, what do we do next?" Aulus asked.

"We wait here, send scouts to track them, and when we are reinforced, we follow and destroy them."

"What if they get away?"

"They won't."

"How can you be so sure?" Aulus asked. Patricia stared at him with all the ice she could muster. After several heartbeats, he finally looked to the ground and grumbled, "My Queen."

"Because I know what awaits them on the other side of the desert," she said and turned away from the brothers.

Aulus and Gnaeus turned to each other, each of them communicating silently through their expressions. Finally, Aulus shrugged and turned away from Seir's woman and walked back to his camp. Gnaeus followed only a few steps behind.

Patricia stared out to the town and then the great plains beyond, contemplating how best to free her daughter.

She knew she could not free her of the bond, but she would kill the Demigod who controlled her, even if it meant Tyla's death, at least she would die free.

A fate she could only dream of happening for herself.

That thought alone caused pain to spread through her head like the worst of migraines. She quickly suppressed her thoughts once again to something that would make the bond approve. She raised her hand and summoned the personal guard she had gotten from the brothers. While she could not trust them fully, she would happily use them to make her life somewhat easier.

"Make sure my personal tent is set up and have Einestra meet me there."

"Yes, my Queen," the guard she never even bothered to look at said as he turned and ran off in search of his task.

Patricia kept her mind as blank as possible as she stood in place. Seir was her master. She freely acknowledged that now. Part of her longed to please him beyond even the compulsion she agreed to, but that was not the whole of who she was. She had to admit she even enjoyed sharing a bed with her long-time lover Josephina again. Those small things made her imprisonment bearable.

But he also created a hierarchy within his own harem. One that allowed her to control those below her. She was now second only to Josephina, and that let her gain autonomy when Seir was not present, for which she was grateful. There were two others in his harem that she knew about, each of them having their own assignments that carried them far away from their shared master.

She would meet them soon enough as well, as long as she maintained her current path. She was sure there would be a small power struggle at first, but she was confident she could prevail against them.

Sounds of a man running behind her got her attention. She never turned, as she knew it was just the guard coming back.

"Your tent is ready, my Queen. Einestra awaits your pleasure."

"She does indeed," Patricia said with a smile, turning and walking towards the camp. "Return to your duties. Have someone attend my tent within an hour."

"Yes, Queen," he said and bowed as she passed by.

She moved to her well-appointed tent in the center of the camp and walked through the open curtains, never bothering to close them. She did not care who watched. They could not touch her nor could she allow them to touch her.

The pain at that would be enough to kill her outright. The lesser pain she was feeling now could only be removed by giving power back to her master. It was another of his gifts to ensure that his women pleased him. But at least the duty was one that she did not mind. Einestra was really good at giving pleasure after all.

The blond woman was kneeling on a rug set in the middle of the tent, completely devoid of any clothing, her hands behind her back as she waited for her senior wife to arrive. Beneath the blond woman, on the carpet, was a wet spot spreading from directly below her crotch, telling Patricia that Einestra looked forward to the duties expected of her.

Patricia pulled the cord that kept her traveling robe in place and let it fall from her shoulders as she passed the submissive blond woman. As soon as the clothing left her, it revealed her naked body in all its glory.

"I have to admit," Patricia said. "I understand the appeal this has to Josephina and Seir."

Patricia sat in the chair that was provided, directly in front of Einestra. "You may begin."

She opened her legs wide to allow the blonde access.

Einestra smiled as she leaned forward, putting her hands down on the carpet and walking forward like a cat about to pounce on its prey. She put her face directly in front of Patricia's entrance and breathed in the scent deeply as she shuddered.

"Be thorough," Patricia said as the tongue of the blonde girl darted out and started to taste her elder wife.

Patricia placed her head against the back of her chair, closed her eyes, and used the power generated from Einestra's carnal acts to cover her thoughts while she plotted how best to save her daughter.

CHAPTER 26

——— ❖ ———

EPILOGUE

"How much longer should we play this game, Controller?" Tarkus asked, sitting across from the two other Grand Senators.

"A few weeks," the Controller replied simply.

"We put ourselves and our interests on habitat Four five two at great risk doing this for you," Rilro added.

"The favor was sworn and called. You agreed it was worth this price when I helped you over four thousand years ago."

"We were both desperate then," Tarkus said.

"And now you have the power you asked for. What I am asking is worth less than what I risked then," the controller replied.

"I don't understand how what we are doing helps you," Rilro said as he wiped his large green hand over his hairless head. "Why must we play these cat and mouse games with the overseer? We risk his wrath for no gain for ourselves. How does this help you with your schemes?"

"My schemes are my own, the oath does not hold you to secrecy. But I will tell you that all I need is time. I do not need you to defeat the overseer's pawn, just hold him to the north while I complete my own preparations. After that, my hold on you ceases and you may conduct your affairs as you see fit."

Both of his fellow Grand Senators eyed him with anger. They obviously were hoping for more, so they could negotiate a truce with the Overseer and save themselves from the repercussions of their actions against the most powerful being in the Empire short of the Emperor himself.

"Sooth yourselves, the Overseer will want to deal with me before he acts against you. I suggest you keep your pieces on the board from acting too harshly and risk his or his pawns' ire for now."

"Baldr can handle Seir," Tarkus said.

"The dwarves are fierce warriors, but Baldr was a poor choice to lead them. He wastes their talents and lives in battle," Rilro chided.

"Landas cannot follow simple orders. All he had to do was to surprise Seir's humans from the rear and they could have defeated them. But he was seen before he reached one hundred miles. The Elves are experts at stealth. It should have been easy!" Tarkus yelled.

"Brothers, please," the Controller said, raising his hands up at each of them in the small room with only three chairs and no windows or doors. "You did exactly what I needed as per my favor. For that, I thank you. Very soon, no more than three weeks at most, I will release you and you can have your armies retreat and address their... lackluster performances."

The small jibe against their hand-picked agents ruffled both, but neither spoke their thoughts. "At that point, I will have everything I need in place. You may even choose to negotiate alliances with the Overseer and chase me down if you want. I care not."

Both Senators looked at each other quickly but tried to keep their calm facades. The Controller smiled as he confirmed his suspicions. "I will not hold it against you."

"This is the last of the great favors we both owe you," Tarkus said. "We do not support your desires or plans."

"I know," the Controller said. "This makes our slates clean... When you finish."

"Three weeks, not a single day more," Rilro said and stood up. "If I do not hear from you before then, I will consider the compact finished and my slate clean."

"Mine as well," Tarkus added.

"Very well," the Controller said. "Your forces will hold Seir in place, not attacking or retreating until the three weeks are complete. In exchange, I will consider my favor returned and all pacts complete, on my word."

A glow surrounded the Controller as he said this, a pact the central construct of Heaven would enforce with death should it be broken. The glow broke into two points and quickly shot out to his two fellow Grand Senators who accepted the terms.

"Our business is concluded," Tarkus said and disappeared in particles of light.

"Have a good day, Rilro. Say hello to your wives for me," the Controller said and bowed to his one-time friend.

"They haven't spoken to me in over four hundred years, and I doubt they would care," Rilro replied then followed Tarkus into nothingness.

The Controller smiled and drifted away from the small room himself, but his destination was not his home province. He entered the in between space of the great Heaven construct and felt himself compress into a tiny point in between that of energy and matter.

He passed through thousands of security protocols and hundreds of gate keeper constructs, designed to protect his destination from just such entry. Each one of the things designed to stop him never even noticing him as he passed through their domains.

The pain of his entry was great, it took all of his mental fortitude developed over his ten-thousand-year life to ignore the sensation of being destroyed a thousand times as he made his dangerous journey.

When he finally arrived, he let out a deep breath, sweat that should not have been possible on his immortal body found its way out of pores that had not existed since his ascension.

"You look like hell, old friend," the Roxannez before him said. "Did they agree?"

The controller wheezed as he fell to one knee, struggling to regain his composure. After a few seconds, his body normalized, and all signs of his weakened state disappeared as his body reset itself. Only then did he get back to his feet, take a deep breath, and nod at his new companion. "They did. They will give us the time we need. You took a great risk intervening like that."

"It had to be done," the Emperor said. "We do not have time or the resources to activate another one of your pieces on the board. We may have given him too much power."

"You may be right, but we have held him back as much as we did to avoid the worst of it. His lack of knowledge on how to use his power is to our advantage for now. My Assistant has created the perfect tool to help him now."

"That also took me a great deal of influence to achieve. To save a human from a habitat world like that... it goes against a lot of ancient laws."

"What we intend to do will make all those laws pointless, my Emperor."

"Please Jabari, call me by the name from our youth," the Emperor said, his voice more solemn than he had heard it in a very long time.

"As you wish, Kai," the Controller said, surprised at the sudden turn of conversation. He had not heard his original name spoked since they both ascended. "What brought this on?"

"I feel old," Kai said. "I know we never age, never falter, never get sick, but today I feel old and ready to leave this world. Follow our Ancestors and parents into the great beyond and find whatever mysteries still elude us."

"I agree with you," Jabari said, sitting in the nearby chair next to his friend. "But our tasks are not yet finished."

"I never should have let them talk me into allowing our people to rise above death. I should have listened to you."

"You know, my dearest and oldest friend. I only ascended so that one day you could say those words to me. Now I can finally end my existence and feel complete."

Kai laughed deeply and naturally. Jabari joined him as the walls around them shook from the first laughter heard in them in hundreds of years.

"I do not look forward to destroying our people, but I see no other way to fix it," Kai finally said when the laughter had died down.

"I have a plan for that, but it will be tricky. I will have our loyal people and family transported to the nature preserves before it begins."

"Good, I am sure that those working against us will act similarly."

"I hope... that they do not see the full extent of our plans until it is too late. Then they will not be able to corrupt the various preserve worlds before we can set up our own people to counter them."

"We will do what we can," Kai said after some thought. "But first we must win on Timeria. It will be the spark that starts the flame."

"I have faith in my choice." Jabari said.

"And I have faith in you, old friend."

Both reached out, grasping each other's wrists, and shook. "I shall prepare the next phase then," the Controller said as he stood to his full height once more, preparing to leave the same way that he came.

"Goodbye. I hope to see you like this again before it is time."

"I will do my best," the Controller said as he dissipated once again, keeping himself just barely from screaming from the agony that enveloped him as he crept through the in-between space out of the Emperor's personal domain.

— • —

AFTERWORD

Thanks for reading!

If you enjoyed this book, please leave a rating or review on Amazon or Goodreads—Independent authors like me live and die by them. They even make it really simple to do from your iPhone or Android now, no text needed anymore. Just scroll all the way to the end of the book and when the review option comes up, just hit the stars you want and then close the book. No more needed. Thanks so much.

So, about Book 3? It's in draft, started April 1st after another project I finished. I hope that I can finish it by the end of May and done with editing by the end of June and published sometime in late July or early August. I plan to put it up for pre-release the day this book here goes live for six months out. However, I will move up the date as soon as I can.

Special thanks! Speaking of editing, I got two editors now and I hope the quality of my book has improved as a result. Even had book 1 cleaned up since release. I would like to personally thank both of them for their time and effort in helping me make a better book!

Also, I want to send a special thanks to my fellow author who helped peer review the first draft. If you haven't checked him out, Stoham Baginbott is a great guy and fellow author who volunteered his time to help me fix the first draft of the story and plug any plot holes along the way. He has his own books that I highly recommend checking out at his amazon page here. https://www.amazon.com/Stoham-Baginbott/e/B08ZBHRQRQ

Early reads of book 3: For those that do not care about polish and just want to read it as soon as I am done. I will probably put the pre-edited version on Kindle Vella like I did for Gambit. So if anyone wants a sneak peek, you can sign up for my email list at my linktree (below) or follow my Facebook page here for the announcement. https://www.facebook.com/Patrick.Underwood.Writes. As of right now, Vella is only available for those in the US, but we hope it will go international soon. I tried to do a Patreon but honestly dont feel like I am providing enough content yet like the big guys for me to take your money each month. However, feel free to contact me via FB if that is something you are interested in and I will reconsider if there is enough interest.

Find my mailing list and all of my other socials here at my microsite https://linktr.ee/Patrick_Underwood (For those with print copies of the book, go to QR code on the last page and scan it and it will bring you to the same place!)

Beta readers wanted! I am trying to get my books up to the quality that I feel they should be. But I am not perfect by any means. With two editors I have a good start, but for book 3 I hope to bring in beta readers to help with the final polish (and eventually some alpha readers). This is a common practice for most authors and want to incorporate it as a final touch. You get early access to the book, all you need is a Gmail account and access to google docs, plus the willingness to tell the truth and give opinions when you read it. This includes spelling errors, grammatical mistakes, and things you like or did not like and why. Don't worry about being perfect or wondering if you are qualified. Just do your best as you get a free read of the book before almost everyone else.

This is how I got started out before writing my own books and highly recommend it. I plan on having up to ten beta readers total. Anyone that is interested after the list is full, I will add you to the wait list as it is fairly common for people to drop out over time. If this is something yo may be interested in, all you have to do is go to my linktree page and use the 'contact me' form or message me on Facebook. Either way works.

Thanks again for all your time. I appreciate it.

About The Author

I'm a fantasy author with a twist! Currently, I have a secret identity career that requires me to pen under Patrick Underwood.

What can I share? Well, I have the perfect wife, three amazing kids, two dogs, two cats (one in particular that likes to sit on my keyboard while I write), and all the fun and daily stress that comes with that.

Join the Community!

Find thousands of your fellow harem fantasy fans in any of the following social media communities:

Facebook Groups:

Harem Lit | Dukes of Harem | HaremLit Readers | Temple of the Storm

Harem Gamelit

Reddit Subs:

r/haremfantasynovels | r/Haremlit

Discord:

HaremLit Discord

— • —

My Socials

Get all of my socials here by scanning this QR Code. This will take you to my linktree page.

Patrick Underwood

— • —

COPYRIGHT

Made in the USA
Monee, IL
12 January 2024

51672108R00150